Gene Wolfe is American, a mechanical engineer engaged for the past seventeen years in research and development. But he is known to a wide and appreciative audience as an author of science-fiction stories and novellas, many of them nominated for Hugo and Nebula Awards. This is his first full-length work available to English readers outside the United States.

Composed of three linked but independent novellas, it is a novel of strange, dreamlike power and convincing, cunning invention.

'A deeply felt *tour de force* ... written with a delicacy that accentuates the savagery of its conclusion' – *The Times*

'Strange, imaginative and compelling' – *Oxford Times*

THE FIFTH HEAD
OF CERBERUS
Three Novellas

Ω ————————————————————

GENE WOLFE

QUARTET BOOKS LONDON

Published by Quartet Books Limited 1975
27 Goodge Street, London W1P 1FD

First published in Great Britain by
Victor Gollancz Limited 1973

Copyright © 1972 by Gene Wolfe

The novella entitled 'The Fifth Head of Cerberus' appeared
first in *Orbit*. Copyright © 1972 by Damon Knight

ISBN 0 704 31176 3

Printed in Great Britain by
Hunt Barnard Printing Ltd, Aylesbury, Bucks

To Damon Knight, who one well-remembered
June evening in 1966 grew me from a bean.

THE FIFTH HEAD
OF CERBERUS

THE FIFTH HEAD
OF CERBERUS

When the ivy-tod is heavy with snow,
And the owlet whoops to the wolf below,
That eats the she-wolf's young.

Samuel Taylor Coleridge –
'The Rime of the Ancient Mariner'

When I was a boy my brother David and I had
to go to bed early whether we were sleepy or not. In summer
particularly, bedtime often came before sunset; and because our
dormitory was in the east wing of the house, with a broad window
facing the central courtyard and thus looking west, the hard,
pinkish light sometimes streamed in for hours while we lay staring
out at my father's crippled monkey perched on a flaking parapet,
or telling stories, one led to another, with soundless gestures.

Our dormitory was on the uppermost floor of the house, and
our window had a shutter of twisted iron which we were forbidden to open. I suppose the theory was that a burglar might, on
some rainy morning (this being the only time he could hope to
find the roof, which was fitted out as a sort of pleasure garden,
deserted) let down a rope and so enter our room unless the
shutter was closed.

The object of this hypothetical and very courageous thief
would not, of course, be merely to steal us. Children, whether

1

boys or girls, were extraordinarily cheap in Port-Mimizon; and indeed I was once told that my father who had formerly traded in them no longer did so because of the poor market. Whether or not this was true, everyone – or nearly everyone – knew of some professional who would furnish what was wanted, within reason, at a low price. These men made the children of the poor and the careless their study, and should you want, say, a brown-skinned, red-haired little girl or one who was plump or who lisped, a blond boy like David or a pale, brown-haired, brown-eyed boy such as I, they could provide one in a few hours.

Neither, in all probability, would the imaginary burglar seek to hold us for ransom, though my father was thought in some quarters to be immensely rich. There were several reasons for this. Those few people who knew that my brother and I existed knew also, or at least had been led to believe, that my father cared nothing at all for us. Whether this was true or not, I cannot say; certainly I believed it, and my father never gave me the least reason to doubt it, though at the time the thought of killing him had never occurred to me.

And if these reasons were not sufficiently convincing, anyone with an understanding of the stratum in which he had become perhaps the most permanent feature would realize that for him, who was already forced to give large bribes to the secret police, to once disgorge money in that way would leave him open to a thousand ruinous attacks; and this may have been – this and the fear in which he was held – the real reason we were never stolen.

The iron shutter is (for I am writing now in my old dormitory room) hammered to resemble in a stiff and oversymmetrical way the boughs of a willow. In my boyhood it was overgrown by a silver trumpet vine (since dug up) which had scrambled up the wall from the court below, and I used to wish that it would close the window entirely and thus shut out the sun when we were trying to sleep; but David, whose bed was under the window, was forever reaching up to snap off branches so that he could whistle through the hollow stem, making a sort of panpipe of four or five. The piping, of course, growing louder as David grew bolder, would in time attract the attention of Mr Million, our tutor. Mr Million would enter the room in perfect silence, his wide wheels gliding across the uneven floor while David pretended sleep. The panpipe might by this time be concealed under his pillow, in the sheet, or even under the mattress, but Mr Million would find it.

What he did with those little musical instruments after confiscating them from David I had forgotten until yesterday;

although in prison, when we were kept in by storms or heavy snow, I often occupied myself by trying to recall it. To have broken them, or dropped them through the shutter on to the patio below would have been completely unlike him; Mr Million never broke anything intentionally, and never wasted anything. I could visualize perfectly the half-sorrowing expression with which he drew the tiny pipes out (the face which seemed to float behind his screen was much like my father's) and the way in which he turned and glided from the room. But what became of them?

Yesterday, as I said (this is the sort of thing that gives me confidence), I remembered. He had been talking to me here while I worked, and when he left it seemed to me – as my glance idly followed his smooth motion through the doorway – that something, a sort of flourish I recalled from my earliest days, was missing. I closed my eyes and tried to remember what the appearance had been, eliminating any skepticism, any attempt to guess in advance what I 'must' have seen; and I found that the missing element was a brief flash, the glint of metal, over Mr Million's head.

Once I had established this, I knew that it must have come from a swift upward motion of his arm, like a salute, as he left our room. For an hour or more I could not guess the reason for that gesture, and could only suppose it, whatever it had been, to have been destroyed by time. I tried to recall if the corridor outside our dormitory had, in that really not so distant past, held some object now vanished: a curtain or a windowshade, an appliance to be activated, anything that might account for it. There was nothing

I went into the corridor and examined the floor minutely for marks indicating furniture. I looked for hooks or nails driven into the walls, pushing aside the coarse old tapestries. Craning my neck, I searched the ceiling. Then, after an hour, I looked at the door itself and saw what I had not seen in the thousands of times I had passed through it: that like all the doors in this house, which is very old, it had a massive frame of wooden slabs, and that one of these, forming the lintel, protruded enough from the wall to make a narrow shelf above the door.

I pushed my chair into the hall and stood on the seat. The shelf was thick with dust in which lay forty-seven of my brother's pipes and a wonderful miscellany of other small objects. Objects many of which I recalled, but some of which still fail to summon any flicker of response from the recesses of my mind . . .

The small blue egg of a songbird, speckled with brown. I suppose the bird must have nested in the vine outside our window, and that David or I despoiled the nest only to be robbed ourselves by Mr Million. But I do not recall the incident.

And there is a (broken) puzzle made of the bronzed viscera of some small animals, and – wonderfully evocative – one of those large and fancifully decorated keys, sold annually, which during the year of its currency will admit the possessor to certain rooms of the city library after hours. Mr Million, I suppose, must have confiscated it when, after expiration, he found it doing duty as a toy; but what memories!

My father had his own library, now in my possession; but we were forbidden to go there. I have a dim memory of standing – at how early an age I cannot say – before that huge carved door. Of seeing it swing back, and the crippled monkey on my father's shoulder pressing itself against his hawk face, with the black scarf and scarlet dressing gown beneath and the rows and rows of shabby books and notebooks behind them, and the sick-sweet smell of formaldehyde coming from the laboratory beyond the sliding mirror.

I do not remember what he said or whether it had been I or another who had knocked, but I do recall that after the door had closed, a woman in pink whom I thought very pretty, stooped to bring her face to the level of my own and assured me that my father had written all the books I had just seen, and that I doubted it not at all.

*

My brother and I, as I have said, were forbidden this room; but when we were a little older Mr Million used to take us, about twice a week, on expeditions to the city library. These were very nearly the only times we were allowed to leave the house, and since our tutor disliked curling the jointed length of his metal modules into a hire cart, and no sedan chair would have withstood his weight or contained his bulk, these forays were made on foot.

For a long time this route to the library was the only part of the city I knew. Three blocks down Saltimbanque Street where our house stood, right at the Rue d'Asticot to the slave market and a block beyond that to the library. A child, not knowing what is extraordinary and what commonplace, usually lights midway between the two, finds interest in incidents adults consider

4

beneath notice and calmly accepts the most improbable occurrences. My brother and I were fascinated by the spurious antiques and bad bargains of the Rue d'Asticot, but often bored when Mr Million insisted on stopping for an hour at the slave market.

It was not a large one, Port-Mimizon not being a center of the trade, and the auctioneers and their merchandise were frequently on a most friendly basis – having met several times previously as a succession of owners discovered the same fault. Mr Million never bid, but watched the bidding, motionless, while we kicked our heels and munched the fried bread he had bought at a stall for us. There were sedan chairmen, their legs knotted with muscle, and simpering bath attendants; fighting slaves in chains, with eyes dulled by drugs or blazing with imbecile ferocity; cooks, house servants, a hundred others – yet David and I used to beg to be allowed to proceed alone to the library.

This library was a wastefully large building which had held government offices in the French-speaking days. The park in which it had once stood had died of petty corruption, and the library now rose from a clutter of shops and tenements. A narrow thoroughfare led to the main doors, and once we were inside, the squalor of the neighbourhood vanished, replaced by a kind of peeling grandeur. The main desk was directly beneath the dome, and this dome, drawing up with it a spiraling walkaway lined with the library's main collection, floated five hundred feet in the air: a stony sky whose least chip falling might kill one of the librarians on the spot.

While Mr Million browsed his way majestically up the helix, David and I raced ahead until we were several full turns in advance and could do what we liked. When I was still quite young it would often occur to me that, since my father had written (on the testimony of the lady in pink) a roomful of books, some of them should be here; and I would climb resolutely until I had almost reached the dome, and there rummage. Because the librarians were very lax about reshelving, there seemed always a possibility of finding what I had failed to find before. The shelves towered far above my head, but when I felt myself unobserved I climbed them like ladders, stepping on books when there was no room on the shelves themselves for the square toes of my small brown shoes, and occasionally kicking books to the floor where they remained until our next visit and beyond, evidence of the staff's reluctance to climb that long, coiled slope.

The upper shelves were, if anything, in worse disorder than those more conveniently located, and one glorious day when I attained the highest of all I found occupying that lofty, dusty position (besides a misplaced astronautics text, *The Mile-Long Spaceship*, by some German) only a lorn copy of *Monday or Tuesday* leaning against a book about the assassination of Trotsky, and a crumbling volume of Vernor Vinge's short stories that owed its presence there, or so I suspect, to some long-dead librarian's mistaking the faded *V. Vinge* on the spine for 'Winge'.

I never found any books of my father's, but I did not regret the long climbs to the top of the dome. If David had come with me, we raced up together, up and down the sloping floor – or peered over the rail at Mr Million's slow progress while we debated the feasibility of putting an end to him with one cast of some ponderous work. If David preferred to pursue interests of his own farther down I ascended to the very top where the cap of the dome curved right over my head; and there, from a rusted iron catwalk not much wider than one of the shelves I had been climbing (and I suspect not nearly so strong), opened in turn each of a circle of tiny piercings – piercings in a wall of iron, but so shallow a wall that when I had slid the corroded cover plates out of the way I could thrust my head through and feel myself truly outside, with the wind and the circling birds and the lime-spotted expanse of the dome curving away beneath me.

To the west, since it was taller than the surrounding houses and marked by the orange trees on the roof, I could make out our house. To the south, the masts of the ships in the harbor, and in clear weather – if it was the right time of day – the whitecaps of the tidal race Sainte Anne drew between the peninsulas called First Finger and Thumb. (And once, as I very well recall, while looking south I saw the great geyser of sunlit water when a star-crosser splashed down.) To east and north spread the city proper, the citadel and the grand market and the forests and mountains beyond.

But sooner or later, whether David had accompanied me or gone off on his own, Mr Million summoned us. Then we were forced to go with him to one of the wings to visit this or that science collection. This meant books for lessons. My father insisted that we learn biology, anatomy, and chemistry thoroughly, and under Mr Million's tutelage, learn them we did – he never considering a subject mastered until we could discuss every topic mentioned in every book catalogued under the heading. The life sciences were my own favorites, but David preferred languages, literature, and law; for we got a smattering of these as well as anthropology, cybernetics, and psychology.

6

When he had selected the books that would form our study for the next few days and urged us to choose more for ourselves, Mr Million would retire with us to some quiet corner of one of the science reading rooms, where there were chairs and a table and room sufficient for him to curl the jointed length of his body or align it against a wall or bookcase in a way that left the aisles clear. To designate the formal beginning of our class he used to begin by calling roll, my own name always coming first.

I would say, 'Here,' to show that he had my attention.

'And David.'

'Here.' (David has an illustrated *Tales From the Odyssey* open on his lap where Mr Million cannot see it, but he looks at Mr Million with bright, feigned interest. Sunshine slants down to the table from a high window, and shows the air as warm with dust.)

'I wonder if either of you noticed the stone implements in the room through which we passed a few moments ago?'

We nod, each hoping the other will speak.

'Were they made on Earth, or here on our own planet?'

This is a trick question, but an easy one. David says, 'Neither one. They're plastic.' And we giggle.

Mr Million says patiently, 'Yes, they're plastic reproductions, but from where did the originals come?' His face, so similar to my father's, but which I thought of at this time as belonging only to him, so that it seemed a frightening reversal of nature to see it on a living man instead of his screen, was neither interested, nor angry, nor bored; but coolly remote.

David answers, 'From Sainte Anne.' Sainte Anne is the sister planet to our own, revolving with us about a common center as we swing around the sun. 'The sign said so, and the aborigines made them – there weren't any abos here.'

Mr Million nods, and turns his impalpable face toward me. 'Do you feel these stone implements occupied a central place in the lives of their makers? Say no.'

'No.'

'Why not?'

I think frantically, not helped by David, who is kicking my shins under the table. A glimmering comes.

'Talk. Answer at once.'

'It's obvious, isn't it?' (Always a good thing to say when you're not even sure 'it' is even possible.) 'In the first place, they can't have been very good tools, so why would the abos have relied on them? You might say they needed those obsidian arrowheads and bone fishhooks for getting food, but that's not true. They could poison the water with the juices of certain plants, and for primitive people the most effective way to fish is probably with weirs, or with nets of rawhide or vegetable fiber. Just the same way, trapping or driving animals with fire would be more effective than hunting; and anyway stone tools wouldn't be needed at all for gathering berries and the shoots of edible plants and things like that, which were probably their most important foods – those stone things got in the glass case here because the snares and nets rotted away and they're all that's left, so the people that make their living that way pretend they were important.'

'Good. David? Be original, please. Don't repeat what you've just heard.'

David looks up from his book, his blue eyes scornful of both of us. 'If you could have asked them, they would have told you that their magic and their religion, the songs they sang and the traditions of their people were what were important. They killed their sacrificial animals with flails of seashells that cut like razors, and they didn't let their men father children until they had had stood enough fire to cripple them for life. They mated with trees and drowned the children to honor their rivers. That was what was important.'

With no neck, Mr Million's face nodded. 'Now we will debate the humanity of those aborigines. David negative and first.'

(I kick him, but he has pulled his hard, freckled legs up beneath him, or hidden them behind the legs of his chair, which is cheating.) 'Humanity,' he says in his most objectionable voice, 'in the history of human thought implies descent from what we may conveniently call *Adam*; that is, the original Terrestrial stock, and if the two of you don't see that, you're idiots.'

I wait for him to continue, but he is finished. To give myself time to think, I say, 'Mr Million, it's not fair to let him call me names in a debate. Tell him that's not debating, it's *fighting*, isn't it?'

Mr Million says, 'No personalities, David.' (David is already peeking at Polyphemus the Cyclops and Odysseus, hoping I'll go on for a long time. I feel challenged and decide to do so.)

I begin, 'The argument which holds descent from Terrestrial stock pivotal is neither valid nor conclusive. Not conclusive because it is distinctly possible that the aborigines of Sainte Anne were descendants of some earlier wave of human expansion – one, perhaps, even predating *The Homeric Greeks*.'

Mr Million says mildly, 'I would confine myself to arguments of higher probability if I were you.'

I nevertheless gloss upon the Etruscans, Atlantis, and the tenacity and expansionist tendencies of a hypothetical technological culture occupying Gondwanaland. When I have finished Mr Million says, 'Now reverse. David, affirmative without repeating.'

My brother, of course, has been looking at his book instead of listening, and I kick him with enthusiasm, expecting him to be stuck; but he says, 'The abos are human because they're all dead.'

'Explain.'

'If they were alive it would be dangerous to let them be human because they'd ask for things, but with them dead it makes it more interesting if they were, and the settlers killed them all.'

And so it goes. The spot of sunlight travels across the black-streaked red of the tabletop – traveled across it a hundred times. We would leave through one of the side doors and walk through a neglected areaway between two wings. There would be empty bottles there and wind-scattered papers of all kinds, and once a dead man in bright rags over whose legs we boys skipped while Mr Million rolled silently around him. As we left the areaway for a narrow street, the bugles of the garrison at the citadel (sounding so far away) would call the troopers to their evening mess. In the Rue d'Asticot the lamplighter would be at work, and the shops shut behind their iron grilles. The sidewalks magically clear of old furniture would seem broad and bare.

Our own Saltimbanque Street would be very different, with the first revelers arriving. White-haired, hearty men guiding very young men and boys, men and boys handsome and muscular but a shade overfed; young men who made diffident jokes and smiled with excellent teeth at them. These were always the early ones, and when I was a little older I sometimes wondered if they were early only because the white-haired men wished to have their pleasure and yet a good night's sleep as well, or if it were because they knew the young men they were introducing to my father's establishment would be drowsy and irritable after midnight, like children who have been kept up too late.

Because Mr Million did not want us to use the alleys after dark we came in the front entrance with the white-haired men and their nephews and sons. There was a garden there, not much bigger than a small room and recessed into the windowless front of the house. In it were beds of ferns the size of graves; a little fountain whose water fell upon rods of glass to make a continual tinkling, and which had to be protected from the street boys; and,

9

with his feet firmly planted, indeed almost buried in moss, an iron statue of a dog with three heads.

It was this statue, I suppose, that gave our house its popular name of *Maison du Chien*, though there may have been a reference to our surname as well. The three heads were sleekly powerful with pointed muzzles and ears. One was snarling and one, the center head, regarded the world of garden and street with a look of tolerant interest. The third, the one nearest the brick path that led to our door, was – there is no other term for it – frankly grinning; and it was the custom for my father's patrons to pat this head between the ears as they came up the path. Their fingers had polished the spot to the consistency of black glass.

*

This, then, was my world at seven of our world's long years, and perhaps for half a year beyond. Most of my days were spent in the little classroom over which Mr Million presided, and my evenings in the dormitory where David and I played and fought in total silence. They were varied by the trips to the library I have described or, very rarely, elsewhere. I pushed aside the leaves of the silver trumpet vine occasionally to watch the girls and their benefactors in the court below, or heard their talk drifting down from the roof garden, but the things they did and talked of were of no great interest to me. I knew that the tall, hatchet-faced man who ruled our house and was called 'Maître' by the girls and servants was my father. I had known for as long as I could remember that there was somewhere a fearsome woman – the servants were in terror of her – called 'Madame,' but that she was neither my mother nor David's, nor my father's wife.

That life and my childhood, or at least my infancy, ended one evening after David and I, worn out with wrestling and silent arguments, had gone to sleep. Someone shook me by the shoulder and called me, and it was not Mr Million but one of the servants, a hunched little man in a shabby red jacket. 'He wants you,' this summoner informed me. 'Get up.'

I did, and he saw that I was wearing nightclothes. This I think had not been covered in his instructions, and for a moment during which I stood and yawned, he debated with himself. 'Get dressed,' he said at last. 'Comb your hair.'

I obeyed, putting on the black velvet trousers I had worn the day before, but (guided by some instinct) a new clean shirt. The room to which he then conducted me (through tortuous corridors now emptied of the last patrons; and others, musty, filthy with the excrement of rats, to which patrons were never admitted) was my father's library – the room with the great carved door before which I had received the whispered confidences of the woman in pink. I had never been inside it, but when my guide rapped discreetly on the door it swung back, and I found myself within, almost before I realized what had happened.

My father, who had opened the door, closed it behind me; and leaving me standing where I was, walked to the most distant end of that long room and threw himself down in a huge chair. He was wearing the red dressing gown and black scarf in which I had most often seen him, and his long, sparse hair was brushed straight back. He stared at me, and I remember that my lip trembled as I tried to keep from breaking into sobs.

'Well,' he said, after we had looked at one another for a long time, 'and there you are. What am I going to call you?'

I told him my name, but he shook his head. 'Not that. You must have another name for me – a private name. You may choose it yourself if you like.'

I said nothing. It seemed to me quite impossible that I should have any name other than the two words which were, in some mystic sense I only respected without understanding, *my name*.

'I'll choose for you then,' my father said. 'You are Number Five. Come here, Number Five.'

I came, and when I was standing in front of him, he told me, 'Now we are going to play a game. I am going to show you some pictures, do you understand? And all the time you are watching them, you must talk. Talk about the pictures. If you talk you win, but if you stop, even for just a second, I do. Understand?'

I said I did.

'Good. I know you're a bright boy. As a matter of fact, Mr Million has sent me all the examinations he has given you and the tapes he makes when he talks with you. Did you know that? Did you ever wonder what he did with them?'

I said, 'I thought he threw them away,' and my father, I noticed, leaned forward as I spoke, a circumstance I found flattering at the time.

'No, I have them here.' He pressed a switch. 'Now remember, you must not stop talking.'

But for the first few moments I was much too interested to talk.

There had appeared in the room, as though by magic, a boy considerably younger than I, and a painted wooden soldier almost

11

as large as I was myself, which when I reached out to touch them proved as insubstantial as air. 'Say something,' my father said. 'What are you thinking about, Number Five?'

I was thinking about the soldier, of course, and so was the younger boy, who appeared to be about three. He toddled through my arm like mist and attempted to knock it over.

They were holographs – three-dimensional images formed by the interference of two wave fronts of light – things which had seemed very dull when I had seen them illustrated by flat pictures of chessmen in my physics book; but it was some time before I connected those chessmen with the phantoms who walked in my father's library at night. All this time my father was saying, 'Talk! Say something! What do you think the little boy is feeling?'

'Well, the little boy likes the big soldier, but he wants to knock him down if he can, because the soldier's only a toy, really, but it's bigger than he is . . . ' And so I talked, and for a long time, hours I suppose, continued. The scene changed and changed again. The giant soldier was replaced by a pony, a rabbit, a meal of soup and crackers. But the three-year-old boy remained the central figure. When the hunched man in the shabby coat came again, yawning, to take me back to my bed, my voice had worn to a husky whisper and my throat ached. In my dreams that night I saw the little boy scampering from one activity to another, his personality in some way confused with my own and my father's so that I was both at once observer, observed, and a third presence observing both.

The next night I fell asleep almost at the moment Mr Million sent us up to bed, retaining consciousness only long enough to congratulate myself on doing so. I woke when the hunched man entered the room, but it was not me whom he roused from the sheets but David. Quietly, pretending I still slept (for it had occurred to me, and seemed quite reasonable at the time, that if he were to see I was awake he might take both of us), I watched as my brother dressed and struggled to impart some sort of order to his tangle of fair hair. When he returned I was sound asleep, and had no opportunity to question him until Mr Million left us alone, as he sometimes did, to eat our breakfast. I had told him my own experiences as a matter of course, and what he had to tell me was simply that he had had an evening very similar to mine. He had seen holographic pictures, and apparently the same pictures: the wooden soldier, the pony. He had been forced to talk constantly, as Mr Million had so often made us do in debates and verbal examinations. The only way in which his interview with our father had differed from mine, as nearly as I could determine, appeared when I asked him by what name he had been called.

He looked at me blankly, a piece of toast half-raised to his mouth.

I asked again, 'What name did he call you by when he talked to you?'

'He called me David. What did you think?'

With the beginning of these interviews the pattern of my life changed, the adjustments I assumed to be temporary becoming imperceptibly permanent, settling into a new shape of which neither David nor I were consciously aware. Our games and stories after bedtime stopped, and David less and less often made his panpipes of the silver trumpet vine. Mr Million allowed us to sleep later and we were in some subtle way acknowledged to be more adult. At about this time too, he began to take us to a park where there was an archery range and provision for various games. This little park, which was not far from our house, was bordered on one side by a canal. And there, while David shot arrows at a goose stuffed with straw or played tennis, I often sat staring at the quiet, only slightly dirty water; or waiting for one of the white ships – great ships with bows as sharp as the scalpel-bills of kingfishers and four, five, or even seven masts – which were, infrequently, towed up from the harbor by ten or twelve spans of oxen.

*

In the summer of my eleventh or twelfth year – I think the twelfth – we were permitted for the first time to stay after sundown in the park, sitting on the greasy, sloped margin of the canal to watch a fireworks display. The first preliminary flight of rockets had no sooner exhausted itself half a mile above the city than David became ill. He rushed to the water and vomited, plunging his hands half up to the elbows in muck while the red and white stars burned in glory above him. Mr Million took him up in his arms, and when poor David had emptied himself we hurried home.

His disease proved not much more lasting than the tainted sandwich that had occasioned it, but while our tutor was putting him to bed I decided not to be cheated of the remainder of the

13

display, parts of which I had glimpsed between the intervening houses as we made our way home; I was forbidden the roof after dark, but I knew very well where the nearest stair was. The thrill I felt in penetrating that prohibited world of leaf and shadow while fireflowers of purple and gold and blazing scarlet overtopped it affected me like the aftermath of a fever, leaving me short of breath, shaking, and cold in the midst of summer.

There were a great many more people on the roof than I had anticipated, the men without cloaks, hats or sticks (all of which they had left in my father's checkrooms), and the girls, my father's employees, in costumes that displayed their rouged breasts in enclosures of twisted wire like birdcages or gave them the appearance of great height (dissolved only when someone stood very close to them), or gowns whose skirts reflected their wearers' faces and busts as still water does the trees standing near it, so that they appeared, in the intermittent colored flashes, like the queens of strange suits in a tarot deck.

I was seen, of course, since I was much too excited to conceal myself effectively; but no one ordered me back, and I suppose they assumed I had been permitted to come up to see the fireworks.

These continued for a long time. I remember one patron, a heavy, square-faced, stupid-looking man who seemed to be someone of importance, who was so eager to enjoy the company of his protégée – who did not want to go inside until the display was over – that, since he insisted on privacy, twenty or thirty bushes and small trees had to be rearranged on the parterre to make a little grove around them. I helped the waiters carry some of the smaller tubs and pots, and managed to duck into the structure as it was completed. Here I could still watch the exploding rockets and 'aerial bombs' through the branches, and at the same time the patron and his *nymphe du bois*, who was watching them a good deal more intently than I.

My motive, as well as I can remember, was not prurience but simple curiosity. I was at that age when we are passionately interested, but the passion is one of science. Mine was nearly satisfied when I was grasped by the shirt by someone behind me and drawn out of the shrubbery.

When I was clear of the leaves I was released, and I turned expecting to see Mr Million, but it was not. My captor was a little gray-haired woman in a black dress whose skirt, as I noticed even at the time, fell straight from her waist to the ground. I suppose I bowed to her, since she was clearly no servant, but she

14

returned no salutation at all, staring intently into my face in a way that made me think she could see as well in the intervals between the bursting glories as by their light. At last, in what must have been the finale of the display, a great rocket rose screaming on a river of flame, and for an instant she consented to look up. Then, when it had exploded in a mauve orchid of unbelievable size and brilliance, this formidable little woman grabbed me again and led me firmly toward the stairs.

While we were on the level stone pavement of the roof garden she did not, as nearly as I could see, walk at all, but rather seemed to glide across the surface like an onyx chessman on a polished board; and that, in spite of all that has happened since, is the way I still remember her: as the Black Queen, a chess queen neither sinister nor beneficient, and Black only as distinguished from some White Queen I was never fated to encounter.

When we reached the stairs, however, this smooth gliding became a fluid bobbing that brought two inches or more of the hem of her black skirt into contact with each step, as if her torso were descending each as a small boat might a rapids – now rushing, now pausing, now almost backing in the crosscurrents.

She steadied herself on these steps by holding on to me and grasping the arm of a maid who had been waiting for us at the stairhead and assisted her from the other side. I had supposed, while we were crossing the roof garden, that her gliding motion had been the result, merely, of a marvelously controlled walk and good posture, but I now understood her to be in some way handicapped; and I had the impression that without the help the maid and I gave her she might have fallen headfirst.

Once we had reached the bottom of the steps her smooth progress was resumed. She dismissed the maid with a nod and led me down the corridor in the direction opposite to that in which our dormitory and classroom lay until we reached a stairwell far toward the back of the house, a corkscrew, seldom-used flight, very steep, with only a low iron banister between the steps and a six-story drop into the cellars. Here she released me and told me crisply to go down. I went down several steps, then turned to see if she was having any difficulty.

She was not, but neither was she using the stairs. With her long skirt hanging as straight as a curtain she was floating suspended, watching me, in the center of the stairwell. I was so startled I stopped, which made her jerk her head angrily, then began to run. As I fled around and around the spiral she revolved with me, turning toward me always a face extraordinarily like my father's,

15

one hand always on the railing. When we had descended to the second floor she swooped down and caught me as easily as a cat takes charge of an errant kitten, and led me through rooms and passages where I had never been permitted to go until I was as confused as I might have been in a strange building. At last we stopped before a door in no way different from any other. She opened it with an old-fashioned brass key with an edge like a saw and motioned for me to go in.

The room was brightly lit, and I was able to see clearly what I had only sensed on the roof and in the corridors: that the hem of her skirt hung two inches above the floor no matter how she moved, and that there was nothing between the hem and the floor at all. She waved me to a little footstool covered with needlepoint and said, 'Sit down,' and when I had done so, glided across to a wing-backed rocker and sat facing me. After a moment she asked, 'What's your name?' and when I told her she cocked an eyebrow at me and started the chair in motion by pushing gently with her fingers at a floor lamp that stood beside it. After a long time she said, 'And what does he call you?'

'He?' I was stupid, I suppose, with lack of sleep.

She pursed her lips. 'My brother.'

I relaxed a little. 'Oh,' I said, 'you're my aunt then. I thought you looked like my father. He calls me Number Five.'

For a moment she continued to stare, the corners of her mouth drawing down as my father's often did. Then she said, 'That number's either far too low or too high. Living, there are he and I, and I suppose he's counting the simulator. Have you a sister, Number Five?'

Mr Million had been having us read *David Copperfield*, and when she said this she reminded me so strikingly and unexpectedly of Aunt Betsey Trotwood that I shouted with laughter.

'There's nothing absurd about it. Your father had a sister – why shouldn't you? You have none?'

'No ma'am, but I have a brother. His name is David.'

'Call me Aunt Jeannine. Does David look like you, Number Five?'

I shook my head. 'His hair is curly and blond instead of like mine. Maybe he looks a little like me, but not a lot.'

'I suppose,' my aunt said under her breath, 'he used one of my girls.'

'Ma'am?'

'Do you know who David's mother was, Number Five?'

'We're brothers, so I guess she would be the same as mine, but Mr Million says she went away a long time ago.'

16

'Not the same as yours,' my aunt said. 'No. I could show you a picture of your own. Would you like to see it?' She rang a bell, and a maid came curtsying from some room beyond the one in which we sat; my aunt whispered to her and she went out again. When my aunt turned back to me she asked, 'And what do you do all day, Number Five, besides run up to the roof when you shouldn't? Are you taught?'

I told her about my experiments (I was stimulating unfertilized frogs' eggs to a sexual development and then doubling the chromosomes by a chemical treatment so that a further asexual generation could be produced) and the dissections Mr Million was by then encouraging me to do, and while I talked, happened to drop some remark about how interesting it would be to perform a biopsy on one of the aborigines of Sainte Anne if any were still in existence, since the first explorers' descriptions differed so widely and some pioneers there had claimed the abos could change their shapes.

'Ah,' my aunt said, 'you know about them. Let me test you, Number Five. What is Veil's Hypothesis?'

We had learned that several years before, so I said, 'Veil's Hypothesis supposes the abos to have possessed the ability to mimic mankind perfectly. Veil thought that when the ships came from Earth the abos killed everyone and took their places and the ships, so they're not dead at all, we are.'

'You mean the Earth people are,' my aunt said. 'The human beings.'

'Ma'am?'

'If Veil was correct, then you and I are abos from Sainte Anne, at least in origin; which I suppose is what you meant. Do you think he was right?'

'I don't think it makes any difference. He said the imitation would have to be perfect, and if it is, they're the same as we were anyway.' I thought I was being clever, but my aunt smiled, rocking more vigorously. It was very warm in the close, bright little room.

'Number Five, you're too young for semantics, and I'm afraid you've been led astray by that word *perfectly*. Dr Veil, I'm certain, meant to use it loosely rather than as precisely as you seem to think. The imitation could hardly have been exact, since human beings don't possess that talent and to imitate them *perfectly* the abos would have to lose it.'

'Couldn't they?'

'My dear child, abilities of every sort must evolve. And when they do they must be utilized or they atrophy. If the abos had been able to mimic so well as to lose the power to do so, that would have been the end of them, and no doubt it would have come long before the first ships reached them. Of course there's not the slightest evidence they could do anything of the sort. They simply died off before they could be thoroughly studied, and Veil, who wants a dramatic explanation for the cruelty and irrationality he sees around him, has hung fifty pounds of theory on nothing.'

This last remark, especially as my aunt seemed so friendly, appeared to me to offer an ideal opportunity for a question about her remarkable means of locomotion, but as I was about to frame it we were interrupted, almost simultaneously, from two directions. The maid returned carrying a large book bound in tooled leather, and she had no sooner handed it to my aunt than there was a tap at the door. My aunt said absently, 'Get that,' and since the remark might as easily have been addressed to me as to the maid I satisfied my curiosity in another form by racing her to answer the knock.

Two of my father's demimondaines were waiting in the hall, costumed and painted until they seemed more alien than any abos, stately as Lombardy poplars and inhuman as specters, with green and yellow eyes made to look the size of eggs and inflated breasts pushed almost shoulder high; and though they maintained an inculcated composure I was pleasantly aware that they were startled to find me in the doorway. I bowed them in, but as the maid closed the door behind them my aunt said absently, 'In a moment, girls. I want to show the boy here something, then he's going to leave.'

The 'something' was a photograph utilizing, as I supposed, some novelty technique which washed away all color save a light brown. It was small, and from its general appearance and crumbling edges very old. It showed a girl of twenty-five or so, thin and as nearly as I could judge rather tall, standing beside a stocky young man on a paved walkway and holding a baby. The walkway ran along the front of a remarkable house, a very long wooden house only a story in height, with a porch or veranda that changed its architectural style every twenty or thirty feet so as to give almost the impression of a number of exceedingly narrow houses constructed with their side walls in contact. I mention this detail, which I hardly noticed at the time, because I have so often since my release from prison tried to find some trace of this house. When I was first shown the picture I was much more in-

18

terested in the girl's face, and the baby's. The latter was in fact scarcely visible, he being nearly smothered in white wool blankets. The girl had large features and a brilliant smile which held a suggestion of that rarely seen charm which is at once careless, poetic, and sly. Gypsy, was my first thought, but her complexion was surely too fair for that. Since on this world we are all descended from a relatively small group of colonists we are rather a uniform population, but my studies had given me some familiarity with the original Terrestrial races, and my second guess, almost a certainty, was Celtic. 'Wales,' I said aloud. 'Or Scotland. Or Ireland.'

'What?' my aunt said. One of the girls giggled; they were seated on the divan now, their long, gleaming legs crossed before them like the varnished staffs of flags.

'It doesn't matter.'

My aunt looked at me acutely and said, 'You're right. I'll send for you and we'll talk about this when we've both more leisure. For the present my maid will take you to your room.'

I remember nothing of the long walk the maid and I must have had back to the dormitory, or what excuses I gave Mr Million for my unauthorized absence. Whatever they were I suppose he penetrated them, or discovered the truth by questioning the servants, because no summons to return to my aunt's apartment came, although I expected it daily for weeks afterward.

That night – I am reasonably sure it was the same night – I dreamed of the abos of Sainte Anne, abos dancing with plumes of fresh grass on their heads and arms and ankles, abos shaking their shields of woven rushes and their nephrite-tipped spears until the motion affected my bed and became, in shabby red cloth, the arms of my father's valet come to summon me, as he did almost every night, to his library.

That night, and this time I am quite certain it was the same night, that is, the night I first dreamed of the abos, the pattern of my hours with him, which had come over the four of five years past to have a predictable sequence of conversation, holographs, free association, and dismissal – a sequence I had come to think inalterable – changed. Following the preliminary talk designed, I feel sure, to put me at ease (at which it failed, as it always did), I was told to roll up a sleeve and lie down upon an old examining table in a corner of the room. My father then made me look at the wall, which meant at the shelves heaped with ragged notebooks. I felt a needle being thrust into the inner part of my arm but my head was held down and my face turned away, so that I could neither sit up nor look at what he was doing. Then the needle was withdrawn and I was told to lie quietly.

After what seemed a very long time, during which my father occasionally spread my eyelids to look at my eyes or took my pulse, someone in a distant part of the room began to tell a very long and confusingly involved story. My father made notes of what was said, and occasionally stopped to ask questions I found it unnecessary to answer, since the storyteller did it for me.

The drug he had given me did not, as I had imagined it would, lessen its hold on me as the hours passed. Instead it seemed to carry me progressively further from reality and the mode of consciousness best suited to preserving the individuality of thought. The peeling leather of the examination table vanished under me, and was now the deck of a ship, now the wing of a dove beating far above the world; and whether the voice I heard reciting was my own or my father's I no longer cared. It was pitched sometimes higher, sometimes lower, but then I felt myself at times to be speaking from the depths of a chest larger than my own, and his voice, identified as such by the soft rustling of the pages of his notebook, might seem the high, treble cries of the racing children in the streets as I heard them in summer when I thrust my head through the windows at the base of the library dome.

*

With that night my life changed again. The drugs – for there seemed to be several, and although the effect I have described was the usual one there were also times when I found it impossible to lie still, but ran up and down for hours as I talked, or sank into blissful or indescribably frightening dreams – affected my health. I often wakened in the morning with a headache that kept me in agony all day, and I became subject to periods of extreme nervousness and apprehensiveness. Most frightening of all, whole sections of days sometimes disappeared, so that I found myself awake and dressed, reading, walking, and even talking, with no memory at all of anything that had happened since I had lain muttering to the ceiling in my father's library the night before.

The lessons I had had with David did not cease, but in some sense Mr Million's role and mine were now reversed. It was I, now, who insisted on holding our classes when they were held at all; and it was I who chose the subject matter and, in most cases, questioned David and Mr Million about it. But often when they were at the library or the park I remained in bed reading, and I believe there were many times when I read and studied from the time I found myself conscious in my bed until my father's valet came for me again.

David's interviews with our father, I should note here, suffered the same changes as my own and at the same time; but since they were less frequent – and they became less and less frequent as the hundred days of summer wore away to autumn and at last to the long winter – and he seemed on the whole to have less adverse reactions to the drugs, the effect on him was not nearly as great.

If at any single time, it was during this winter that I came to the end of childhood. My new ill health forced me away from childish activities, and encouraged the experiments I was carrying out on small animals, and my dissections of the bodies Mr Million supplied in an unending stream of open mouths and staring eyes. Too, I studied or read, as I have said, for hours on end; or simply lay with my hands behind my head while I struggled to recall, perhaps for whole days together, the narratives I had heard myself give my father. Neither David nor I could ever remember enough even to build a coherent theory of the nature of the questions asked us, but I have still certain scenes fixed in my memory which I am sure I have never beheld in fact, and I believe these are my visualizations of suggestions whispered while I bobbed and dove through those altered states of consciousness.

My aunt, who had previously been so remote, now spoke to me in the corridors and even visited our room. I learned that she controlled the interior arrangements of our house, and through her I was able to have a small laboratory of my own set up in the same wing. But I spent the winter, as I have described, mostly at my enamel dissecting table or in bed. The white snow drifted half up the glass of the window, clinging to the bare stems of the silver trumpet vine. My father's patrons, on the rare occasions I saw them, came in with wet boots, the snow on their shoulders and their hats, puffing and red-faced as they beat their coats in the foyer. The orange trees were gone, the roof garden no longer used, and the courtyard under our window only late at night when half a dozen patrons and their protégées, whooping with hilarity and wine, fought with snowballs – an activity invariably concluded by stripping the girls and tumbling them naked in the snow.

*

Spring surprised me, as she always does those of us who remain most of our lives indoors. One day, while I still thought, if I thought about the weather at all, in terms of winter, David threw open the window and insisted that I go with him into the park – and it was April. Mr Million went with us, and I remember that as we stepped out the front door into the little garden that opened into the street, a garden I had last seen banked with the snow shoveled from the path, but which was now bright with early bulbs and the chiming of the fountain, David tapped the iron dog on its grinning muzzle and recited: 'And thence the dog/With fourfold head brought to these realms of light.'

I made some trivial remark about his having miscounted.

'Oh, no. Old Cerberus has four heads, don't you know that? The fourth's her maidenhead, and she's such a bitch no dog can take it from her.' Even Mr Million chuckled, but I thought afterward, looking at David's ruddy good health and the foreshadowing of manhood already apparent in the set of his shoulders, that if, as I had always thought of them, the three heads represented Maître, Madame, and Mr Million, that is, my father, my aunt (David's *maidenhead*, I suppose), and my tutor, then indeed a fourth would have to be welded in place soon for David himself.

The park must have been a paradise for him, but in my poor health I found it bleak enough and spent most of the morning huddled on a bench, watching David play squash. Toward noon I was joined, not on my own bench, but on another close enough for there to be a feeling of proximity, by a dark-haired girl with one ankle in a cast. She was brought there, on crutches, by a sort of nurse or governess who seated herself, I felt sure deliberately, between the girl and me. This unpleasant woman was, however, too straight-backed for her chaperonage to succeed completely. She sat on the edge of the bench, while the girl, with her injured leg thrust out before her, slumped back and thus gave me a good view of her profile, which was beautiful; and occasionally, when she turned to make some remark to the creature with her, I could study her full face – carmine lips and violet eyes, a round rather than an oval face, with a broad point of black hair dividing the forehead; archly delicate black eyebrows and long, curling lashes. When a vendor, an old woman, came selling Cantonese egg rolls (longer than your hand, and still so hot from the boiling fat that they needed to be eaten with great caution as though they were in some way alive), I made her my messenger and, as well as buying one for myself, sent her with two scalding delicacies to the girl and her attendant monster.

22

The monster, of course, refused; the girl, I was charmed to see, pleaded; her huge eyes and bright cheeks eloquently proclaiming arguments I was unfortunately just too far away to hear but could follow in pantomime: it would be a gratuitous insult to a blameless stranger to refuse; she was hungry and had intended to buy an egg roll in any event – how thriftless to object when what she had wished for was tendered free! The vending woman, who clearly delighted in her role as go-between, announced herself on the point of weeping at the thought of being forced to refund my gold (actually a bill of small denomination nearly as greasy as the paper in which her wares were wrapped, and considerably dirtier), and eventually their voices grew loud enough for me to hear the girl's, which was a clear and very pleasing contralto. In the end, of course, they accepted; the monster conceded me a frigid nod, and the girl winked at me behind her back.

Half an hour later when David and Mr Million, who had been watching him from the edge of the court, asked if I wanted lunch, I told them I did, thinking that when we returned I could take a seat closer to the girl without being brazen about it. We ate, I (at least so I fear) very impatiently, in a clean little café close to the flower market; but when we came back to the park the girl and her governess were gone.

We returned to the house, and about an hour afterward my father sent for me. I went with some trepidation, since it was much earlier than was customary for our interview – before the first patrons had arrived, in fact, while I usually saw him only after the last had gone. I need not have feared. He began by asking about my health, and when I said it seemed better than it had been during most of the winter he began, in a self-conscious and even pompous way, as different from his usual fatigued incisiveness as could be imagined, to talk about his business and the need a young man had to prepare himself to earn a living. He said, 'You are a scientific scholar, I believe.'

I said I hoped I was in a small way, and braced myself for the usual attack upon the uselessness of studying chemistry or biophysics on a world like ours where the industrial base was so small, of no help at the civil service examinations, does not even prepare one for trade, and so on. He said instead, 'I'm glad to hear it. To be frank, I asked Mr Million to encourage you in that as much as he could. He would have done it anyway I'm sure; he did with me. These studies will not only be of great satisfaction to you, but will . . . ' he paused, cleared his throat, and massaged his face and scalp with his hands, 'be valuable in all sorts

of ways. And they are, as you might say, a family tradition
I said, and indeed felt, that I was very happy to hear that.

'Have you seen my lab? Behind the big mirror there?'

I hadn't, though I had known that such a suite of rooms ex
isted beyond the sliding mirror in the library, and the servan
occasionally spoke of his 'dispensary' where he compounde
doses for them, examined monthly the girls we employed, an
occasionally prescribed treatment for 'friends' of patrons, me
recklessly imprudent who had failed (as the wise patrons had no
to confine their custom to our establishment exclusively. I tol
him I should very much like to see it.

He smiled. 'But we are wandering from our topic. Science is c
great value; but you will find, as I have, that it consumes mor
money than it produces. You will want apparatus and books an
many other things, as well as a livelihood for yourself. We have
not unprofitable business here, and though I hope to live a lon
time – thanks in part to science – you are the heir, and it will b
yours in the end ...'

(So I was older than David!)

' ... every phase of what we do. None of them, believe me, ar
unimportant.'

I had been so surprised, and in fact elated, by my discovery tha
I had missed a part of what he said. I nodded, which seemed safe

'Good. I want you to begin by answering the front door. On
of the maids has been doing it, and for the first month or so she'
stay with you, since there's more to be learned there than yo
think. I'll tell Mr Million, and he can make the arrangements.'

I thanked him, and he indicated that the interview was over b
opening the door of the library. I could hardly believe, as I wer
out, that he was the same man who devoured my life in the earl
hours of almost every morning.

*

I did not connect this sudden elevation in status with the even
in the park. I now realize that Mr Million who has, quite literally
eyes in the back of his head must have reported to my father tha
I had reached the age at which desires in childhood subliminall
fastened to parental figures begin, half consciously, to grop
beyond the family.

In any event that same evening I took up my new duties and
became what Mr Million called the 'greeter' and David (ex

24

plaining that the original sense of the word was related to *portal*) the 'porter', of our house – thus assuming in a practical way the functions symbolically executed by the iron dog in our front garden. The maid who had previously carried them out, a girl named Nerissa who had been selected because she was not only one of the prettiest but one of the tallest and strongest of the maids as well, a large-boned, long-faced, smiling girl with shoulders broader than most men's, remained, as my father had promised, to help. Our duties were not onerous, since my father's patrons were all men of some position and wealth, not given to brawling or loud arguments except under unusual circumstances of intoxication; and for the most part they had visited our house already dozens, and in a few cases even hundreds of times. We called them by nicknames that were used only here (of which Nerissa informed me *sotto voce* as they came up the walk), hung up their coats, and directed them – or if necessary conducted them – to the various parts of the establishment. Nerissa flounced (a formidable sight, as I observed, to all but the most heroically proportioned patrons), allowed herself to be pinched, took tips, and talked to me afterward, during slack periods, of the times she had been 'called upstairs' at the request of some connoisseur of scale, and the money she had made that night. I laughed at jokes and refused tips in such a way as to make the patrons aware that I was a part of the management. Most patrons did not need the reminder, and I was often told that I strikingly resembled my father.

When I had been serving as a receptionist in this way for only a short time, I think on only the third or fourth night, we had an unusual visitor. He came early one evening, but it was the evening of so dark a day, one of the last really wintry days, that the garden lamps had been lit for an hour or more and the occasional carriages that passed on the street beyond, though they could be heard, could not be seen. I answered the door when he knocked, and as we always did with strangers, asked him politely what he wished.

He said, 'I should like to speak to Dr Aubrey Veil.'

I am afraid I looked blank.

'This is 666 Saltimbanque?'

It was of course; and the name of Dr Veil, though I could not place it, touched a chime of memory. I supposed that one of our patrons had used my father's house as an *adresse d'accommodation*, and since this visitor was clearly legitimate, and it was not desirable to keep anyone arguing in the doorway despite the

25

partial shelter afforded by the garden, I asked him in; then I sent Nerissa to bring us coffee so that we might have a few moments of private talk in the dark little receiving room that opened off the foyer. It was a room very seldom used, and the maids had been remiss in dusting it, as I saw as soon as I opened the door. I made a mental note to speak to my aunt about it, and as I did I recalled where it was that I had heard Dr Veil mentioned. My aunt, on the first occasion I had ever spoken to her, had referred to his theory that we might in fact be the natives of Sainte Anne, having murdered the original Terrestrial colonists and displaced them so thoroughly as to forget our own past.

The stranger had seated himself in one of the musty, gilded armchairs. He wore a beard, very black and more full than the current style, was young, I thought, though of course considerably older than I, and would have been handsome if the skin of his face – what could be seen of it – had not been of so colorless a white as almost to constitute a disfigurement. His dark clothing seemed abnormally heavy, like felt, and I recalled having heard from some patron that a starcrosser from Sainte Anne had splashed down in the bay yesterday, and asked if he had perhaps been on board it. He looked startled for a moment, than laughed. 'You're a wit, I see. And living with Dr Veil you'd be familiar with his theory. No, I'm from Earth. My name is Marsch.' He gave me his card, and I read it twice before the meaning of the delicately embossed abbreviations registered on my mind. My visitor was a scientist, a doctor of philosophy in anthropology, from Earth.

I said: 'I wasn't trying to be witty. I thought you might really have come from Sainte Anne. Here, most of us have a kind of planetary face, except for the gypsies and the criminal tribes, and you don't seem to fit the pattern.'

He said, 'I've noticed what you mean; you seem to have it yourself.'

'I'm supposed to look a great deal like my father.'

'Ah,' he said. He stared at me. Then, 'Are you cloned?'

'Cloned?' I had read the term, but only in conjunction with botany, and as has happened to me often when I have especially wanted to impress someone with my intelligence, nothing came. I felt like a stupid child.

'Parthenogenetically reproduced, so that the new individual – or individuals, you can have a thousand if you want – will have a genetic structure identical to the parent. It's antievolutionary, so it's illegal on Earth, but I don't suppose things are as closely watched out here.'

'You're talking about human beings?'

He nodded.

'I've never heard of it. Really I doubt if you'd find the necessary technology here; we're quite backward compared to Earth. Of course, my father might be able to arrange something for you.'

'I don't want to have it done.'

Nerissa came in with the coffee then, effectively cutting off anything further Dr Marsch might have said. Actually, I had added the suggestion about my father more from force of habit than anything else, and thought it very unlikely that he could pull off any such biochemical tour de force, but there was always the possibility, particularly if a large sum were offered. As it was, we fell silent while Nerissa arranged the cups and poured, and when she had gone Marsch said appreciatively, 'Quite an unusual girl.' His eyes, I noticed, were a bright green, without the brown tones most green eyes have.

I was wild to ask him about Earth and the new developments there, and it had already occurred to me that the girls might be an effective way of keeping him here, or at least of bringing him back. I said: 'You should see some of them. My father has wonderful taste.'

'I'd rather see Dr Veil. Or is Dr Veil your father?'

'Oh, no.'

'This is his address, or at least the address I was given. Number 666 Saltimbanque Street, Port-Mimizon, Department de la Main, Sainte Croix.'

He appeared quite serious, and it seemed possible that if I told him flatly that he was mistaken he would leave. I said: 'I learned about Veil's Hypothesis from my aunt; she seemed quite conversant with it. Perhaps later this evening you'd like to talk to her about it.'

'Couldn't I see her now?'

'My aunt sees very few visitors. To be frank, I'm told she quarreled with my father before I was born, and she seldom leaves her own apartments. The housekeepers report to her there and she manages what I suppose I must call our domestic economy, but it's very rare to see Madame outside her rooms, or for any stranger to be let in.'

'And why are you telling me this?'

'So that you'll understand that with the best will in the world it may not be possible for me to arrange an interview for you. At least, not this evening.'

'You could simply ask her if she knows Dr Veil's present address, and if so what it is.'

27

'I'm trying to help you, Dr Marsch. Really I am.'

'But you don't think that's the best way to go about it?'

'No.'

'In other words if your aunt were simply asked, without being given a chance to form her own judgment of me, she wouldn' give me information even if she had it?'

'It would help if we were to talk a bit first. There are a grea many things I'd like to learn about Earth.'

For an instant I thought I saw a sour smile under the black beard. He said, 'Suppose I ask you first – '

He was interrupted – again – by Nerissa, I suppose because she wanted to see if we required anything further from the kitchen. could have strangled her when Dr Marsch halted in midsentence and said instead, 'Couldn't this girl ask your aunt if she would see me?'

I had to think quickly. I had been planning to go myself and, after a suitable wait, return and say that my aunt would receive Dr Marsch later, which would have given me an additional opportunity to question him while he waited. But there was at least a possibility (no doubt magnified in my eyes by my eagerness to hear of new discoveries from Earth) that he would not wait – or that, when and if he did eventually see my aunt, he might mention the incident. If I sent Nerissa I would at least have him to myself while she ran her errand, and there was an excellent chance – or at least so I imagined – that my aunt would in fact have some business which she would want to conclude before seeing a stranger. I told Nerissa to go, and Dr Marsch gave her one of his cards after writing a few words on the back.

'Now,' I said, 'what was it you were about to ask me?'

'Why this house, on a planet that has been inhabited less than two hundred years, seems so absurdly old.'

'It was built a hundred and forty years ago, but you must have many on Earth that are far older.'

'I suppose so. Hundreds. But for every one of them there are ten thousand that have been up less than a year. Here, almost every building I see seems nearly as old as this one.'

'We've never been crowded here, and we haven't had to tear down; that's what Mr Million says. And there are fewer people here now than there were fifty years ago.'

'Mr Million?'

I told him about Mr Million, and when I finished he said, 'It sounds as if you've got a ten nine unbound simulator here, which should be interesting. Only a few have ever been made.'

'A ten nine simulator?'

'A billion, ten to the ninth power. The human brain has several billion synapses, of course; but it's been found that you can simulate its action pretty well –'

It seemed to me that no time at all had passed since Nerissa had left, but she was back. She curtsied to Dr Marsch and said, 'Madame will see you.'

I blurted, 'Now?'

'Yes,' Nerissa said artlessly, 'Madame said right now.'

'I'll take him then. You mind the door.'

I escorted Dr Marsch down the dark corridors, taking a long route to have more time, but he seemed to be arranging in his mind the questions he wished to ask my aunt, as we walked past the spotted mirrors and warped little walnut tables, and he answered me in monosyllables when I tried to question him about Earth.

At my aunt's door I rapped for him. She opened it herself, the hem of her black skirt hanging emptily over the untrodden carpet, but I do not think he noticed that. He said, 'I'm really very sorry to bother you, Madame, and I only do so because your nephew thought you might be able to help me locate the author of Veil's Hypothesis.'

My aunt said, 'I am Dr Veil, please come in,' and shut the door behind him, leaving me standing open-mouthed in the corridor.

            *

I mentioned the incident to Phaedria the next time we met, but she was more interested in learning about my father's house. Phaedria, if I have not used her name before now, was the girl who had sat near me while I watched David play squash. She had been introduced to me on my next visit to the park by no one less than the monster herself, who had helped her to a seat beside me and, miracle of miracles, promptly retreated to a point which, though not out of sight, was at least beyond earshot. Phaedria had thrust her broken ankle in front of her, halfway across the graveled path, and smiled a most charming smile. 'You don t object to my sitting here?' She had perfect teeth.

'I'm delighted.'

'You're surprised too. Your eyes get big when you're surprised, did you know that?'

'I am surprised. I've come here looking for you several times, but you haven't been here.'

'We've come looking for you, and you haven't been here either, but I suppose one can't really spend a great deal of time in a park.'

'I would have,' I said, 'if I'd known you were looking for me. I went here as much as I could anyway. I was afraid that she ...' I jerked my head at the monster, 'wouldn't let you come back. How did you persuade her?'

'I didn't,' Phaedria said. 'Can't you guess? Don't you know anything?'

I confessed that I did not. I felt stupid, and I was stupid, at least in the things I said, because so much of my mind was caught up not in formulating answers to her remarks but in committing to memory the lilt of her voice, the purple of her eyes, even the faint perfume of her skin and the soft, warm touch of her breath on my cool cheek.

'So you see,' Phaedria was saying, 'that's how it is with me. When Aunt Uranie – she's only a poor cousin of mother's, really – got home and told him about you he found out who you are, and here I am.'

'Yes,' I said, and she laughed.

Phaedria was one of those girls raised between the hope of marriage and the thought of sale. Her father's affairs, as she herself said, were 'unsettled'. He speculated in ship cargoes, mostly from the south – textiles and drugs. He owed, most of the time, large sums which the lenders could not hope to collect unless they were willing to allow more to recoup. He might die a pauper, but in the meanwhile he had raised his daughter with every detail of education and plastic surgery attended to. If when she reached marriageable age he could afford a good dowry, she would link him with some wealthy family. If he were pressed for money instead, a girl so reared would bring fifty times the price of a common street child. Our family, of course, would be ideal for either purpose.

'Tell me about your house,' she said. 'Do you know what the kids call it? "The Cave Canem", or sometimes just "The Cave". The boys all think it's a big thing to have been there and they lie about it. Most of them haven't.'

But I wanted to talk about Dr Marsch and the sciences of Earth, and I was nearly as anxious to find out about her own world, 'the kids' she mentioned so casually, her school and family as she was to learn about us. Also, although I was willing to detail the services my father's girls rendered their benefactors, there were some things, such as my aunt's floating down the stairwell, that I was adverse to discussing. But we bought egg rolls from the same old woman to eat in the chill sunlight and exchanged confidences and somehow parted not only lovers but friends, promising to meet again the next day.

At some time during the night, I believe at almost the same time that I returned – or to speak more accurately *was returned* since I could scarcely walk – to my bed after a session of hours with my father, the weather changed. The musked exhalation of late spring or early summer crept through the shutters, and the fire in our little grate seemed to extinguish itself for shame almost at once. My father's valet opened the window for me and there poured into the room that fragrance that tells of the melting of the last snows beneath the deepest and darkest evergreens on the north sides of mountains. I had arranged with Phaedria to meet at ten, and before going to my father's library I had posted a note on the escritoire beside my bed, asking that I be awakened an hour earlier; and that night I slept with the fragrance in my nostrils and the thought – half-plan, half-dream – in my mind that by some means Phaedria and I would elude her aunt entirely and find a deserted lawn where blue and yellow flowers dotted the short grass.

When I woke, it was an hour past noon, and rain drove in sheets past the window. Mr Million, who was reading a book on the far side of the room, told me that it had been raining like that since six, and for that reason he had not troubled to wake me. I had a splitting headache, as I often did after a long session with my father, and took one of the powders he had prescribed to relieve it. They were gray, and smelled of anise.

'You look unwell,' Mr Million said.

'I was hoping to go to the park.'

'I know.' He rolled across the room toward me, and I recalled that Dr Marsch had called him an 'unbound' simulator. For the first time since I had satisfied myself about them when I was quite small, I bent over (at some cost to my head) and read the almost obliterated stampings on his main cabinet. There was only the name of a cybernetics company on Earth and, in French as I had always supposed, his name: M.Million – 'Monsieur' or 'Mister' Million. Then, as startling as a blow from behind to a man musing in a comfortable chair, I remembered that a dot was employed in some algebras for multiplication. He saw my change of expression at once. 'A thousand million word core capacity,' he said. 'An English billion or a French milliard, the M being the Roman numeral for one thousand, of course. I thought you understood that some time ago.'

'You are an unbound simulator. What is a bound simulator, and whom are you simulating – my father?'

'No.' The face in the screen, Mr Million's face as I had always thought of it, shook its head. 'Call me, call the person simulated, at least, your great-grandfather. He – I – am dead. In order to achieve simulation, it is necessary to examine the cells of the brain, layer by layer, with a beam of accelerated particles so that the neural patterns can be reproduced, we say "core imaged", in the computer. The process is fatal.'

I asked after a moment, 'And a bound simulator?'

'If the simulation is to have a body that looks human the mechanical body must be linked – "bound" – to a remote core, since the smallest billion word core cannot be made even approximately as small as a human brain.' He paused again, and for an instant his face dissolved into myriad sparkling dots, swirling like dust motes in a sunbeam. 'I am sorry. For once you wish to listen but I do not wish to lecture. I was told, a very long time ago, just before the operation, that my simulation – this – would be capable of emotion in certain circumstances. Until today I had always thought they lied.' I would have stopped him if I could, but he rolled out of the room before I could recover from my surprise.

For a long time, I suppose an hour or more, I sat listening to the drumming of the rain and thinking about Phaedria and about what Mr Million had said, all of it confused with my father's questions of the night before, questions which had seemed to steal their answers from me so that I was empty, and dreams had come to flicker in the emptiness, dreams of fences and walls and the concealing ditches called ha-has, that contain a barrier you do not see until you are about to tumble on it. Once I had dreamed of standing in a paved court fenced with Corinthian pillars so close set that I could not force my body between them, although in the dream I was only a child of three or four. After trying various places for a long time, I had noticed that each column was carved with a word – the only one that I could remember was *carapace* – and that the paving stones of the courtyard were mortuary tablets like those set into the floors in some of the old French churches, with my own name and a different date on each.

This dream pursued me even when I tried to think of Phaedria, and when a maid brought me hot water – for I now shaved twice a week – I found that I was already holding my razor in my hand, and had in fact cut myself with it so that the blood had streaked my nightclothes and run down on to the sheets.

32

The next time I saw Phaedria, which was four or five days afterward, she was engrossed by a new project in which she enlisted both David and me. This was nothing less than a theatrical company, composed mostly of girls her own age, which was to present plays during the summer in a natural amphitheatre in the park. Since the company, as I have said, consisted principally of girls, male actors were at a premium, and David and I soon found ourselves deeply embroiled. The play had been written by a committee of the cast, and – inevitably – revolved about the loss of political power by the original French-speaking colonists. Phaedria, whose ankle would not be mended in time for our performance, would play the crippled daughter of the French governor; David, her lover (a dashing captain of chasseurs); and I, the governor himself – a part I accepted readily because it was a much better one than David's, and offered scope for a great deal of fatherly affection toward Phaedria.

The night of our performance, which was early in June, I recall vividly for two reasons. My aunt, whom I had not seen since she had closed the door behind Dr Marsch, notified me at the last moment that she wished to attend and that I was to escort her. And we players had grown so afraid of having an empty house that I had asked my father if it would be possible for him to send some of his girls – who would thus lose only the earliest part of the evening, when there was seldom much business in any event. To my great surprise (I suppose because he felt it would be good advertising) he consented, stipulating only that they should return at the end of the third act if he sent a messenger saying they were needed.

Because I would have to arrive at least an hour early to make up, it was no more than late afternoon when I called for my aunt. She showed me in herself, and immediately asked my help for her maid, who was trying to wrestle some heavy object from the upper shelf of a closet. It proved to be a folding wheelchair, and under my aunt's direction we set it up. When we had finished she said abruptly, 'Give me a hand in, you two,' and taking our arms lowered herself into the seat. Her black skirt, lying emptily against the leg boards of the chair like a collapsed tent, showed legs no thicker than my wrists; but also an odd thickening, almost like a saddle, below her hips. Seeing me staring she snapped, 'Won't be needing that until I come back, I suppose. Lift me up a little. Stand behind and get me under the arms.'

I did so, and her maid reached unceremoniously under my aunt's skirt and drew out a little leather padded device on which

33

she had been resting. 'Shall we go?' my aunt sniffed. 'You'll be late.

I wheeled her into the corridor, her maid holding the door for us. Somehow, learning that my aunt's ability to hang in the air like smoke was physically, indeed mechanically, derived, made it more disturbing than ever. When she asked why I was so quiet, I told her and added that I had been under the impression that no one had yet succeeded in producing working antigravity.

'And you think I have? Then why wouldn't I use it to get to your play?'

'I suppose because you don't want it to be seen.'

'Nonsense. It's a regular prosthetic device. You buy them at the surgical stores. She twisted around in her seat until she could look up at me, her face so like my father's, and her lifeless legs like the sticks David and I used as little boys when, doing parlor magic, we wished Mr Million to believe us lying prone when we were in fact crouched beneath our own supposed figures. 'Puts out a superconducting field, then induces eddy currents in the reinforcing rods in the floors. The flux of the induced currents oppose the machine's own flux and I float, more or less. Lean forward to go forward, straighten up to stop. You look relieved.'

'I am. I suppose antigravity frightened me.'

'I used the iron banister when I went down the stairs with you once; it has a very convenient coil shape.'

Our play went smoothly enough, with predictable cheers from members of the audience who were, or at least wished to be thought, descended from the old French aristocracy. The audience, in fact, was better than we had dared hope, five hundred or so besides the inevitable sprinkling of pickpockets, police, and streetwalkers. The incident I most vividly recall came toward the latter half of the first act, when for ten minutes or so I sat with few lines at a desk, listening to my fellow actors. Our stage faced the west, and the setting sun had left the sky a welter of lurid color: purple-reds striped gold and flame and black. Against this violent ground, which might have been the massed banners of Hell, there began to appear, in ones and twos, like the elongate shadows of fantastic grenadiers crenelated and plumed, the heads, the slender necks, the narrow shoulders, of a platoon of my father's demimondaines; arriving late, they were taking the last seats at the upper rim of our theatre, encircling it like the soldiery of some ancient, bizarre government surrounding a treasonous mob.

They sat at last, my cue came, and I forgot them; and that is

34

ll I can now remember of our first performance, except that at
one point some motion of mine suggested to the audience a man-
nerism of my father's, and there was a shout of misplaced
laughter – and that at the beginning of the second act, Sainte
Anne rose with its sluggish rivers and great grassy meadowmeres clearly visible, flooding the audience with green light; and
at the close of the third I saw my father's crooked little valet
bustling among the upper rows, and the girls, green-edged black
shadows, filing out.

We produced three more plays that summer, all with some
success, and David and Phaedria and I became an accepted part-
nership, with Phaedria dividing herself more or less equally be-
ween us – whether by her own inclination or her parents' orders
I could never be quite sure. When her ankle knit she was a com-
panion fit for David in athletics, a better player of all the ball and
racket games than any of the other girls who came to the park;
but she would as often drop everything and come to sit with me,
where she sympathized with (though she did not actually share)
my interest in botany and biology, and gossiped, and delighted in
showing me off to her friends since my reading had given me a
sort of talent for puns and repartee.

It was Phaedria who suggested, when it became apparent that
the ticket money from our first play would be insufficient for the
costumes and scenery we coveted for our second, that at the close
of future performances the cast circulate among the audience to
take up a collection; and this, of course, in the press and bustle
easily lent itself to the accomplishment of petty thefts for our
cause. Most people, however, had too much sense to bring to our
theater, in the evening, in the gloomy park, more money than was
required to buy tickets and perhaps an ice or a glass of wine
during intermission; so no matter how dishonest we were the
profit remained small, and we, and especially Phaedria and
David, were soon talking of going forward to more dangerous and
lucrative adventures.

At about this time, I suppose as a result of my father's continued and intensified probing of my subconscious, a violent and
almost nightly examination whose purpose was still unclear to
me and which, since I had been accustomed to it for so long, I
scarcely questioned, I became more and more subject to frightening lapses of conscious control. I would, so David and Mr Million
told me, seem quite myself though perhaps rather more quiet
than usual, answering questions intelligently if absently, and then,
suddenly, come to myself, start, and stare at the familiar rooms,

the familiar faces, among which I now found myself, perhaps after the mid-afternoon, without the slightest memory of having awakened, dressed, shaved, eaten, gone for a walk.

Although I loved Mr Million as much as I had when I was a boy, I was never able, after that conversation in which I learned the meaning of the familiar lettering on his side, quite to re-establish the old relationship. I was always conscious, as I am conscious now, that the personality I loved had perished years before I was born; and that I addressed an imitation of it, fundamentally mathematical in nature, responding as that personality might to the stimuli of human speech and action. I could never determine whether Mr Million is really aware in that sense which would give him the right to say, as he always has, 'I think,' and 'I feel.' When I asked him about it he could only explain that he did not know the answer himself, that having no standard of comparison he could not be positive whether his own mental processes represented true consciousness or not; and I, of course, could not know whether this answer represented the deepest medi-tation of a soul somehow alive in the dancing abstractions of the simulation, or whether it was merely triggered, a phonographic response, by my question.

Our theater, as I have said, continued through the summer and gave its last performance with the falling leaves drifting, like obscure, perfumed old letters from some discarded trunk, upon our stage. When the curtain calls were over we who had written and acted the plays of our season were too disheartened to do more than remove our costumes and cosmetics, and drift ourselves, with the last of our departing audience, down the whip-poorwill-haunted paths to the city streets and home. I was pre-pared, as I remember, to take up my duties at my father's door, but that night he had stationed his valet in the foyer to wait for me, and I was ushered directly into the library, where he explained brusquely that he would have to devote the latter part of the evening to business and for that reason would speak to me (as he put it) early. He looked tired and ill, and it occurred to me, I think for the first time, that he would one day die – and that I would, on that day, become at once both rich and free.

What I said under the drugs that evening I do not, of course, recall, but I remember as vividly as I might if I had only this morning awakened from it, the dream that followed. I was on a ship, a white ship like one of those the oxen pull, so slowly the sharp prows make no wake at all, through the green water of the canal beside the park. I was the only crewman, and indeed the only living man aboard. At the stern, grasping the huge wheel in such a flaccid way that it seemed to support and guide and steady *him* rather than he it, stood the corpse of a tall, thin man whose face, when the rolling of his head presented it to me, was the face that floated in Mr Million's screen. This face, as I have said, was very like my father's, but I knew the dead man at the wheel was not he.

I was aboard the ship a long time. We seemed to be running free, with the wind a few points to port and strong. When I went aloft at night, masts and spars and rigging quivered and sang in the wind, and sail upon sail towered above me, and sail upon white sail spread below me, and more masts clothed in sails stood before me and behind me. When I worked on deck by day, spray wet my shirt and left tear-shaped spots on the planks which dried quickly in the bright sunlight.

I cannot remember ever having really been on such a ship, but perhaps, as a very small child, I was, for the sounds of it, the creaking of the masts in their sockets, the whistling of the wind in the thousand ropes, the crashing of the waves against the wooden hull were all as distinct, and as real, as much *themselves*, as the sounds of laughter and breaking glass overhead had been when, as a child, I had tried to sleep; or the bugles from the citadel which sometimes, then, woke me in the morning.

I was about some work, I do not know just what, aboard this ship. I carried buckets of water with which I dashed clotted blood from the decks, and I pulled at ropes which seemed attached to nothing – or rather, firmly tied to immovable objects still higher in the rigging. I watched the surface of the sea from bow and rail, from the mastheads, and from atop a large cabin amidships, but when a starcrosser, its entry shields blinding-bright with heat, plunged hissing into the sea far off I reported it to no one.

And all this time the dead man at the wheel was talking to me. His head hung limply, as though his neck were broken, and the jerkings of the wheel he held, as big waves struck the rudder, sent it from one shoulder to the other, or back to stare at the sky or down. But he continued to speak, and the few words I caught suggested that he was lecturing upon an ethical theory whose postulates seemed even to him doubtful. I felt a dread of hearing this talk and tried to keep myself as much as possible toward the bow, but the wind at times carried the words to me with great clarity, and whenever I looked up from my work I found myself much nearer the stern, sometimes in fact almost touching the dead steersman, than I had supposed.

37

After I had been on this ship a long while, so that I was very tired and very lonely, one of the doors of the cabin opened and my aunt came out, floating quite upright about two feet above the tilted deck. Her skirt did not hang vertically as I had always seen it, but whipped in the wind like a streamer, so that she seemed on the point of blowing away. For some reason I said, 'Don't get close to that man at the wheel, Aunt. He might hurt you.'

She answered, as naturally as if we had met in the corridor outside my bedroom, 'Nonsense. He's far past doing anyone any good, Number Five, or any harm either. It's my brother we have to worry about.'

'Where is he?'

'Down there.' She pointed at the deck as if to indicate that he was in the hold. 'He's trying to find out why the ship doesn't move.'

I ran to the side and looked over, and what I saw was not water but the night sky. Stars – innumerable stars were spread at an infinite distance below me, and as I looked at them I realized that the ship, as my aunt had said, did not make headway or even roll, but remained heeled over, motionless. I looked back at her and she told me, 'It doesn't move because he has fastened it in place until he finds out why it doesn't move,' and at this point I found myself sliding down a rope into what I supposed was the hold of the ship. It smelled of animals. I had awakened, though at first I did not know it.

My feet touched the floor, and I saw that David and Phaedria were beside me. We were in a huge, loftlike room, and as I looked at Phaedria, who was very pretty but tense and biting her lips, a cock crowed.

David said, 'Where do you think the money is?' He was carrying a tool kit.

And Phaedria, who I suppose had expected him to say something else, or in answer to her own thoughts, said, 'We'll have lots of time; Marydol is watching.' Marydol was one of the girls who appeared in our plays.

'If she doesn't run away. Where do you think the money is?'

'Not up here. Downstairs behind the office.' She had been crouching, but she rose now and began to creep forward. She was all in black, from her ballet slippers to a black ribbon binding her black hair, with her white face and arms in striking contrast, and her carmine lips an error, a bit of color left by mistake. David and I followed her.

Crates were scattered, widely separated, on the floor; and as we passed them I saw that they held poultry, a single bird in each. It was not until we were nearly to the ladder which plunged down a hatch in the floor at the opposite corner of the room that I realized that these birds were gamecocks. Then a shaft of sun from one of the skylights struck a crate and the cock rose and stretched himself, showing fierce red eyes and plumage as gaudy as a macaw's. 'Come on,' Phaedria said, 'the dogs are next,' and we followed her down the ladder. Pandemonium broke out on the floor below.

The dogs were chained in stalls, with dividers too high for them to see the dogs on either side of them and wide aisles between the rows of stalls. They were all fighting dogs, bu of every size from ten-pound terriers to mastiffs larger than small horses, brutes with heads as misshapen as the growths that appear on old trees and jaws that could sever both a man's legs at a mouthful. The din of the barking was incredible, a solid substance that shook us as we descended the ladder, and at the bottom I took Phaedria's arm and tried to indicate by signs – since I was certain that we were wherever we were without permission – that we should leave at once. She shook her head and then, when I was unable to understand what she said even when she exaggerated the movements of her lips, wrote on a dusty wall with her moistened forefinger: 'They do this all the time – a noise in the street – anything.'

Access to the floor below was by stairs, reached through a heavy but unbolted door which I think had been installed largely to exclude the din. I felt better when we had closed it behind us even though the noise was still very loud. I had fully come to myself by this time, and I should have explained to David and Phaedria that I did not know where I was or what we were doing there, but shame held me back. And in any event I could guess easily enough what our purpose was. David had asked about the location of money, and we had often talked – talk I had considered at the time to be more than half empty boasting – about a single robbery that would free us from the necessity of further petty crime.

Where we were I discovered later when we left; and how we had come to be there I pieced together from casual conversations. The building had been originally designed as a warehouse, and stood on the Rue des Egouts close to the bay. Its owner supplied those enthusiasts who staged combats of all kinds for sport, and was credited with maintaining the largest assemblage of these creatures in the Department. Phaedria's father had happened to hear that this man had recently put some of his most valuable stock on ship, had taken Phaedria when he called on him, and, since the place was known not to open its doors until after the last Angelus, we had come the next day a little after the second and entered through one of the skylights.

I find it difficult to describe what we saw when we descended from the floor of the dogs to the next, which was the second floor of the building. I had seen fighting slaves many times before when Mr Million, David, and I had traversed the slave market to reach the library; but never more than one or two together, heavily manacled. Here they lay, sat, and lounged everywhere, and for a moment I wondered why they did not tear one another to pieces, and the three of us as well. Then I saw that each was held by a short chain stapled to the floor, and it was not difficult to tell from the scraped and splintered circles in the boards just how far the slave in the center could reach. Such furniture as they had, straw pallets and a few chairs and benches, was either too light to do harm if thrown or very stoutly made and spiked down. I had expected them to shout and threaten us as I had heard they threatened each other in the pits before closing, but they seemed to understand that as long as they were chained, they could do nothing. Every head turned toward us as we came down the steps, but we had no food for them, and after that first examination they were far less interested in us than the dogs had been.

'They aren't people, are they?' Phaedria said. She was walking erectly as a soldier on parade now, and looking at the slaves with interest; studying her, it occurred to me that she was taller and less plump than the 'Phaedria' I pictured to myself when I thought of her. She was not just a pretty, but a beautiful girl. 'They're a kind of animal, really,' she said.

From my studies I was better informed, and I told her that they had been human as infants – in some cases even as children or older – and that they differed from normal people only as a result of surgery (some of it on their brains) and chemically induced alterations in their endocrine systems. And of course in appearance because of their scars.

'Your father does that sort of thing to little girls, doesn't he? For your house?'

David said, 'Only once in a while. It takes a lot of time, and most people prefer normals, even when they prefer pretty odd normals.'

'I'd like to see some of them. I mean the ones he's worked on.'

40

I was still thinking of the fighting slaves around us and said, 'Don't you know about these things? I thought you'd been here before. You knew about the dogs.'

'Oh, I've seen them before, and the man told me about them. I suppose I was just thinking out loud. It would be awful if they were still people.'

Their eyes followed us, and I wondered if they could understand her.

The ground floor was very different from the ones above. The walls were paneled, there were framed pictures of dogs and cocks and of the slaves and curious animals. The windows, opening toward Egouts Street and the bay, were high and narrow and admitted only slender beams of the bright sunlight to pick out of the gloom the arm alone of a rich-leather chair, a square of maroon carpet no bigger than a book, a half-full decanter. I took three steps into this room and knew that we had been discovered. Striding toward us was a tall, high-shouldered young man – who halted, with a startled look, just when I did. He was my own reflection in a gilt-framed pier glass, and I felt the momentary dislocation that comes when a stranger, an unrecognized shape, turns or moves his head and is some familiar friend glimpsed, perhaps for the first time, from outside. The sharp-chinned, grim-looking boy I had seen when I did not know him to be myself had been myself as Phaedria and David, Mr Million and my aunt, saw me.

'This is where he talks to customers,' Phaedria said. 'If he's trying to sell something he has his people bring them down one at a time so you don't see the others, but you can hear the dogs bark even from way down here, and he took Papa and me upstairs and showed us everything.'

David asked, 'Did he show you where he keeps the money?'

'Behind. See that tapestry? It's really a curtain, because while Papa was talking to him, a man came who owed him for something and paid, and he went through there with it.'

The door behind the tapestry opened on a small office, with still another door in the wall opposite. There was no sign of a safe or strongbox. David broke the lock on the desk with a pry bar from his tool kit, but there was only the usual clutter of papers, and I was about to open the second door when I heard a sound, a scraping or shuffling, from the room beyond.

For a minute or more none of us moved. I stood with my hand on the latch. Phaedria, behind me and to my left, had been looking under the carpet for a cache in the floor – she remained

41

crouched, her skirt a black pool at her feet. From somewhere near the broken desk I could hear David's breathing. The shuffling came again, and a board creaked. David said very softly, 'It's an animal.'

I drew my fingers away from the latch and looked at him. He was still gripping the pry bar and his face was pale, but he smiled. 'An animal tethered in there, shifting its feet. That's all.'

I said, 'How do you know?'

'Anybody in there would have heard us, especially when I cracked the desk. If it were a person he would have come out, or if he were afraid he'd hide and be quiet.'

Phaedria said, 'I think he's right. Open the door.'

'Before I do, if it isn't an animal?'

David said, 'It is.'

'But if it isn't?'

I saw the answer on their faces; David gripped his pry bar, and I opened the door.

The room beyond was larger than I had expected, but bare and dirty. The only light came from a single window high in the farther wall. In the middle of the floor stood a big chest, of dark wood bound with iron, and before it lay what appeared to be a bundle of rags. As I stepped from the carpeted office the rags moved and a face, a face triangular as a mantis's, turned toward me. Its chin was hardly more than an inch from the floor, but under deep brows the eyes were tiny scarlet fires.

'That must be it,' Phaedria said. She was looking not at the face but at the iron-banded chest. 'David, can you break into that?'

'I think so,' David said, but he, like me, was watching the ragged thing's eyes. 'What about that?' he said after a moment, and gestured toward it. Before Phaedria or I could answer, its mouth opened showing long, narrow teeth, gray-yellow. 'Sick,' it said.

None of us, I think, had thought it could speak. It was as though a mummy had spoken. Outside, a carriage went past, its iron wheels rattling on the cobbles.

'Let's go,' David said. 'Let's get out.'

Phaedria said, 'It's sick. Don't you see, the owner's brought it down here where he can look in on it and take care of it. It's sick.'

'And he chained his sick slave to the cashbox?' David cocked an eyebrow at her.

'Don't you see? It's the only heavy thing in the room. All you have to do is go over there and knock the poor creature in the head. If you're afraid, give me the bar and I'll do it myself.'

'I'll do it.'

I followed him to within a few feet of the chest. He gestured at the slave imperiously with the steel pry bar. 'You! Move away from there.'

The slave made a gurgling sound and crawled to one side, dragging his chain. He was wrapped in a filthy, tattered blanket and seemed hardly larger than a child, though I noticed that his hands were immense.

I turned and took a step toward Phaedria, intending to urge that we leave if David were unable to open the chest in a few minutes. I remember that before I heard or felt anything I saw her eyes open wide, and I was still wondering why when David's kit of tools clattered on the floor and David himself fell with a thud and a little gasp. Phaedria screamed, and all the dogs on the third floor began to bark.

All this, of course, took less than a second. I turned to look almost as David fell. The slave had darted out an arm and caught my brother by the ankle, and then in an instant had thrown off his blanket and bounded – that is the only way to describe it – on top of him.

I caught him by the neck and jerked him backward, thinking that he would cling to David and that it would be necessary to tear him away, but the instant he felt my hands he flung David aside and writhed like a spider in my grip. *He had four arms.*

I saw them flailing as he tried to reach me, and I let go of him and jerked back, as if a rat had been thrust at my face. That instinctive repulsion saved me; he drove his feet backward in a kick which, if I had still been holding him tightly enough to give him a fulcrum, would have surely ruptured my liver or spleen and killed me.

Instead it shot him forward and me, gasping for breath, back. I fell and rolled, and was outside the circle permitted him by his chain; David had already scrambled away, and Phaedria was well out of his reach.

For a moment, while I shuddered and tried to sit up, the three of us simply stared at him. Then David quoted wryly:

Arms and the man I sing, who forc'd by fate,
And haughty Juno's unrelenting hate,
Expell'd and exil'd, left the Trojan shore.

Neither Phaedria nor I laughed, but Phaedria let out her breath in a long sigh and asked me, 'How did they do that? Get him like that?'

I told her I supposed they had transplanted the extra pair after suppressing his body's natural resistance to the implanted foreign tissue, and that the operation had probably replaced some of his ribs with the donor's shoulder structure. 'I've been teaching myself to do the same sort of thing with mice – on a much less ambitious scale, of course – and the striking thing to me is that he seems to have full use of the grafted pair. Unless you've got identical twins to work with, the nerve endings almost never join properly, and whoever did this probably had a hundred failures before he got what he wanted. That slave must be worth a fortune.'

David said, 'I thought you threw your mice out. Aren't you working with monkeys now?'

I wasn't, although I hoped to; but whether I was or not, it seemed clear that talking about it wasn't going to accomplish anything. I told David that.

'I thought you were hot to leave.'

I had been, but now I wanted something else much more. I wanted to perform an exploratory operation on that creature much more than David or Phaedria had ever wanted money. David liked to think that he was bolder than I, and I knew when I said, 'You may want to get away, but don't use me as an excuse, Brother,' that that would settle it.

'All right, how are we going to kill him?' He gave me an angry look.

Phaedria said: 'It can't reach us. We could throw things at it.'

'And he could throw the ones that missed back.'

While we talked, the thing, the four-armed slave, was grinning at us. I was fairly sure it could understand at least a part of what we were saying, and I motioned to David and Phaedria to indicate that we should go back into the room where the desk was. When we were there I closed the door. 'I didn't want him to hear us. If we had weapons on poles, spears of some kind, we might be able to kill him without getting too close. What could we use for the sticks? Any ideas?'

David shook his head, but Phaedria said, 'Wait a minute, I remember something.' We both looked at her and she knitted her brows, pretending to search her memory and enjoying the attention.

'Well?' David asked.

She snapped her fingers. 'Window poles. You know, long things with a little hook on the end. Remember the windows out there where he talks to customers? They're high up in the wall,

44

and while he and Papa were talking one of the men who works for him brought one and opened a window. They ought to be around somewhere.'

We found two after a five-minute search. They looked satisfactory: about six feet long and an inch and a quarter in diameter, of hard wood. David flourished his and pretended to thrust at Phaedria, then asked me, 'Now what do we use for points?'

The scalpel I always carried was in its case in my breast pocket, and I fastened it to the rod with electrical tape from a roll David had fortunately carried on his belt instead of in the tool kit, but we could find nothing to make a second spearhead for him until he himself suggested broken glass.

'You can't break a window.' Phaedria said, 'they'd hear you outside. Besides, won't it just snap off when you try to get him with it?'

'Not if it's thick glass. Look here, you two.'

I did, and saw – again – my own face. He was pointing toward the large mirror that had surprised me when I came down the steps. While I looked his shoe struck it, and it shattered with a crash that set the dogs barking again. He selected a long, almost straight, triangular piece and held it up to the light, where it flashed like a gem. 'That's about as good as they used to make them from agate and jasper on Sainte Anne, isn't it?'

*

By prior agreement we approached from opposite sides. The slave leaped to the top of the chest, and from there, watched us quite calmly, his deep-set eyes turning from David to me until at last when we were both quite close, David rushed him.

He spun around as the glass point grazed his ribs and caught David's spear by the shaft and jerked him forward. I thrust at him but missed, and before I could recover he had dived from the chest and was grappling with David on the far side. I bent over it and jabbed down at him, and it was not until David screamed that I realized I had driven my scalpel into his thigh. I saw the blood, bright arterial blood, spurt up and drench the shaft, and let it go and threw myself over the chest on top of them.

He was ready for me, on his back and grinning, with his legs and all four arms raised like a dead spider's. I am certain he would have strangled me in the next few seconds if it had not been that David, how consciously I do not know, threw one arm across the creature's eyes so that he missed his grip and I fell between those outstretched hands.

*

There is not a great deal more to tell. He jerked free of David, and pulling me to him, tried to bite my throat; but I hooked a thumb in one of his eye sockets and held him off. Phaedria, with more courage than I would have credited her with, put David's glass-tipped spear into my free hand and I stabbed him in the neck – I believe I severed both jugulars and the trachea before he died. We put a tourniquet on David's leg and left without either the money or the knowledge of technique I had hoped to get from the body of the slave. Marydol helped us get David home, and we told Mr Million he had fallen while we were exploring an empty building – though I doubt that he believed us.

There is one other thing to tell about that incident – I mean the killing of the slave – although I am tempted to go on and describe instead a discovery I made immediately afterward that had, at the time, a much greater influence on me. It is only an impression, and one that I have, I am sure, distorted and magnified in recollection. While I was stabbing the slave, my face was very near his and I saw (I suppose because of the light from the high windows behind us) my own face reflected and doubled in the corneas of his eyes, and it seemed to me that it was a face very like his. I have been unable to forget, since then, what Dr Marsch told me about the production of any number of identical individuals by cloning, and that my father had, when I was younger, a reputation as a child broker. I have tried since my release to find some trace of my mother, the woman in the photograph shown me by my aunt; but that picture was surely taken long before I was born – perhaps even on Earth.

The discovery I spoke of I made almost as soon as we left the building where I killed the slave, and it was simply this: that it was no longer autumn, but high summer. Because all four of us – Marydol had joined us by that time – were so concerned about David and busy concocting a story to explain his injury, the shock was somewhat blunted, but there could be no doubt of it. The weather was warm with that torpid, damp heat peculiar to summer. The trees I remembered nearly bare were in full leaf and filled with orioles. The fountain in our garden no longer played, as it always did after the danger of frost and burst pipes had come, with warmed water: I dabbled my hand in the basin as we helped David up the path, and it was as cool as dew.

My periods of unconscious action then, my sleepwalking, had increased to devour an entire winter and the spring, and I felt that I had lost myself.

When we entered the house, an ape which I thought at first was my father's sprang to my shoulder. Later Mr Million told me that it was my own, one of my laboratory animals I had made a pet. I did not know the little beast, but scars under his fur and the twist of his limbs showed he knew me.

(I have kept Popo ever since, and Mr Million took care of him for me while I was imprisoned. He climbs still in fine weather on the gray and crumbling walls of this house; and as he runs along the parapets and I see his hunched form against the sky, I think, for a moment, that my father is still alive and that I may be summoned again for the long hours in his library – but I forgive my pet that.)

*

My father did not call a physician for David, but treated him himself; and if he was curious about the manner in which he had received his injury he did not show it. My own guess – for whatever it may be worth, this late – is that he believed I had stabbed him in some quarrel. I say this because he seemed after this, apprehensive whenever I was alone with him. He was not a fearful man, and he had been accustomed for years to deal occasionally with the worst sort of criminals; but he was no longer at ease with me – he guarded himself. It may have been, of course, merely the result of something I had said or done during the forgotten winter.

Both Marydol and Phaedria, as well as my aunt and Mr Million, came frequently to visit David, so that his sickroom became a sort of meeting place for us all, only disturbed by my father's occasional visits. Marydol was a slight, fair-haired, kindhearted girl, and I became very fond of her. Often when she was ready to go home I escorted her, and on the way back stopped at the slave market, as Mr Million and David and I had once done so often, to buy fried bread and the sweet black coffee and to watch the bidding. The faces of slaves are the dullest in the world; but I would find myself staring into them, and it was a long time, a month at least, before I understood – quite suddenly, when I

47

found what I had been looking for – why I did. A young male, a sweeper, was brought to the block. His face as well as his back had been scarred by the whip, and his teeth were broken; but I recognized him: the scarred face was my own or my father's. I spoke to him and would have bought and freed him, but he answered me in the servile way of slaves and I turned away in disgust and went home.

That night when my father had me brought to the library – as he had not for several nights – I watched our reflections in the mirror that concealed the entrance to his laboratories. He looked younger than he was; I older. We might almost have been the same man, and when he faced me and I, staring over his shoulder, saw no image of my own body, but only his arms and mine, we might have been the fighting slave.

I cannot say who first suggested we kill him. I only remember that one evening, as I prepared for bed after taking Marydol and Phaedria to their homes, I realized that earlier when the three of us, with Mr Million and my aunt, had sat around David's bed, we had been talking of that.

Not openly, of course. Perhaps we had not admitted even to ourselves what it was we were thinking. My aunt had mentioned the money he was supposed to have hidden; and Phaedria, then, a yacht luxurious as a palace; David talked about hunting in the grand style, and the political power money could buy.

And I, saying nothing, had thought of the hours and weeks, and the months he had taken from me; of the destruction of my *self*, which he had gnawed at night after night. I thought of how I might enter the library that night and find myself when next I woke an old man and perhaps a beggar.

Then I knew that I must kill him, since if I told him those thoughts while I lay drugged on the peeling leather of the old table he would kill *me* without a qualm.

While I waited for his valet to come I made my plan. There would be no investigation, no death certificate for my father. I would replace him. To our patrons it would appear that nothing had changed. Phaedria's friends would be told that I had quarreled with him and left home. I would allow no one to see me for a time, and then, in make-up, in a dim room, speak occasionally to some favored caller. It was an impossible plan, but at the time I believed it possible and even easy. My scalpel was in my pocket and ready. The body could be destroyed in his own laboratory.

He read it in my face. He spoke to me as he always had, but I think he knew. There were flowers in the room, something that had never been before, and I wondered if he had not known even earlier and had them brought in, as for a special event. Instead of telling me to lie on the leather-covered table, he gestured toward a chair and seated himself at his writing desk. 'We will have company today,' he said.

I looked at him.

'You're angry with me. I've seen it growing in you. Don't you know who – '

He was about to say something further when there was a tap at the door, and when he called, 'Come in!' it was opened by Nerissa who ushered in a demimondaine and Dr Marsch. I was surprised to see him; and still more surprised to see one of the girls in my father's library. She seated herself beside Marsch in a way that showed he was her benefactor for the night.

'Good evening, Doctor,' my father said. 'Have you been enjoying yourself?'

Marsch smiled, showing large, square teeth. He wore clothing of the most fashionable cut now, but the contrast between his beard and the colorless skin of his cheeks was as remarkable as ever. 'Both sensually and intellectually,' he said. 'I've seen a naked girl, a giantess twice the height of a man, walk through a wall.'

I said, 'That's done with holographs.'

He smiled again. 'I know. And I have seen a great many other things as well. I was going to recite them all, but perhaps I would only bore my audience; I will content myself with saying that you have a remarkable establishment – but you know that.'

My father said, 'It is always flattering to hear it again.'

'And now are we going to have the discussion we spoke of earlier?'

My father looked at the demimondaine; she rose, kissed Dr Marsch, and left the room. The heavy library door swung shut behind her with a soft click.

*

Like the sound of a switch, or old glass breaking.

*

I have thought since, may times, of that girl as I saw her leaving:

the high-heeled platform shoes and grotesquely long legs, the backless dress dipping an inch below the coccyx. The bare nape of her neck; her hair piled and teased and threaded with ribbons and tiny lights. As she closed the door she was ending, though she could not have known it, the world she and I had known.

'She'll be waiting when you come out,' my father said to Marsch.

'And if she's not, I'm sure you can supply others.' The anthropologist's green eyes seemed to glow in the lamplight. 'But now, how can I help you?'

'You study race. Could you call a group of similar men thinking similar thoughts a race?'

'And women,' Marsch said, smiling.

'And here,' my father continued, 'here on Sainte Croix, you are gathering material to take back with you to Earth?'

'I am gathering material, certainly. Whether or not I shall return to the mother planet is problematical.'

I must have looked at him sharply; he turned his smile toward me, and it became, if possible, even more patronizing than before. 'You're surprised?'

'I've always considered Earth the center of scientific thought.' I said. 'I can easily imagine a scientist leaving it to do field work, but – '

'But it is inconceivable that one might want to stay in the field?'

'Consider my position. You are not alone – happily for me – in respecting the mother world's gray hairs and wisdom. As an Earth-trained man I've been offered a department in your university at almost any salary I care to name, with a sabbatical every second year. And the trip from here to Earth requires twenty years of Newtonian time; only six months subjectively for me, of course, but when I return, if I do, my education will be forty years out of date. No, I'm afraid your planet may have acquired an intellectual luminary.'

My father said, 'We're straying from the subject, I think.'

Marsch nodded, then added, 'But I was about to say that an anthropologist is peculiarly equipped to make himself at home in any culture – even in so strange a one as this family has constructed about itself. I think I may call it a family, since there are two members resident besides yourself. You don't object to my addressing the pair of you in the singular?'

He looked at me as if expecting a protest, then when I said nothing: 'I mean your son David – that, and not brother is his real relationship to your continuing personality – and the woman you call your aunt. She is in reality daughter to an earlier – shall we say "version"? – of yourself.'

'You're trying to tell me I'm a cloned duplicate of my father, and I see both of you expect me to be shocked. I'm not. I've suspected it for some time.'

My father said: 'I'm glad to hear that. Frankly, when I was your age the discovery disturbed me a great deal; I came into my father's library – this room – to confront him, and I intended to kill him.'

Dr Marsch asked, 'And did you?'

'I don't think it matters – the point is that it was my intention. I hope that having you here will make things easier for Number Five.'

'Is that what you call him?'

'It's more convenient since his name is the same as my own.'

'He is your fifth clone-produced child?'

'My fifth experiment? No.' My father's hunched, high shoulders wrapped in the dingy scarlet of his old dressing-gown made him look like some savage bird; and I remembered having read in a book of natural history of one called the red-shouldered hawk. His pet monkey, grizzled now with age, had climbed on to the desk. 'No, more like my fiftieth, if you must know. I used to do them for drill. You people who have never tried it think the technique is simple because you've heard it can be done, but you don't know how difficult it is to prevent spontaneous differences. Every gene dominant in myself had to remain dominant, and people are not garden peas – few things are governed by simple Mendelian pairs.'

Marsch asked, 'You destroyed your failures?'

I said: 'He sold them. When I was a child I used to wonder why Mr Million stopped to look at the slaves in the market. Since then I've found out.' My scalpel was still in its case in my pocket; I could feel it.

'Mr Million,' my father said, 'is perhaps a bit more sentimental than I – besides, I don't like to go out. You see, Doctor, your supposition that we are all truly the same individual will have to be modified. We have our little variations.'

Dr Marsch was about to reply, but I interrupted him. 'Why?' I said. 'Why David and me? Why Aunt Jeannine a long time ago? Why go on with it?'

'Yes,' my father said, 'why? We ask the question to ask the question.'

'I don't understand you.'

51

'I seek self-knowledge. If you want to put it this way, *we* seek self-knowledge. You are here because I did and do, and I am here because the individual behind me did – who was himself originated by the one whose mind is simulated in Mr Million. And one of the questions whose answers we seek is why we seek. But there is more than that.' He leaned forward, and the little ape lifted its white muzzle and bright, bewildered eyes to stare into his face. 'We wish to discover why we fail, why others rise and change and we remain here.'

I thought of the yacht I had talked about with Phaedria and said, 'I won't stay here.' Dr Marsch smiled.

My father said, 'I don't think you understand me. I don't necessarily mean here physically, but *here*, socially and intellectually. I have traveled, and you may, but – '

'But you end here,' Dr Marsch said.

'We end at this level!' It was the only time, I think, that I ever saw my father excited. He was almost speechless as he waved at the notebooks and tapes that thronged the walls. 'After how many generations? We do not achieve fame or the rule of even this miserable little colony planet. Something must be changed, but what?' He glared at Dr Marsch.

'You are not unique,' Dr Marsch said, then smiled. 'That sounds like a truism, doesn't it? But I wasn't referring to your duplicating yourself. I meant that since it became possible, back on Earth during the last quarter of the twentieth century, it has been done in such chains a number of times. We have borrowed a term from engineering to describe it, and call it the process of relaxation – a bad nomenclature, but the best we have. Do you know what relaxation in the engineering sense is?'

'No.'

'There are problems which are not directly soluble, but which can be solved by a succession of approximations. In heat transfer, for example, it may not be possible to calculate initially the temperature at every point on the surface of an unusually shaped body. But the engineer, or his computer, can assume reasonable temperatures, see how nearly stable the assumed values would be, then make new assumptions based on the result. As the levels of approximation progress, the successive sets become more and more similar until there is essentially no change. That is why I said the two of you are essentially one individual.'

'What I want you to do,' my father said impatiently, 'is to make Number Five understand that the experiments I have performed on him, particularly the narcotherapeutic examinations

52

resents so much, are necessary. That if we are to become more
[th]an we have been we must find out – ' He had been almost
[sh]outing, and he stopped abruptly to bring his voice under con-
[tr]ol. 'That is the reason he was produced, the reason for David
[to] – I hoped to learn something from an outcrossing.'

'Which was the rationale, no doubt,' Dr Marsch said, 'for the
[ex]istence of Dr Veil as well, in an earlier generation. But as far
[a]s your examinations of your younger self are concerned, it
[w]ould be just as useful for him to examine you.'

'Wait a moment,' I said. 'You keep saying that he and I are
[id]entical. That's incorrect. I can see that we're similar in some
[re]spects, but I'm not really like my father.'

'There are no differences that cannot be accounted for by age.
[Y]ou are what? Eighteen? And you,' he looked toward my father,
[I] should say are nearly fifty. There are only two forces, you see,
[w]hich act to differentiate between human beings: they are hered-
[it]y and environment, nature and nurture. And since the personal-
[it]y is largely formed during the first three years of life, it is the
[en]vironment provided by the home which is decisive. Now every
[p]erson is born into *some* home environment, though it may be
[su]ch a harsh one that he dies of it; and no person, except in this situa-
[ti]on we call anthropological relaxation, provides that environment
[h]imself – it is furnished for him by the preceding generation.'

'Just because both of us grew up in this house – '

'Which you built and furnished and filled with the people you
[ch]ose. But wait a moment. Let's talk about a man neither of you
[h]ave ever seen, a man born in a place provided by parents quite
[d]ifferent from himself: I mean the first of you . . . '

I was no longer listening. I had come to kill my father, and it
[w]as necessary that Dr Marsch leave. I watched him as he leaned
[f]orward in his chair, his long, white hands making incisive little
[g]estures, his cruel lips moving in a frame of black hair; I watched
[h]im and I heard nothing. It was as though I had gone deaf or as
[if] he could communicate only by his thoughts, and I, knowing
[th]e thoughts were silly lies had shut them out. I said, 'You are
[f]rom Sainte Anne.'

He looked at me in surprise, halting in the midst of a senseless
[s]entence. 'I have been there, yes. I spent several years on Sainte
[A]nne before coming here.'

'You were born there. You studied your anthropology there
[f]rom books written on Earth twenty years ago. You are an abo,
[o]r at least half-abo; but we are men.'

Marsch glanced at my father, then said: 'The abos are gone.

53

Scientific opinion on Sainte Anne holds that they have been ex
tinct for almost a century.'

'You didn't believe that when you came to see my aunt.'

'I've never accepted Veil's Hypothesis. I called on everyone
here who had published anything in my field. Really, I don't have
time to listen to this.'

'You are an abo and not from Earth.'

And in a short time my father and I were alone.

*

Most of my sentence I served in a labor camp in the Tattered
Mountains. It was a small camp, housing usually only a hundred
and fifty prisoners – sometimes less than eighty when the winter
deaths had been bad. We cut wood and burned charcoal and
made skis when we found good birch. Above the timberline we
gathered a saline moss supposed to be medicinal and knotted
long plans for rock slides that would crush the stalking machines
that were our guards – though somehow the moment never came,
the stones never slid. The work was hard, and these guards ad-
ministered exactly the mixture of severity and fairness some
prison board had decided upon when they were programmed and
the problem of brutality and favoritism by hirelings was settled
forever, so that only well-dressed men at meetings could be cruel
or kind.

Or so they thought. I sometimes talked to my guards for hours
about Mr Million, and once I found a piece of meat, and once a
cake of hard sugar, brown and gritty as sand, hidden in the
corner where I slept.

A criminal may not profit by his crime, but the court – so I was
told much later – could find no proof that David was indeed my
father's son, and made my aunt his heir.

She died, and a letter from an attorney informed me that by
her favor I had inherited 'a large house in the city of Port-
Mimizon, together with the furniture and chattels appertaining
thereto'. And that this house, 'located at 666 Saltimbanque, is
presently under the care of a robot servitor'. Since the robot
servitors under whose direction I found myself did not allow me
writing materials, I could not reply.

Time passed on the wings of birds. I found dead larks at the
feet of north-facing cliffs in autumn, at the feet of south-facing
cliffs in spring.

I received a letter from Mr Million. Most of my father's girls had left during the investigation of his death; the remainder he had been obliged to send away when my aunt died, finding that as a machine he could not enforce the necessary obedience. David had gone to the capital. Phaedria had married well. Marydol had been sold by her parents. The date on his letter was three years later than the date of my trial, but how long the letter had been in reaching me I could not tell. The envelope had been opened and resealed many times and was soiled and torn.

A seabird, I believe a gannet, came fluttering down into our camp after a storm, too exhausted to fly. We killed and ate it.

One of our guards went berserk, burned fifteen prisoners to death, and fought the other guards all night with swords of white and blue fire. He was not replaced.

I was transferred with some others to a camp farther north where I looked down chasms of red stone so deep that if I kicked a pebble in, I could hear the rattle of its descent grow to a roar of slipping rock – and hear that, in half a minute, fade with distance to silence, yet never strike the bottom lost somewhere in darkness.

I pretended the people I had known were with me. When I sat shielding my basin of soup from the wind, Phaedria sat upon a bench nearby and smiled and talked about her friends. David played squash for hours on the dusty ground of our compound, slept against the wall near my own corner. Marydol put her hand in mine while I carried my saw into the mountains.

In time they all grew dim, but even in the last year I never slept without telling myself, just before sleep, that Mr Million would take us to the city library in the morning; never woke without fearing that my father's valet had come for me.

*

Then I was told that I was to go, with three others, to another camp. We carried our food, and nearly died of hunger and exposure on the way. From there we were marched to a third camp where we were questioned by men who were not prisoners like ourselves but free men in uniforms who made notes of our answers and at last ordered that we bathe, and burned our old clothing, and gave us a thick stew of meat and barley.

I remember very well that it was then that I allowed myself to realize, at last, what these things meant. I dipped my bread into my bowl and pulled it out soaked with the fragrant stock, with bits of meat and grains of barley clinging to it; and I thought then of the fried bread and coffee at the slave market not as something of the past but as something in the future, and my hands shook until I could no longer hold my bowl and I wanted to rush shouting at the fences.

In two more days we, six of us now, were put into a mule cart that drove on winding roads always downhill until the winter that had been dying behind us was gone, and the birches and firs were gone, and the tall chestnuts and oaks beside the road had spring flowers under their branches.

The streets of Port-Mimizon swarmed with people. I would have been lost in a moment if Mr Million had not hired a chair for me, but I made the bearers stop, and bought (with money he gave me) a newspaper from a vendor so that I could know the date with certainty at last.

My sentence had been the usual one of two to fifty years, and though I had known the month and year of the beginning of my imprisonment, it had been impossible to know, in the camps, the number of the current year which everyone counted and no one knew. A man took fever and in ten days, when he was well enough again to work, said that two years had passed or had never been. Then you yourself took fever. I do not recall any headline, any article from the paper I bought. I read only the date at the top, all the way home.

It had been nine years.

I had been eighteen when I had killed my father. I was now twenty-seven. I had thought I might be forty.

*

The flaking gray walls of our house were the same. The iron dog with his three wolf-heads still stood in the front garden, but the fountain was silent, and the beds of fern and moss were full of weeds. Mr Million paid my chairmen and unlocked with a key the door that was always guard-chained but unbolted in my father's day – but as he did so, an immensely tall and lanky woman who had been hawking pralines in the street came running toward us. It was Nerissa, and I now had a servant and might have had a bedfellow if I wished, though I could pay her nothing.

*

And now I must, I suppose, explain why I have been writing this account, which has already been the labor of days; and I must even explain why I explain. Very well then. I have written to disclose myself to myself, and I am writing now because I will, I know, sometimes read what I am now writing and wonder.

Perhaps by the time I do, I will have solved the mystery of myself; or perhaps I will no longer care to know the solution.

It has been three years since my release. This house, when Nerissa and I re-entered it, was in a very confused state, my aunt having spent her last days, so Mr Million told me, in a search for my father's supposed hoard. She did not find it, and I do not think it is to be found; knowing his character better than she, I believe he spent most of what his girls brought him on his experiments and apparatus. I needed money badly myself at first, but the reputation of the house brought women seeking buyers and men seeking to buy. It is hardly necessary, as I told myself when we began, to do more than introduce them, and I have a good staff now. Phaedria lives with us and works too; the brilliant marriage was a failure after all. Last night while I was working in my surgery I heard her at the library door. I opened it and she had the child with her. Someday they'll want us.

'A STORY,'
by John V. Marsch

If you want to possess all,
  you must desire nothing.
If you want to become all,
  you must desire to be nothing.
If you want to know all,
  you must desire to know nothing.

For if you desire to possess
anything, you cannot possess
God as your only treasure.

St John of the Cross

A girl named Cedar Branches Waving lived in
the country of sliding stones where the years are longer, and it
came to her as it comes to women. Her body grew thick and
clumsy, and her breasts grew stiff and leaked milk at the teats.
When her thighs were drenched her mother took her to the place
where men are born, where two outcrops of rock join. There there
is a narrow space smooth with sand, and a new-dropped stone
lying at the joining in a few bushes; and there, where all the unseen is kind to mothers, she bore two boys.

The first came just at dawn, and because a wind rose as he fled
the womb, a cold wind out of the eye of the first light across the
mountains, his mother called him John (which only signifies 'a
man', all boy children being named *John*) Eastwind.

The second came not as they are ordinarily born – that is, head foremost as a man climbs from a lower place into a high – but feet foremost as a man lets himself down into a lower place. His grandmother was holding his brother, not knowing that two were to be born, and for that reason his feet beat the ground for a time with no one to draw him forth. Because of this his mother called him John Sandwalker.

*

She would have stood as soon as her sons were born, but her own mother would not permit it. 'You'll kill yourself,' she said. 'Here, let them suck at once so you won't dry.'

Cedar Branches Waving took one in each arm, one to each breast, and lay back again on the cold sand. Her black hair, as fine as floss, made a dark halo behind her head. There were tear streaks from the pain. Her mother began to scoop the sand with her hands, and when she reached that which still held the strength of the dead day's sun, she heaped it over her daughter's legs.

'Thank you, Mother,' said Cedar Branches Waving. She was looking at the two little faces, still smeared with her blood, that drank of her.

'So my own mother did for me when you were born. So will you do for your daughters.'

'They are boys.'

'You'll have girls too. The first birth kills – or none.'

'We must wash these in the river,' Cedar Branches Waving said, and sat up, and after a moment stood. She was a pretty girl, but because it was newly emptied her body hung shapeless. She staggered but her mother caught her, and she would not lie down again.

The sun was high by the time they reached the river, and there Cedar Branches Waving's mother was drowned in the shallows and Eastwind taken from her.

*

By the time Sandwalker was thirteen he was nearly as tall as a man. The years of his world, where the ships turned back, were long years; and his bones stretched, and his hands – large and strong. There was no fat on him (but there was no fat on anyone

60

in the country of sliding stones) and he was a foodbringer, though he dreamed strange dreams. When his thirteenth year was almost done his mother and old Bloodyfinger and Flying Feet decided to send him to the priest, and so he went out alone into the wide, high country, where the cliffs rise like banks of dark cloud, and all living things are unimportant beside the wind, the sun, the dust, the sand, and the stones. He traveled by day, alone, always south, and at night caught rock-mice to leave with twisted necks before his sleeping place. In the morning these were sometimes gone.

About noon on the fifth day he reached the gorge of Thunder Always, where the priest was. By great good luck he had been able to kill a feign-pheasant to bring as a gift, and he carried this by its hairy legs, with the long naked head and neck trailing behind him as he walked; and he, knowing that he was that day a man, and that he would reach the gorge before the sun set (Flying Feet had told him landmarks and he had passed them) walked proudly but with some fear.

He heard Thunder Always before he saw it. The ground was nearly level, dotted with rock and bush, and held no hint that there was less than stone forever beneath his feet. There was a faint grumbling, a muttering of the air. As he walked on he saw a faint mist rising. This could not indicate the gorge of Thunder Always because he could see plainly farther ground, not far off, through it; and the sound was not loud.

He took three steps more. The sound was a roaring. The earth shook. At his feet a narrow crevice opened down and down to white water far below. He was wet with the spray, and the dust ran from his body. He had been warm and he was chill. The stones were smooth and wet and shook. Carefully he sat, his legs over the darkness and white water far below, and then, feet foremost as a man lets himself down into a lower place, climbed into Thunder Always. Not until he searched just where the water foamed, where the sky was a slot of purple no wider than a finger and sprinkled with day stars, did he find the priest's cave.

*

The mouth was running with spray, and loud with the rushing waters – but the cave sloped up and up on broken stones fallen from the roof. In the dark Sandwalker climbed, climbed on hands and feet like a beast, holding the feign-pheasant in his teeth until

61

his fingers found the priest's feet and his hands the withered legs. Then he laid the feign-pheasant there, feeling like cobweb the hair and feathers and the small, dry bones dropped from earlier offerings, and retreated to the cave mouth.

Night had come, and at the appointed spot he lay down and after a long time slept despite the roaring water; but the ghost of the priest did not come into his dreams. His bed was a raft of rushes floating in a few inches of water. Around him in a circle stood immense trees, each rising from a ring of its own serpentine roots. Their bark was white like the bark of sycamores, and their trunks rose to great heights before vanishing in dark masses of their own leaves. But in his dream he was not looking at these. The circle in which he floated was of such extent that the trees formed only a horizon to it, cutting off the immeasurable concavity of the sky just where it would otherwise have touched earth.

He was, in some way he could not define, changed. His limbs were longer, yet softer; but he did not move them. He stared at the sky, and felt that he fell into it. The raft rocked, with a motion hardly detectable, to the beating of his heart.

It was his fourteenth birthday, and the constellations, therefore, occupied just those positions they had held on the night of his birth. When morning came the sun would rise in Fever; but sisterworld, whose great blue disk now showed a thin paring above the encompassing trees, obscured the two bright stars, the eyes, that were all that could be seen of The Shadow Child. None of the planets were the same. He wiped from his mind the knowledge that The Snow Woman now stood in Five Flowers, and imagined her in the place of Seeing Seed, as he knew she had been on his birthnight. And Swift in the Valley of Milk, Dead Man in the place of Lost Wishes... The Waterfall roared silently across the sky.

Feet splashed close to his head. Eastwind sat up, by long practice imparting only the slightest motion to the tiny raft.

'What have you learned?' It was Lastvoice, the greatest of starwalkers, his teacher.

'Not as much as I wished,' Eastwind said ruefully. 'I fear I slept. I deserve to be beaten.'

'You are honest at least,' Lastvoice said.

'You have told me often that one who would advance must own to every fault.'

'I've told you as well that it is not the offender who passes sentence.'

'Which will be?' asked Eastwind. He strove to keep apprehension from his voice.

'Suspended, for my best acolyte. You slept.'

'Only a moment, I'm sure. I had a curious dream, but I've had these before.'

'Yes.' Serene and commanding, Lastvoice leaned over his pupil. He was very tall, and the blue light of rising sisterworld showed a bloodless face from which the few wisps of beard, as ritual required, were plucked daily. The sides of his head had been seared with brands kindled in the flows of the Mountains of Manhood, so that his hair, thicker than any woman's, grew only in a stiffened crest.

'I dreamed again that I was a hill-man, and I had gone to the source of the river, where I was to receive an oracle in a sacred cave. I lay down, that I might be given it, near rushing water.'

Lastvoice said nothing, and Eastwind continued, 'You hoped I had been walking among the stars; but as you see, it was a dream of no spirit.'

'Perhaps. But what do the stars tell you of the enterprise tomorrow? Will you wind the conch?'

'As my master says.'

*

When Sandwalker woke he was stiff and cold. He had had such dreams before, but they faded quickly and if there was any message in this one he did not understand it, and he knew that Lastvoice was certainly not the priest whose ghost he had invited. For a few minutes he toyed with the idea of staying in the gorge until he was ready to sleep again, but the thought of the clear morning sky above and the warmth of the sun on the plateau decided him against it. It was almost noon when, ravenously hungry, he made the last climb and flung himself down to rest on the warm, dusty ground.

In an hour he was ready to rise again and hunt. He was a good hunter, young and strong, and more patient than the long-toothed bitch cat that waits flattened on a ledge all day, two days, remembering her cubs that weaken as they mew for her and sigh, and sleep, and cry again until she kills. There had been others when Sandwalker was only a year or two younger; not, perhaps, quite so strong as he; others who, after running and stalking and hunting again until the sun was almost down had come back to

the sleeping place with hands empty and slack bellies, hoping fo
leavings and begging their mothers for breasts now belonging t
a younger child. These were dead. They had learned the truth tha
the sleeping place is easily found by a food-bringer, not hard fo
a full belly to find; but shifts and turns before hungry mouth
until it is lost in the stones, and on the third empty day is gon
forever.

And so for two days Sandwalker hunted as only hill-men hunt
seeing everything, gleaning everything, sniffing out the nest o
the owl-mouse to swallow her children like shrimp and chew the
hoarded seeds to sweet pulp; creeping, his skin the cold ston
color of the dust, his wild hair breaking the telltale silhouette o
his head; silent as the fog that reaches into the high country an
is not seen until it touches the cheek (when it blinds).

An hour before full dark of the second day he crossed the trai
of a tick-deer, the hornless little ungulate that lives by licking u
the brown blood drinkers its hoofs' click calls from their hidin
places near water holes. He followed it while sisterworld rose an
ruled, and was still following when she had sunk half her blue
wealth of continents behind the farthest of the smoking mountain
of the west. Then he heard spring up before him the feasting
song the Shadow children sing when they have killed enough fo
every mouth, and he knew that he had lost.

In the great old days of long dreaming, when God was king o
men, men had walked unafraid among the Shadow children by
night, and the Shadow children, unafraid, had sought the company of men by day. But the long dreaming had given its years to
the river long ago, floating down to the clammy meadow-mere
and death. Yet a great hunter, thought Sandwalker, (and ther
because he had held since least boyhood that milk-gift that allows
a man to look from eyes outside his own and laugh he added, *a
great hunter who was very hungry*) might attempt the old way
again. God, surely, orders all things. The Shadow children migh
slay by the right hands and the left while the sun slept, but wha
fools they'd look if they tried to kill him if God did not wish it,
by night or day.

Silently, but proud and straight, he strode on until sisterworld's
blue light showed the place where, like bats around spilled blood,
the Shadow children ringed the tick-deer. Long before he reached
them their heads turned, on stems unhindered as the necks of owls.
'Morning met where much food is,' Sandwalker said politely.

While he walked five paces there was no sound, then a mouth
not human answered, 'Much food indeed.'

Women at the sleeping place, wishing to frighten children still playing when their shadows were longer than themselves, said the Shadow children's teeth dripped poison. Sandwalker did not believe it, but he remembered this when the other spoke. He knew 'much food' did not mean the tick-deer, but he said: 'That is well. I heard your song – you sang of many mouths and all full. It was I who drove your meat to you, and I ask a share – or I kill the largest of you to eat myself, and the rest may dine upon the bones when I have finished. It is all one to me.'

'Men are not as you. Men do not eat the flesh of their kind.'

'You mean yourselves? Only when you are hungry, but you are hungry all the time.'

Several voices said softly, 'No,' drawing out the word.

'A man I know – Flying Feet, a tall man and not afraid of the sun – killed one of you and left the head for night-offering. When he woke, the skull was stripped.'

'Foxes,' said a voice that had not spoken before, 'or it was a native boy of his own get he killed, which is more likely. Mice you left us while you came here, and now you would be repaid in deer's flesh. Dear mice indeed. We should have strangled you while you slept.'

'You would have lost many in the attempt.'

'I could kill you now. I alone. So we butcher your brats that come whimpering to us – quiet them and dine well.' One of the dark figures rose.

'I am no suckling – I have fourteen summers. And I do not come starving. I have eaten today and I will eat again.'

The Shadow Child who had risen took a step forward. Several of the others reached toward him as though to stop him, but did not. 'Come!' Sandwalker said. 'Do you think to call me from the sleeping place to kill among the rocks? Baby killer!' He flexed his knees and hands and felt the strength that lived in his arms. Before making his bold approach he had resolved that if the Shadow children tried to kill him he would flee at once without trying to fight – he was certain that he could quickly outdistance their short legs. But he was equally sure now that whether the poisoned bite was real or not, he could deal with the diminutive figure facing him.

The voice which had spoken to him first said urgently, but so softly it was almost a whisper, 'You must not harm him. He is sacred.'

'I did not come to fight you,' Sandwalker said. 'I only want a fair portion of the tick-deer I drove into your hands. You sing that you have much.'

The Shadow Child who had risen to face him said, 'With my smallest finger, little native animal, I will break your bones until the ends burst through your skin.'

Sandwalker edged away from the talons the other thrust toward him and announced contemptuously, 'If you are his blood, make him squat again – or he is mine.'

'Sacred,' their voices replied. The sound of the word was like the night wind that looks for the sleeping place and never finds it.

His left hand would bat the shrunken claws aside; his right take the small, too-supple throat in the grip that killed. Sandwalker set his feet and waited, crouching, the slight farther advance that would bring the shuffling figure within sure reach. And then, perhaps because at the edge of sight a mile-wide plume of smoke from the Mountains of Manhood had blown aside to reveal her, sisterworld's light fell, in the instant before setting and as quickly as lightning-glare, on The Shadow Child's face. It was dark and weak, huge eyes above sagging flesh, the cheeks sunken, the nose and mouth, from which a thick liquid ran, no larger than an infant's.

But though Sandwalker remembered these things later he did not notice them in the brief flash of blue light. Instead he saw the face of all men, and the strength they think theirs when they are full of meat, and that they are fools to be destroyed with a breath; and because Sandwalker was young he had never seen that thing before. When the talons touched his throat he tore himself away, and, gasping and choking for a reason he could not understand, dodged back toward the knot of dark bodies about the tick-deer.

'Look,' said the voice which had spoken to him first. 'He weeps. Boy, here, quickly, sit with us. Eat.'

Sandwalker squatted, drawn down by their small, dark hands, beside the tick-deer with the others. Someone said to The Shadow Child whose fingers had stretched for his throat a moment before, 'You mustn't hurt him; he's our guest.'

'Ah.'

'It's all right to play with them, of course; it keeps them in their place. But let him eat now.'

Another put a gobbet of the tick-deer's flesh into Sandwalker's hands, and as he always had, he gorged it before it could be snatched away. The Shadow Child who had threatened him laid a hand on his shoulder. 'I'm sorry I frightened you.'

'It's all right.'

Sisterworld had set and, no longer robbed of their brilliance, the constellations blazed across the autumn sky: Burning Hair

Woman, bearded Five Legs, Rose of Amethyst that the people of the meadowmeres, the marshmen, called Thousand Feelers and the Fish. The tick-deer was sweet in Sandwalker's mouth and sweeter in his belly, and he felt a sudden content. The shrunken figures around him were his friends. They had given him to eat. It was good to be sitting thus, with friends and food, while Burning Hair Woman stood on her head in the night sky.

The voice that had addressed him first (he could not, for a time, make out from whose mouth it came) said: 'You are our friend now. It has been a long time since we've taken a shadowfriend from among the native population.'

Sandwalker did not know what was meant, but it seemed polite, and safe, to nod; he did so.

'You say we sing. When you came you said we sang The Song of Many Mouths and All Full. There is a singing in you now, a happy song, though without counterpoint.'

'Who are you?' Sandwalker asked. 'I can't tell which of you is talking.'

'Here.' Two of the Shadow children edged (apparently) aside, and a dark area which Sandwalker had thought was only the star-shadow of a stone straightened and showed a shrunken face and bright eyes.

'Well met,' said Sandwalker, and gave his name.

'I am called the Old Wise One,' said the oldest of the Shadow children. 'Well met truly.' Sandwalker noticed that the stars could be seen faintly through the Old Wise One's back, so he was a ghost; but this did not greatly bother Sandwalker – ghosts (though they most frequently stayed in the dreamworld as who would not if he might) were a fact of life, and a helpful ghost could be a strong ally.

'You think me a shadow of the dead,' said the Old Wise One, 'but it is not so.'

'We are all,' Sandwalker pronounced diplomatically, 'but shadows cast ahead of them.'

'No,' said the Old Wise One, 'I am not that. Since you are a shadowfriend, now I will tell you what I am. You see all these others – your friends as truly as I – gathered about this carcass?'

'Yes.' (Sandwalker had been counting them lest another appear. There were seven.)

'You would say that these sing. There is The Song of Many Mouths and All Full, The Bending Sky-Paths Song that none may come, The Hunting Song, The Song of Ancient Sorrows we sing when the Fighting Lizard is high in the summer sky and we

67

see our old home as a little yellow gem in his tail. And so on. Your people say these songs sometimes disturb your dreams.'

Sandwalker nodded, his mouth full.

'Now when you speak to me, or your own people sing at your sleeping places, that singing is a shaking in the air. When you speak, or one of these others speaks to you, that, too, is a shaking in the air.'

'When the thunder speaks,' said Sandwalker, '*that* is a shaking. And now I feel a small shaking in my throat when I talk to you.'

'Yes, your throat shakes itself and thus the air, as a man shakes a bush by first shaking his arm which holds it. But when *we* sing it is not the air that shakes. We shake extension; and I am the song all the Shadow children sing, their thought when they think as one. Hold your hands before you thus, not touching. Now think of your hands gone. That is what we shake.'

Sandwalker said, 'That is nothing.'

'That which you call nothing is what holds all things apart. When it is gone, all the worlds will come together in a fiery death from which new worlds will be born. But now listen to me. As you are named shadowfriend you must learn before this night is over to call our help when you require it. It is easily done, and it is done this way: when you hear our singing – and you will find now that if you listen well, lying or sitting without motion and bending your thought to us, you may hear us very far off – you, in your mind, must sing the same song. Sing with us, and we will hear the echo of our song in your thought and know you require us. Try it now.'

All about Sandwalker, the Shadow children began singing The Daysleep Song, which tells of the sun's rising; and of the first light; the long, long shadows and the dances the dust-devils do on the hilltops. 'Sing with us,' the Old Wise One urged.

Sandwalker sang. At first he tried to add something of his own to the song, as men do at the sleeping place; but the Shadow children pinched him and frowned. After that he only sang The Daysleep Song as he heard them singing, and soon all of them were dancing around the bones of the tick-deer, showing how the dust-devils would.

He now saw that the Shadow children were not all old men as he had imagined. Two indeed were wrinkled and stiff. One seemed a woman though like the rest she had only wisps of hair; two neither old nor young; and two, little more than boys. Sandwalker watched their faces as he danced, marveling that they seemed at once both young and old – and the faces of the others

…at seemed old yet young. He could see much better than he had …een able to while they were squatting about the tick-deer, and … came to him – both understandings at once, so that surprise …ushed surprise – that in the east the black of the sky was giving …ay to purple, and that there were but seven Shadow children. …he Old Wise One was gone. He turned to face the rising sun – …alf from instinct, half because he thought the Old Wise One …ight have gone that way. When he turned again the Shadow …hildren had scattered behind him, darting among the rocks. Only …vo were visible, then none. His first thought was to pursue them, …ut he felt certain they would not wish it. He called loudly, 'Go …ith God!' and waved his arms.

The first beams of the new sun sent shapes of black and gold …eaping toward him. He looked at the tick-deer; some shreds of …esh remained, and bones that would yield marrow if he could …reak them. Half-humorously he said to these leavings, 'Morning …et where much food is,' then ate again before the ants came.

An hour later, as he picked his teeth with a fingernail, he …ought about his dream of the night before. The Old Wise One, …e felt, might have interpreted it for him. He wished that he had …sked. If he slept now, by daylight, there was little chance that any …ood dream would come, but he was tired and cold. He stretched …imself in the warm sunshine – and noticed that the back of the …voman walking before him looked familiar. He was walking …aster than she and soon could see that it was his mother, but …hen he tried to greet her he found he was unable to do so. Then …e, who had always been so sure of foot, tripped on a stone. He …hrew out his hands to save himself, a shock went through his …vhole body, and he found himself sitting up, alone, and sweating …rom the sun's heat.

He stood, still trembling, brushing at the grit that clung to his …amp limbs and his back. It was only foolishness. There was no …se in sleeping by day – his spirit only left the body at once and …vent wandering, and then if the priest *did* come to him in sleep …here would be no one to receive him. The priest might even …ecome angry with him and not come back. No, he must either …eturn to the cave and try again there, or acknowledge failure and …o away – which would be intolerable. He would return, then, to …he gorge.

But not with empty hands. The feign-pheasant he had brought …efore had proved an inadequate gift. This might be because the …riest was in some way displeased with him; but, as he reflected …vith some satisfaction, it might also be because the priest in-

tended some revelation of great moment, for which the feign
pheasant was insufficient. Another tick-deer, if he could find one
might be satisfactory. He had come from the north and had seen
few signs of game; to go east would mean crossing the river gorge
before he traveled far, and westward, toward the burning moun
tains, stretched a waterless wilderness of stone. He went south.

The land rose slowly as he went. There had been little vegeta
tion, but it became less. The gray rock gave way to red. About
noon, as his tireless stride brought him to the summit of a ridge
he saw something he had seen only twice before in his life: a tiny
watered valley, an oasis of the high desert which had managed to
hold soil enough for real grass, a few wild flowers, and a tree.

Such a place was of great significance, but it was possible to
drink there, and even to stay for a few hours if one dared. And i
was less offensive to the tree, as Sandwalker knew, if one came
alone – an advantage for him. Approaching, as custom dictated
neither swiftly nor slowly, but with an expression of studied
courtesy, he was about to greet it when he saw a girl sitting
holding an infant, among the roots.

For a moment, impolitely, his eyes left the tree. The girl's face
was heart-shaped, timorous, scarcely a woman's yet. Her long
hair (and this was something to which Sandwalker was un-
accustomed) was clean – she had washed it in the pool at the foot
of the tree, and untied the tangles with her fingers so that it now
spread a dark caul upon her brown shoulders. She sat cross-
legged and unmoving, with the baby, a flower thrust in its hair,
asleep on her thighs.

Sandwalker greeted the tree ceremoniously, asking permission
to drink and promising not to stay long. A murmuring of leaves
answered him, and though he could not understand the words
they did not sound angry. He smiled to show his appreciation,
then went to the pool and drank.

He drank long and deep, as desert animals do; and when he
had had his fill and lifted his head from the wind-rippled water
he saw the girl's reflection dancing beside his own. She was
watching him with large, fearful eyes; but she was quite close.
'Morning met,' he said.

'Morning met.'

'I am Sandwalker.' He thought of his journey to the cave, of
the tick-deer and the feign-pheasant and the Old Wise One.
'Sandwalker the far-traveled, the great hunter, the shadowfriend.'

'I am Seven Girls Waiting,' the girl said. 'And this,' she smiled tenderly down at the baby she carried, 'is Mary Pink Butterflies. I called her that because of her little hands, you know. She waves them at me when she's awake.'

Sandwalker, who in his own short life had seen how many children come and how few live, smiled and nodded.

The girl looked down into the pool at the foot of the tree, at the tree, at the flowers and grass, everywhere but at Sandwalker's face. He saw her small, white teeth creep out like snowmice to touch her lips, then flee again. The wind made patterns on the grass, and the tree said something he could not understand – though Seven Girls Waiting, perhaps, did. 'Will you,' she asked hesitantly, 'make this your sleeping place tonight?'

He knew what she meant and answered as gently as he could, 'I have no food to share. I'm sorry. I hunt, but what I find I must keep for a gift for the priest in Thunder Always. Doesn't anyone sleep where you sleep?'

'There was nothing anywhere. Pink Butterflies was new, and I could not walk far . . . We slept up there, beyond the bent rock.' She made a wretched little gesture with her shoulders.

'I have never known that,' Sandwalker said, laying a hand on her arm, 'but I know how it must feel, sitting alone, waiting for them to come when no one comes. It must be a terrible thing.'

'You are a man. It will not come to you until you are old.'

'I didn't mean to make you angry.'

'I'm not angry. I'm not alone either – Pink Butterflies is with me all the time, and I have milk for her. Now we sleep here.'

'Every night?'

The girl nodded, half-defiantly.

'It isn't good to sleep where a tree is for more than one night.'

'Pink Butterflies is his daughter. I know because he told me in a dream a long time before she was born. He likes having her here.'

Sandwalker said carefully, 'We were all engendered in women by trees. But they seldom want us to stay by them for more than a single night.'

'He's good to us! I thought . . . ' the girl's voice dropped until it was barely audible above the rustling of the wind in the grass, 'when you came he might have sent you to bring us something to eat.'

Sandwalker looked at the little pool. 'Are there fish here?'

The girl said humbly, as though confessing some misdemeanor, 'I haven't been able to find any for . . . for . . . '

'How long?'

'For the last three days. That's how we were living. I ate the fish from the pool, and I had milk for Pink Butterflies. I still have milk.' She looked down at the baby, then up again at Sandwalker, her wide eyes begging him to believe her. 'She just drank. There was enough milk.'

Sandwalker was looking at the sky. 'It's going to be cold,' he said. 'See how clear it is.'

'You will make this your sleeping place tonight?'

'Any food I find must go toward my gift.' He told her about the priest, and his dream.

'But you will come back?'

Sandwalker nodded, and she described the best places to hunt – the places where her people had found game, when they had found game.

The long, rocky slope above the tree and pool and little circle of living grass took the better part of an hour to climb. At the bent rock – a crooked finger of stone left pointing skyward after some calamity of erosion – he found the sleeping place her people had used: the rocks that had sheltered the sleepers from wind, a few scuffed tracks the weather had not yet erased, the gleaming bones of small animals. But the sleeping place was of no use or interest to him.

He hunted until sisterworld rose, and found nothing, and would have liked to sleep where he was; but he had promised the girl he would come back, and there was already an icy spirit in the air. He found her, as he had expected, lying with her arms around the baby among the tangled roots of the tree.

Exhausted, he flung himself down beside her. The sound of his breathing and the warmth of his body woke her; she started, then looked at him and smiled, and he was suddenly glad he had come back. 'Did you catch anything?' she said.

He shook his head.

'I did. Look. I thought you might like to have it for your gift.' She held up a small fish, now stiff and cold.

Sandwalker took it, then shook his head. If the feign-pheasant had been inadequate, this would certainly not be acceptable. 'A fish would spoil before I got it there,' he said. He started a hole in the belly with his teeth, then widened it with his fingers until he could scrape out the intestines and lift away most of the bones, leaving two little strips of flesh. He gave one to the girl.

'Good,' she said, swallowing. Then, 'Where are you going?'

Sandwalker had risen, still chewing the fish, and stood stretching his tired, cold muscles in sisterworld's blue light. 'Hunting,' he answered. 'Before, I was looking for something large, something I could take for a gift. Now I'm going to look for something small, just something for us to eat tonight. Rock-mice, maybe.'

Then he was gone, and the girl lay hugging her child, looking through the leaves at the bright band of The Waterfall and the broad seas and scattered storms of sisterworld. Then her eyes closed, and she could pull sisterworld from the tree. She put the blue rind to her lips and tasted sweetness. Then she woke again, the sweet juice still in her mouth. Someone was bending over her, and for a moment she was afraid.

'Come on.' It was he, Sandwalker. 'Wake up, I've got something.' He touched her lips again with his fingers; they were sticky, and fragrant with a piercing perfume of fruit, flowers, and earth.

She stood, holding Pink Butterflies pressed against her, her jutting breasts warming Pink Butterflies's stomach and legs (that was what they were for, besides milk), her arms wrapped about the little body, shivering.

Sandwalker pulled her. 'Come on.'

'Is it far?'

'No, not very far.' (It was far, and he wanted to offer to carry Pink Butterflies, but he knew Seven Girls Waiting would fear he might harm her.)

The way lay north by east, almost on the margin of the earliest beginning of the river. Seven Girls Waiting was stumbling by the time they reached it: a small dark hole where Sandwalker had kicked in the ground with his heel. 'Here,' he said. 'I stopped to rest here, and with my ears close I could hear them talking.' He ripped up the seemingly solid ground with strong fingers, tossing away the clods; then a clod, dark as the others in sisterworld's blue light, came up dripping. There was a soft murmuring. He broke the clotted stuff in two, thrusting half into his own mouth, half into hers. She knew, suddenly, that she was starving and chewed and swallowed frantically, spitting out the wax.

'Help me,' he said. 'They won't sting you. It's too cold. You can just brush them off.'

He was digging again and she joined him, laying Pink Butterflies in a safe place and smearing her little mouth with honey to lick, and her hands so that she could lick her fingers. They ate not only the honey but the fat, white larva, digging and eating until their arms and faces, their entire bodies, were sticky and powdered with the bee-rotten soil; Sandwalker, thrusting his choice finds into the girl's mouth and she, her best discoveries into his,

73

brushing aside the stupefied bees and digging and eating again until they fell back happy and surfeited in one another's arms. She pressed against him, feeling her stomach hard and round as a melon beneath her ribs and against his skin. Her lips were on his face, and it was dirty and sweet.

He moved her shoulders gently. 'No,' she said, 'not on top of me. I'd split. I'd be sick. Like this.' His tree had grown large, and she wrapped it with her hands. Afterward they put Pink Butterflies between their perspiring bodies to keep her warm and slept the remainder of the night, the three of them, pressed in a tangle of legs and sighs.

The roaring of Thunder Always came to Sandwalker's ears. He rose and went into the priest's cave, but this time, though it was as dark as before, he could see everything. He had found the power, he did not know where, to see without eyes and without light; the cave stretched to either side of him and ahead of him – a jumble of fallen slabs.

He went forward and upward. It was drier. The floor became gritty clay. Icicles of stone hung from the coldly sweating rocks overhead and lifted from the floor at his feet until he walked as if in the mouth of a beast. Drier still, and there were no more stone teeth, only the rough tongue of clay and the vaulted throat growing smaller and smaller. Then he saw the bed of the priest with the bones of gifts all around it, and the priest rose on his bed to look at him.

'I am sorry,' Sandwalker told him, 'you are hungry and I've brought you nothing.' Then he held out his hands and saw he held a dripping comb in one and a mass of fat larva cemented with honey in the other. The priest took them, smiling, and bending down chose from among the litter of bones an animal's skull, which he held out to Sandwalker.

Sandwalker took it; it was dry and old, but the priest's hand had stained it with fresh blood, and as he watched, the blood brought life to it: the bone becoming new and wet, then marble with dark veins, then wrapped in skin and fur. It was the head of an otter. The eyes, liquid and living, looked into Sandwalker's face.

In them he saw the river, where the otter had been born; the river trickling past the despoiled hive; saw the water dive through the high hills seeking the true surface of the world; saw it rush in torrents through Thunder Always and slow from plunging rapids to a swift stream and at last to a broad halfmile, winding almost without current through the meadowmeres. He saw the stiff

74

light of hair-herons and aigrettes, yellow frogs wrestling for the possession of the wind; and through the slow, green water, as though he were swimming in it himself twenty feet down among the stones and gravel and mountain-born sand of the bottom, the figure of the otter. With brown fur that was nearly black it threaded the waters like a snake until, close to him, it turned broad side on and he could see its short strong legs paddling – clear of the sandy bottom by a finger-width, but seeming to walk along it.

'What?' he said. 'What?' Pink Butterflies was squirming against him. Sleepily he helped her until she reached one of her mother's breasts, then cupped his hand about the other. He was cold and thought of his dream, but it seemed hardly to have ended.

He stood beside the broad river, his feet in mud. It was not yet quite sunrise, but the stars were dimming. Rushes rippled in the dawn wind, the waves running to the edge of the world. Calf-deep in the river, with slow eddies circling their legs, stood Flying Feet, old Bloodyfinger, Leaves-you-can-eat, the girl Sweetmouth, and Cedar Branches Waving.

From behind him stepped two men. The people of the meadow-meres, he knew, drove their young men from women until fire from the mountains proved their manhood and left their thigh and shoulders puckered with scars. These men had such scars, and their hair had been knotted in locks, and they wore grass about their wrists and waxy blossoms at their necks. A man with a scarred head chanted, then ended. He saw Flying Feet see that the man's eyes were on him and step backward – and so doing, into a place where the river was suddenly deeper. Flying Feet sank, floundering. The scarred man seized him. The water churned with his strugglings, but the scarred men, themselves now waist-deep, bent over him, thrusting him down. The strugglings grew less, and Sandwalker, knowing he dreamed – Sandwalker asleep beside Seven Girls Waiting – thought as he dreamed that were he Flying Feet he would feign death until they brought him to the air again. Meantime Flying Feet's churning of the river had ceased. The silt his kicking had raised floated away, leaving the water clear. In it his arms and legs lay lifeless, and his long hair trailed behind him like weed. The dream Sandwalker strode to him, feet lifting high, scarcely splashing when they came down. He looked at the blank white face under the water, and as he looked, the eyes opened, and the mouth opened, and there was an agony in them which faded and became slack, the eyes no longer seeing.

75

Sandwalker could not breathe. He sat up trembling, gulping air, a pressure on his chest. He stood, feeling he must thrust his head higher than water he could not see. Seven Girls Waiting stirred, and Pink Butterflies waked and whimpered.

He left them and walked to the top of a small knoll. As in his dream the sun was coming, and the east was rose and purple with the reflection of his face.

When Seven Girls Waiting had drunk from the river and was feeding Pink Butterflies he explained his dream to her: 'Flying Feet thought as I. He would pretend death. But the marshmen had seen that trick, and . . . ' Sandwalker shrugged.

'You said he couldn't get up,' she said practically, 'so he would have died anyway.'

'Yes.'

'Will you hunt today? You still need a gift, and since we didn't stay at the tree last night you could sleep there tonight.'

'I don't think the priest requires another gift of me,' Sandwalker said slowly. 'I thought he was not helping me, but now I see that the dream I dreamed in his cave of floating and watching the stars was by his help, and the dream I dreamed by daylight of walking with my mother and the others was by his help, and the dream I dreamed last night. Truly, the men of the marsh have taken my people.'

Seven Girls Waiting sat down, holding Pink Butterflies on her lap and not looking at his face. 'It is a long way to the marshes,' she said.

'Yes, but my dream has shown me how I may travel swiftly.' Sandwalker walked to the edge of the little stream which would become the great river and looked down into it. The water was very clear, and hip-deep. The bottom was sand and stones. He plunged in.

The current, fast even here, took him. For a moment he raised his head from the water. Seven Girls Waiting was already far away, a small figure shining in the new sun; she waved and held up Pink Butterflies so that she could see, and he knew that she was calling, 'Go with God.'

The water took him again and he spun on to his belly and thought of the otter, imagining that he too had nostrils close to the top of his head and short, powerful swimming legs in place of his long limbs. He stroked and shot ahead, stroked and shot ahead, occasionally pausing to listen for the roar of a falls.

*

He passed many, leaving the river and circling them on foot. The lesser rapids he swam, growing more skillful at each. Through half the gorge of Thunder Always he carried a large fish to leave as an offering in the priest's cave. In deep pools the currents sent him swirling toward the bottom until, with their force spent, he hung suspended in the green light, his hair a cloud about his face – then streaming straight out behind it as he followed the waters to the surface again among crystal spheres of air.

Late that day, though he could only guess it, he passed through the country most familiar to him, the rocky hills where his own people roved, having come farther north since morning than he had traveled southward on the way to Thunder Always in five days. Evening came, and, from a stretch of the river quieter than most, he crawled onto a sandy bank, finding himself almost too tired to drag his body from the water. He slept on the sand in the shelter of high grass, and did not look at the stars at all.

The next morning he walked for half an hour along the little beach before slipping, hungry, into the water again. Everything was easier now. Fish were more plentiful and he caught a fine one, then a dabduck by swimming under water, eyes open and limbs scarcely moving, until he could grasp the unlucky bird's feet.

The river, too, was quieter; and if he did not rush along as swiftly, his progress was less exhausting. It flowed smoothly among wooded hills; then, much broader, slipped through lowlands where great trees sank roots in the water and arched branches fifty feet toward mid-channel from either side. At last it seemed to stagnate in a flatland where reeds, dotted with trees and brush, spread without limit; and the cold, unliving water acquired, by means Sandwalker did not comprehend, faintly, the taste of sweat.

Now night came again, but there was no friendly bank. Cautiously he picked his way half a mile over the reeking mud to reach a tree. Waterfowl circled overhead, calling to each other and sometimes crying – as though the death of the sun meant terror and death for them as well, a night of fear.

He spoke to the tree when he reached it, but it did not reply and he felt that whatever power dwelt in the lonely oasis trees of his own land was absent here; that this tree spoke to the unseen no more than to him, engineering no babes in women. After begging permission (he might, after all, be wrong) he climbed into a high fork to sleep. A few insects found him, but they were torpid in the cold. The sky was streaked with clouds through which sisterworld's bloodless light shone only fitfully. He slept, then woke; and first smelled, then heard, then in the wanton beams saw, a ghoul-bear lope by – huge, thick-limbed, and stinking.

Almost he slept again. *Sorrow, sorrow, sorrow.*

Not sorrow, he thought, though when he remembered Seven Girls Waiting and Pink Butterflies and the living, thinking tree ruling kindly its little lake and flowered lawn in the country of sliding stones, something hurt.

Sorrow, sorrow, sorrow, sang the night wind, throbbing.

Not sorrow, Sandwalker thought to himself, hate. The marsh-men had killed Flying Feet, who had sometimes out of his plenty given him to eat when he was small. They would kill Bloody-finger and Leaves-you-can-eat, Sweetmouth and his mother.

Sorrow, sing sorrow.

Not sorrow, he thought, the wind, the tree. He sat up, listening to convince himself that it was only the sighing of the wind he heard, or perhaps the tree murmuring of better places. Whatever it was – perhaps, indeed, he had been wrong about this lonely, reed-hemmed tree – it was not an angry sound. It was . . . nothing.

The lost wind sighed, but not in words. The leaves around him scarcely trembled. Far overhead and far away thunder boomed. *Sorrow,* sang many voices. *Sorrow, sorrow, sorrow. Loneliness, and the night coming that will never go.*

Not the wind; not the tree. Shadow children. Somewhere. Forming the words sof^tly, Sandwalker said, 'Morning met. I am not lonely or sad, but I will sing with you.' *Sorrow, sorrow, sorrow.* He remembered that the Old Wise One had said, 'As you are named shadowfriend, you must learn before this night is over to call for our help when you require it.' He had hoped, with a boy's optimism, to free his people by his own strength, but if the Shadow children would help him he was very willing that they should. '*Loneliness,*' he sang with them, and then, closing his lips and unfolding his mind to the clouds and the empty miles of water and reeds, *and the night coming that will never go.*

Sorrow, sorrow, sorrow, sang again the Shadow children (somewhere), but the mind-song seemed now something less an expression of feeling and something more a ritual, a song tradi-tional to their circumstances. They had heard him. *Come to us, shadowfriend. Aid us in our sorrow.*

He tried to ask questions, and discovered he could not. As soon as his thought was no longer the thought of the song, as long as it no longer swayed and pleaded with the others, the touching was broken and he was alone.

78

Aid us, aid us, sang the Shadow children. *Help us.*

Sandwalker climbed down from the tree, shuddering at the thought of the ghoul-bear. Far off in the night a bird chuckled fiendishly. Not only was it difficult to tell from whence the song came, but activity submerged the impression of it in his own mind's motions. He stopped, first standing, then leaning against the bole of the tree, finally closing his eyes and throwing back his head. *Sorrow, sorrow, sorrow.* A direction – perhaps – north by west; diagonally away from the main channel of the river. He looked at the sky, hoping to take a bearing from the Eye of Cold – but the clouds, rank upon serried rank, allowed no star more than an instant.

He walked and splashed, then halted, embarrassed by his own noise. Around him the marsh seemed to listen. He tried again, and in a few hundred steps developed a method of walking which was reasonably silent. Knees high, he moved his feet quickly across the water and put them down with the whole foot arched like a diver. Like a wading bird, he thought. He remembered the times he had seen the long-limbed, plumed frog-spearers stalking the margins of the river. I am Sandwalker truly.

But there was mud underfoot now. Several times he was afraid he would be mired, and small animals he recognized as somehow akin to the rockrats scuttled away at his approach or dove into ponds. Something he could never see whistled at him from thickets of reeds and the black mouths of burrows.

Sorrow, sorrow, sorrow, sang the Shadow children, closer now. The ground, though still soft, was no longer covered with standing water. Sandwalker moved from shadow to shadow, immobile when the clouds leaked sisterworld's light. A voice – a Shadow child's thin voice, but a real voice that came to the ears – said (at some distance, but distinctly), 'They are waiting to take him.'

'They will not take him,' answered a second, much less clearly. 'He's our friend. He ... we ... will kill them all.'

Sandwalker crouched among rushes. For five minutes, ten minutes, he did not move. Overhead the clouds flew east and were replaced by more. The wind swayed the reeds and whispered. After a long time a voice, not a Shadow child's said: 'They've gone. If there ever were any. They heard them.'

A second voice grunted. Ahead of him a hundred paces or more something moved; he heard rather than saw it. After another five minutes he began to circle to his left.

An hour later he knew that there were four men waiting in a rough square, and suspected that the Shadow children were in

79

the center. To be hunted was no new experience – twice as a child he had been hunted by starving men – and it would be simple now to melt away and find a new sleeping place or return to his old one. He crept forward instead, at once frightened and excited.

'Light soon,' one of the men said, and another answered him, 'More might still come; be quiet.' Sandwalker had almost reached the center of the square.

Slowly he crept forward. His hand touched air. The earth was no longer level in front of him. He groped. It fell away. Not straight down, but down at a steep slope, very soft. He peered into the darkness, and a reedy Shadow voice whispered: 'We see you. A little further, if you can, and hold out your hands.'

They were taken by diminutive, skeletal fingers, tugged, and there was a small, dark shape beside him; tugged again and there was another. Three, but already the first had faded into the rushes. Four, but only the newcomer beside him. Five, and he and the fifth were alone. Holding his body close to the ground, he turned and began to creep away the way he had come. There were stealthy noises around him, and one of the hunters said, almost (it seemed) in his ear, 'Go look.' Then there was a crash as a hundred reeds snapped, and a confusion of thrashing sound. To his right a man stood up and began to run. The Shadow child beside him threw himself at the marshman's ankles as he passed and he came crashing down.

Sandwalker was upon him almost before he hit, his thumbs merciless as stones as they drove into the neck. Lightning flashed, and he saw the contorted face, and two small hands that reached down to pluck out the marshman's eyes.

Then he was up; it was blind dark, and the marshmen were yelling and a thin voice screaming. A man loomed in front of him and Sandwalker kicked him expertly, then drove the head down with his hands to meet his knees; he took a step backward and a Shadow child was on the man's shoulders, his fleshless legs locked around the throat and his fingers plunged into the hair. 'Come,' Sandwalker said urgently, 'we have to get away.'

'Why?' The Shadow child sounded calm and happy. 'We're winning.' The man he rode, who had been doubled over in agony, straightened up and tried to free himself; the Shadow child's legs tightened, and as Sandwalker watched, the marshman fell to his knees. It was suddenly quiet – much quieter, in fact, than it had been before they had been discovered, because the insects and night birds were mute. The wind no longer stirred the reeds. A

Shadow child's voice said: 'That's over. They're a fine lot, aren't they?'

Sandwalker, who was not equally sure that there would be no more fighting, answered, 'I'm certain your people are brave, but it was I who overcame two of these wetlanders.'

The marshman who had dropped to his knees a moment before rose shakily, and guided by the Shadow child on his shoulders staggered away. 'I didn't mean us,' the voice talking to Sandwalker said. 'I meant them. We have enough here for a number of feasts. Now everyone's meeting by the hole where they kept us. Go over there and you can see.'

'Aren't you coming?' Sandwalker had been looking for the speaker, and could not locate him.

There was no answer. He turned, and guided by a well-developed sense of direction went back to the pit. The four men were there, three of them with riders on their shoulders, the fourth moaning and swaying, scrubbing with bloodied hands at the bleeding sockets of his eyes. Two more Shadow children crouched in the trampled marsh grass.

A voice from behind Sandwalker said, 'We should eat the blind one tonight. The rest we can drive into the hills to share with friends.' The blind man moaned.

'I wish I could see you,' Sandwalker said. 'Are you the same Old Wise One I talked to three nights ago?'

'No.' A sixth Shadow child stepped from somewhere. In the faint light (even Sandwalker's eyes had difficulty seeing more than half-shapes and outlines; the ridden men were bulks more felt than seen) he seemed completely solid, but older than any of the others.

The starlight, when the clouds permitted starlight, glittered on his head as on frost. 'We knew you as a shadow friend only by your singing. You are very young. Was it only three nights ago that you became one of us?'

'I am your friend,' Sandwalker said carefully, 'but I do not think I am one of you.'

'In the mind. Only the mind is significant.'

'The stars.' It was the blind man, and his voice might have been the voice of a wound, speaking through livid lips with a tongue of running blood. 'If Lastvoice our starwalker were here he would explain to you. Leaving the body behind to rove the stars and straddle the back of the Fighting Lizard. Seeing what God sees to know what he knows and what he must do.'

'There are those in my country who speak thus,' said Sandwalker, 'and we drive them to the edges of the cliffs – and beyond.'

'The stars tell God,' the blind prisoner mumbled stubbornly, 'and the river tells the stars. Those who look into the nightwaters may see, in the ripples, the shifting stars coming. We give them the lives of you ignorant hillsmen, and if a star leaves its place we darken the water with the starwalker's blood.'

The Old Wise One seemed to have gone away – Sandwalker could no longer see him among the silently waiting Shadow children – but his voice said, 'Enough talk. We hunger.'

'A few moments more. I want to ask about my mother and my friends. They are prisoners of these people.'

The blind man said, 'Make the not-men go, first.'

Sandwalker said, 'Go away,' and the two Shadow children who were not riding men moved their feet to make a trampling in the grass, but remained where they were. 'They are gone,' Sandwalker said. 'Now what of the prisoners?'

'Was it you who blinded me?'

'No, a Shadow child; mine were the hands at your throat.'

'Their singing brought you.'

'Yes.'

'Thus we keep them where no other men are, near the hills. And often their singing brings more of the kind – until sometimes we have as many as twenty, for they do not care if their friends may be eaten if they themselves may escape. But sometimes instead, as now, we lose what we have – though I never thought this should come to me. But I have never known of the singing to bring a boy.'

'I am a man. I have known woman, and dreamed great dreams. You drowned Flying Foot, defiling God's purity with death. What of the others?'

'You will try to save them, Fingers at My Throat?'

'My name is Sandwalker. Yes, if I can.'

'They are far north of here,' said the terrible voice of the blind man. 'Near the great observatory of The Eye. In the pit called The Other Eye. But my own eye is gone, and my other eye also; tell me, how stand the stars now? I must know when it is time to die.'

Sandwalker glanced up, though the racing clouds covered everything; and as he did, the blind man lunged. In an instant the Shadow children were on him like ants on carrion, and Sandwalker kicked him in the face. The other prisoners bolted.

'Will you eat this meat with us?' the Old Wise One asked when the blind man had been subdued. 'As a shadowfriend you are one of us, and may eat this meat without disgrace.' He had re-appeared, though he took no part in the struggle with the blind man – at least, one of the dim figures seemed to be he.

'No,' Sandwalker said. 'I ate well yesterday. But will you not pursue those who fled?'

'Later. Burdened with this one, we would never retrieve them, and he would flee too – blind or not – if we were to leave him alone. It would be possible to break his legs, but there is a ghoul-bear near; we winded him before you came.'

Sandwalker nodded. 'I too.'

'Would you see this one's death?'

'I might start the trail of the others,' Sandwalker said. To himself he reflected that they would run north, downstream. Toward the pit call The Other Eye.

'That is a good thought.'

Sandwalker turned away. He had not taken ten steps before the rain came; through its drumming he heard the blind man's death rattle.

*

Day came, clear and cold. By the time the sun stood a hand's width above the horizon the last clouds were gone, leaving the sky a blue touched with black and dotted with faint stars. In the meadowmeres the reeds bent and creaked in the wind, and an occasional bird, riding the turbulent air as Sandwalker had ridden the river's thundering waters, crossed heaven from end to end while he watched.

The trail of the three who had fled had not been difficult. The marshmen were fishers, fighters, finders of small game – but not hunters, as hunting was understood in the mountains. He had not yet seen them, but a hundred clues told him they were not far ahead: a broken herb still struggling to rise as he passed, footprints in mud still filling with water. And the signs of other men were there as well. The hunted ran now on paths that were more than game trails, and there was a presence in the land as there had not been in the empty miles at the highland's feet, a presence cruel and detached, thinking deep thoughts, contemptuous of everything below the clouds.

At the same time he was conscious of the Shadow children be-hind him. In the last hours of the night he had heard their song of Many Mouths and All Full, and then The Daysleep Song; now they were quiet, but their quiet was a presence.

The three who had fled were tired – their steps, as the mud showed, stumbled and dragged. But there was nothing to be gained by overtaking them without the Shadow children, and indeed they were of no use to him at all except as a lure to bring the Shadow children deep into the wetlands where they might help him. He was exhausted himself, and finding a spot dry enough to grow a few shrubs he slept.

*

Where is he?' said Lastvoice, and Eastwind, who had seen everything, told him. 'Ah!' said Lastvoice.

*

They took Sandwalker at twilight, a great ring of them. They had come behind him and closed from all sides, big, scarred men with ugly eyes. He ran from one part of their circle to another, from end to end, finding no escape, the marshmen always closer until they were shoulder to shoulder, he hoping for dark but caught (at last) in the dark. He fought hard and they hurt him.

For five days they held him, then all night drove him before them, and at first light, cast him into that pit which is called The Other Eye. There were four there already. They were his mother, Cedar Branches Waving; Leaves-you-can-eat; old Bloodyfinger; and the girl Sweetmouth.

'My son!' said Cedar Branches Waving, and she wept. She was very thin.

For half a day Sandwalker tried to climb the walls of The Other Eye. He made Leaves-you-can-eat and the girl Sweetmouth push him, and he persuaded old Bloodyfinger to lean against the sloping sand while Leaves-you-can-eat climbed upon his shoulders so that he, Sandwalker, might climb upon both and so escape; but the walls of the pit called The Other Eye are of so soft a sand that they fade under the feet and hands, and the more they are pulled down, the less they can be climbed. Bloodyfinger floundered and Sandwalker fell, and they were the same as before.

At about an hour after the noon, another Sandwalker appeared at the rim of the pit, and stood a long time looking down.

Sandwalker, in the pit, stared up at himself. Then men, the big men of the meadowmeres with their scars, brought a long liana, and holding one end of this woody vine flung the other down. 'That one,' said the Sandwalker who stood in the high place, and he pointed to the real Sandwalker.

Sandwalker shook his head. *No.*

'You are not to be sacrificed – not yet. Climb up.'

'Am I to be freed?'

The other laughed.

'Then if you would speak to me, Brother, you must come down.'

Eastwind looked at the men holding the liana, shrugged in a way that was half a joke, and with his hands on the vine slid down. 'I wish to see you better,' he said to Sandwalker. 'You have my face.'

'You are my brother,' Sandwalker said. 'I have dreamed of you, and my mother told me of you. Two of us were born, and at the washing she held me and her own mother you. The marsh-men came and forced your name from her mother's mouth that they might have power over you, then killed her.'

'I know all that,' Eastwind said. 'Lastvoice, my teacher, has told me.'

Sandwalker hoped for some advantage by drawing their mother into the talk, so he said, 'What was her name, mother? Your mother, whom they drowned? I have forgotten.' But Cedar Branches Waving was weeping and would not answer.

'You are to be killed,' said Eastwind, 'that you may carry our messages to the river, who tells the stars, who tell God. Lastvoice has warned me that there may be some danger to me in your death. We are, perhaps, but one person.'

Sandwalker shook his head and spat.

'It is an honor for you. You are a hill-boy like ten others – but in the stars you will be greater than I, who learn to read the in-structions the river writes God.'

'You are really not so much like me,' Sandwalker said, 'and you have no beard.' He touched his lip where the bristles were beginning to sprout. Unexpectedly the girl Sweetmouth, who had been (with Leaves-you-can-eat and old Bloodyfinger) watching them silently, began to giggle. Sandwalker looked at her angrily and she pointed at Eastwind, unable to contain her laughter.

'When I was an infant,' Eastwind said. 'We bind those things tightly with a woman's hair, and they putrefy. It is not painful, and only a few of those who will be starwalkers die. I had wished to say that Lastvoice has warned me that we are one. You will die before I, and go to the river and the stars. I am not afraid of that. In my dreams I shall float with you in places of power; I came to tell you that in your dreams you may yet walk as a living man.'

A voice from the rim of the pit hailed Eastwind. 'Scholar of the Sky, there are more. Do you wish to come up?'

Sandwalker looked up and saw the small forms of Shadow children, hemmed on three sides by the marshmen.

'No,' said Eastwind. 'If I am not afraid of these – these are at least men – should I fear those?'

'Perhaps,' Sandwalker said.

The Shadow children came tumbling down the soft slope. In the bright sunlight they looked far smaller than they had by night, bloodless and crook-legged. Sandwalker thought real children looking so would soon die.

'We will soon die,' one of the Shadow children (Sandwalker was not certain which) said. 'And be eaten by these. You too.'

Eastwind said: 'The ritual eating of gifts given the river is very different from feasting, little mock-men. We shall feast on you.'

The marshman who had called to Eastwind, apparently a man of some importance among them, announced from his place at the rim, 'Five, Scholar of the Sky.' He rubbed his hands. 'And there's no sweeter meat than Shadow child's.'

'Six,' Eastwind corrected him.

'This pit was not dug by hands,' said one of the Shadow children. Several of them were by now poking about, sifting the fine sand through their fingers.

'These are your followers,' Eastwind said to Sandwalker. 'Would you care to explain their new home to them?'

'I would if I could, but no one knows why the world is as it is, save that it conforms to the will of God.'

'Learn, then, where you stand. Here – a few hundred paces east – the river widens forever. It is as a stem widens to the flower, save that the flower of the river, which is called Ocean, widens without limit.'

'I don't believe it,' Sandwalker said.

'Don't you understand yet? Don't you know why the river exceeds in holiness both God and the stars? Why children at the beginning of their lives must be washed by it, and its waters muddied with the blood of the very starwalkers should a star fall? The river is Time, and it ends at this sacred place in Ocean, which is the past and extends forever. On the east bank, where the ground

86

is low and the water sometimes sweet and sometimes salt, is the Eye, the great circle from which the starwalkers go forth. On this west bank it has pleased Ocean to build this Other Eye to contain the gifts that will in time be his. Lastvoice, who has thought much on all things, says that the hands of Ocean, which strike the beaches forever, draw forth the sand on which we stand even as more slips down to replace it – having been returned by him to the beaches. Thus it is that The Other Eye is never empty and can never be filled.'

'We wash our children in the river,' Sandwalker said, 'because it signifies the purity of God. The root-earth of the trees, their fathers is still upon them and should be washed away. As for the rest of your nonsense, I think it no better than that about our being the same person.'

'Lastvoice has opened the bodies of women . . . ' Eastwind began, then seeing the disgust on Sandwalker's face he turned on his heel, grasped the liana, and signaled the men waiting to pull him up. At the rim he waved briefly and called, 'Good-by, Mother. Good-by, Brother,' then was gone.

Old Bloodyfinger said in his snarling voice, 'You might have got something from him – but he won't be back.'

Sandwalker shrugged and said: 'Do they let us go up to drink? I'm thirsty and there are no pools in this place.'

There was no shade either, but the Shadow children were lying down on the side of the pit which would be shaded first, curling into small, dark balls. Bloodyfinger said, 'About sundown they'll throw down stalks that don't have much flavor but a lot of juice. That's all the drink you'll get. All the food too.' He jerked a thumb at the Shadow children. 'But butchering those vermin would give us food and juicy drink. Three of us, five of them, that's not bad, and they won't fight well while the sun is high.'

'Two of you, six of us. And Leaves-you-can-eat won't fight if I fight him.'

For a moment Bloodyfingers looked angry, and Sandwalker remembering those big fists, readied himself to dodge and kick. Then Bloodyfinger grinned his gap-toothed grin – 'Just you and I, huh, boy? Bruising each other while the rest watch and yell. If you win, your friends eat, and if I do – why they come for me after dark. No. In a few days you'll be hungry – if any of us are alive. I'll talk to you again then.'

Sandwalker shook his head, but smiled. He had been driven all night by his captors and had spent the morning struggling with the slipping walls, so when Bloodyfinger turned away he scooped a place in the sand near the Shadow children and lay down. After a time the girl Sweetmouth came and lay beside him.

*

At sunset, as Bloodyfinger had said, the stems of plants were thrown down to them. The Shadow children were beginning to stir, and brought two for Sweetmouth and Sandwalker. Sweetmouth took hers, but she was frightened by the Shadow children's gleaming eyes. She went to the other side of the pit to sit with Cedar Branches Waving.

The Old Wise One came to sit beside Sandwalker, who noticed that he had no water stalk. Sandwalker said, 'Well, what do we do now?'

'Talk,' said the Old Wise One.

'Why?'

'Because there is no opportunity to act. It is always wise to talk a great deal, discussing what has been done and what may be done, when nothing can be done. All the great political movements of history were born in prisons.'

'What are political movements, and history?'

'Your forehead is high and your eyes are far apart,' the Old Wise One said. 'Unfortunately like all your species you have your brain in your thorax – ' (he tapped Sandwalker's hard, flat belly, or at least made the gesture of doing so, though his finger had no substance) 'so neither of those indications of mental capacity is valid.'

Sandwalker said tactfully, 'All of us have our brains in our stomachs when we are hungry.'

'You mean minds,' the Old Wise One told him. 'It is possible for the mind to float fourteen thousand feet or more above the head.'

'The starwalkers of these wetlanders say their minds – perhaps they mean their souls – leave the ground, tumble through space, kick off from sisterworld, and, drawn by the tractive universe, glide, soar, sweep, and whirl among the constellations until dawn, reading everything and tending the whole. So they told me in my captivity.'

The Old Wise One made a spitting sound and asked Sandwalker, 'Do you know what a starcrosser is?'

Sandwalker shook his head.

88

'Have you ever seen a log floating in the river? I mean high in the hills, where the water rushes between stones and the log with it.'

'I rode the river myself that way. That's how I came to the meadowmeres so quickly.'

'Better yet.' The Old Wise One lifted his head to stare at the night sky. 'There,' he said, pointing. 'There. What do you call that?'

Sandwalker was trying to follow the direction of his shadowy finger. 'Where?' he said. Burning Hair Woman watched with calm, unseeing eyes through the Old Wise One's hand.

'There, spread across all the heavens from end to end.'

'Oh, that,' Sandwalker said. 'That's the Waterfall.'

'Exactly. Now think of a hollow log big enough for men to get into. That would be a starcrosser.'

'I see.'

'Now humans – my race – actually traveled in those, cruising among the stars before the long dreaming days. We came here that way.'

'I thought you were always here,' Sandwalker said.

The Old Wise One shook his head. 'We either came recently or a long, long time ago. I'm not sure which.'

'Don't your songs tell?'

'We had no songs when we came here – that was one of the reasons we stayed, and why we lost the starcrosser.'

'You couldn't have gone back in it anyway,' Sandwalker said. He was thinking of going upstream on a river.

'We know. We've changed too much. Do you think we look like you, Sandwalker?'

'Not very much. You're too small and you don't look healthy, and your ears are too round and you don't have enough hair.'

'True,' said the Old Wise One, and fell silent. In the quiet that followed, Sandwalker could hear softly a sound he had never heard before, a sound rising and falling: it was Ocean smoothing the beach a quarter-mile away with his wet hands, but Sandwalker did not know this.

'I didn't mean to be insulting,' Sandwalker said at last. 'I was just pointing these things out.'

'It is thought,' the Old Wise One said, 'that makes things so. We do not conceive of ourselves as you have described us, and so we are not actually that way. However, it's sobering to hear how another thinks of us.'

'I'm sorry.'

'In any event, we once looked just as you do now.'

'Ah,' said Sandwalker. When he was younger, Cedar Branches Waving had often told him stories with names like 'How the Mule-Cat Got His Tail' (stole it from the lack-lizard, who had it for a tongue) and 'Why the Neagle Never Flies' (doesn't want the other animals to see his ugly feet, so he hides them in the grass unless he's using them to kill something). He thought the Old Wise One's story was going to be something like these, and since he hadn't heard it before he was quite willing to listen.

'We came either recently or a long, long time ago, as I said. Sometimes we try to recall the name of our home as we sit staring at each other's faces in the dawn, before we raise the Day-sleep Song. But we hear also the mind-singing of our brothers – who do not sing – as they pass up and down between the stars; we bend their thinking then, making them go back, but these thoughts come into our songs. It is possible that our home was named Atlantis or Mu – Gondwanaland, Africa, Poictesme, or The Country Of Friends. I, for five, remember all these names.'

'Yes,' said Sandwalker. He had enjoyed the names, but the Old Wise One's referring to himself as five had reminded him of the other Shadow children. They all seemed to be awake and listening, but sitting far off in various places around the pit. Two, so it appeared, had attempted to climb the shifting walls, and now waited where they had abandoned the effort – one a quarter way, one almost halfway up. All the humans except himself slept. The blue radiance of sisterworld was sifting over the rim.

'When we came we looked as you do now – ' began the Old Wise One.

'But you took off your appearance to bathe,' Sandwalker continued for him, thinking of the feathers and flowers his own people sometimes thrust into their hair, 'and we stole it from you and have worn it ever since.' Cedar Branches Waving had once told him some similar story.

'No. It was not necessary for us to lose our appearance for you to gain it. You come of a race of shape-changers – like those we called werewolves in our old home. When we came some of you looked like every beast, and some were of fantastic forms inspired by the clouds – or by lava flows, or water. But we walked among you in power and majesty and might, hissing like a thousand serpents as we splashed down in your sea, stepping like conquerors when we strode ashore with burning lights in our fists, and flame.'

'Ah!' said Sandwalker, who was enjoying the story.

'Of flame and light,' repeated the Old Wise One, rocking back and forth. His eyes were half-shut, and his jaws moved vigorously as though he were eating.

'Then what happened?' asked Sandwalker.

'That is the end. We so impressed your kind that you became like us, and have so remained ever since. That is, as we were.'

'That can't be the end,' said Sandwalker. 'You told how we became the same, but you haven't told yet how we became different. I am taller already than any of you, and my legs are straight.'

'We are taller than you, and stronger,' said the Old Wise One. 'And wrapped in terrible glory. It is true that we no longer have the things of flame and light, but our glance withers, and we sing death to our enemies. Yes, and the bushes drop fruit into our hands, and the earth yields the sons of flying mothers do we but turn a stone.'

'Ah,' said Sandwalker again. He wanted to say, *Your bones are bent and weak and your faces ill; you run from men and the light,* but he did not. He had called himself a shadowfriend – besides, there was no point in quarreling now. So he said, 'But we're still not the same, since my own people do not have those powers; neither do our songs come on the night wind to disturb sleep.'

The Old Wise One nodded and said, 'I will show you.' Then looking down he coughed into his hands and held them out to Sandwalker.

Sandwalker tried to see what it was he held, but sisterworld was shining brightly now and the Old Wise One's hands were cobweb. There was something – a dark mass – but though he bent close Sandwalker could see nothing more, and when he tried to touch what the Old Wise One held, his fingers passed through the hands as well as what they contained, making him feel suddenly foolish and alone, a boy who sat muttering to empty air when he might have slept.

'Here,' the Old Wise One said, and motioned. A second Shadow child came and squatted beside him, solid and real. 'Is it you I'm talking to, really?' Sandwalker asked, but the other did not answer or meet his eyes. After a moment he coughed into his hands as the Old Wise One had done and held them out.

'You talk to all of us when you talk to me,' the Old Wise One said. 'Mostly to us five here; but also to all Shadow children. Though weak, their songs come from far away to help shape what I am. But look at what this one is showing you.'

For a moment Sandwalker looked instead at the Shadow child.

He might have been young, but the dark face was silent and closed. The eyes were nearly shut, yet through the lids Sandwalker sensed his stare, friendly, embarrassed, and afraid.

'Take some,' invited the Old Wise One. Sandwalker prodded the chewed stuff with a finger and sniffed – vile.

'For this we have given up everything, because this is more than anything, though it is only a herb of this world. The leaves are wide, warty, and gray; the flowers yellow, the seed pink prickled eggs.'

'I have seen it,' Sandwalker said. 'Leaves-you-can-eat warned me of it when I was young. It is poisoned.'

'So your kind believes, and so it is if swallowed – though to die in that way might be better than life. But once, between the full face of sisterworld and her next, a man may take the fresh leaves, and folding them tightly carry them in his cheek. Then there is no woman for him, nor any meat; he is sacred then, for God walks in him.'

'I met such a one,' Sandwalker said softly. 'I would have killed him save that I pitied him.'

He had not meant to speak aloud and he expected the Old Wise One to be angry, but he only nodded. 'We too pity such a one,' he said, 'and envy him. He is God. Understand that he pitied you as well.'

'He would have killed me.'

'Because he saw you for what you are, and seeing felt your shame. But only once, until sisterworld appears again as she did, may a man search out the plant and pluck new leaves, spitting away then that which he has carried and chewed until it comforts him no longer. If he takes the fresh leaves more often, he will die.'

'But the plant is harmless as you use it?'

'All of us have been warmed by it since we were very young, and we are healthy as you see us. Didn't we fight well? We live to a great age.'

'How long?' Sandwalker was curious.

'What does it matter? It is great in terms of experience – we feel many things. When we die at last we have been greater than God and less than the beasts. But when we are not great, that which we carry in our mouths comforts us. It is flesh when we hunger and there is no fish, milk when we thirst and there is no water. A young man seeks a woman and finds her and is great and dies to the world. Afterward he is never as great again, but the woman is a comfort to him, reminding him of the time that was.

and he is a little again with her what once he was wholly. Just so with us until our wives that were are white when we spit them into our palms, and without comfort. Then we watch sister-world's face to see how great the time has been, and when the phase comes again we find new wives, and are young, and God.'

Sandwalker said, 'But you no longer look as we look now.'

'We were that, and have exchanged for this. Long ago in our home, before a fool struck fire, we were so – roaming without whatever may be named save the sun, the night, and each other. Now we are so again, for are gods, and things made by hands do not concern us. And as we are, so are you – because you walk only as you see us walk, doing as we do.'

The thought of his own people imitating the Shadow children whom they by day despised amused Sandwalker; but he only said, 'Now it is late, and I must rest. I thank you for all your kindness.'

'You will not taste?'

'Not now.'

The silent Shadow child, who seemed less real than the gossamer figure he crouched beside, returned the chewed fiber to his mouth and wandered away. Sandwalker stretched himself and wished Sweetmouth would come again to lie with him. The Old Wise One, without having left, was gone; and there were evil dreams: every part of him had vanished, so that he saw without eyes and felt without skin, hanging, a naked worm of consciousness amid blazing glories. Someone screamed.

They screamed again, and he came up fighting nothing, his arms flailing but his legs bound, his mouth full of grit. Cedar Branches Waving was screaming, and Leaves-you-can-eat and old Bloodyfinger seized his arms and pulled until he thought he must break. Around him in a circle the Shadow children watched, and Sweetmouth was crying.

'This dirt at the bottom goes down,' Bloodyfinger said when they had pulled him free, 'and sometimes it goes down fast.'

Cedar Branches Waving said, 'When you were still small but thought you were grown, you wouldn't sleep beside me any longer, and I used to get up in the night and go over and see if you were all right. I woke and thought of that tonight.'

'Thank you.' He was still gagging and spitting sand.

From the shadows a voice told him, 'We did not know. In the future, unsleeping eyes will watch you.'

'Thank you all,' Sandwalker said. 'I have many friends.'

There was more talk until, one by one, the humans returned to their resting places and lay down again. Sandwalker moved for a time around the floor of the pit, testing the footing and listening for the crawling of the sand. He heard only Ocean, and at last tried to sleep again. *'This cannot be true,'* Lastvoice was saying. *'Look again!' 'I cannot . . . a cloud –' Ahead the oily surface of the river stretched away beneath the night sky; black, glistening, broadening, it showed no stars, nothing but its own water and bits of floating weed. 'Look again!' Long hands, soft yet bony, gripped his shoulders.*

Someone shook him, and it was not yet light. For a moment he felt that he was sinking into the sand once more, but it was not so. Bloodyfinger and Sweetmouth were beside him, and behind them other, unfamiliar, figures. He sat up and saw that these were marshmen with scarred shoulders and knotted hair. Sweetmouth said, 'We have to go.' Her large, foolish eyes looked everywhere at no one.

There was a liana to help them climb, and with the marshmen behind they floundered up, Sandwalker and Bloodyfinger first, then Leaves-you-can-eat, then the two women and the Shadow children. 'Who?' Sandwalker asked Bloodyfinger, but the older man only shrugged.

At the river Lastvoice stood with his feet in the shallows and the dawnlight behind him. There was a chaplet of white flowers on his head, hiding the scars where his hair had been burned away; and another garland, of red blossoms that looked black in the pale light, upon his shoulders. Eastwind stood near him, watching, and on the bank several hundred people waited – silent figures light-stained early morning colors of yellow and red, their features growing clearer, individuals, a man here, a child there, standing suddenly contrasted from the mass with mask-like, immobile faces. Sandwalker ignored them and stared at Lastvoice; it was the first time he had seen the starwalker beyond the dream-world.

Their guards drove them into the water until it reached their knees. Then Lastvoice lifted his arms and, facing the fading stars, began to chant. The chant was blasphemy, and after a few moments Sandwalker closed his ears to it, begging God that he might dive, swim deep, and so escape; but then the others would be left behind, and there were so many marshmen on the bank, and he had always heard that they were good swimmers. He asked the priest to help him, but the priest was not there. Then Lastvoice had finished, long before he expected it.

There was a silence, and Lastvoice stabbed the air with both hands. A sound, a moan that might have been of pleasure, came

rom the watchers. Men surged forward and seized old Bloody-
inger and Leaves-you-can-eat, forcing them into deeper water.
Sandwalker sprang to help them, but was at once struck down
rom behind; he floundered, fighting, expecting that they would
ry to hold him under, but no one molested him further. He got
is feet beneath him and stood, coughing and wiping his long
air from his eyes. Men were still clustered around Leaves-you-
an-eat and old Bloodyfinger, but the water was still, the ripples
gold-tipped by the rising sun.

'Two today,' someone said behind Sandwalker. 'The people
are delighted.' He turned and saw Eastwind, who pushed past
im and stalked away with the high-kneed hair-heron gait.
Back to the pit,' one of the guards announced, and with Cedar
Branches Waving and Sweetmouth, Sandwalker turned and
splashed back toward shore, the Shadow children following. He
had just left the water when he heard the snap of breaking bone,
and turning saw that two of the Shadow children were dead,
their heads lolling as marshmen carried them away. He stopped,
angry in a way he had not been at the other deaths. A guard
pushed him.

'Why did you kill them?' Sandwalker said. 'They weren't even
part of the ceremony.'

Two grabbed him and bent his arms behind him. One said:
'They're not people. We can eat them anytime.' The other added,
'Big feast tonight.'

'Let him go.' It was Eastwind, who took his elbow. 'No use
fighting, Brother. They'll just break your arms.'

'All right.' Sandwalker's shoulders had been close to breaking
already. He swung his arms back and forth.

Eastwind was saying: 'We usually sacrifice only one at a time
– that's why the people are excited now. With the two men and
the two others there will be enough for a large piece for everyone,
so they're happy.'

'The stars were kind, then,' said Sandwalker.

'When the stars are kind,' Eastwind answered in a flat voice
that was yet like an echo of his own, 'we don't send the river any
messengers at all.'

They had reached the pit before Sandwalker realized it was
near. He strode to the edge determined to climb down rather
than be pushed. Someone, a small figure that seemed to hold a
smaller one, was already there; he stopped in surprise, was
straight-armed from behind, and tumbled ignominiously down.

The newcomer was Seven Girls Waiting.

That night the Old Wise One and the other remaining Shadow children sang the Tear Song for their dead friends. Sandwalker lay on his back and tried to read the stars to see if the message old Bloodyfinger and Leaves-you-can-eat had carried had had any effect, but he was not learned and they seemed only the familiar constellations. Seven Girls Waiting had spent the day telling all of them how she had followed him down the river and been caught, and the sorrow he had felt at first in seeing her had turned, as he listened, to a kind of weak anger at her foolishness. Seven Girls Waiting herself seemed more happy than frightened, having found in the pit substitutes for the companions who had deserted her. Sandwalker reminded himself that she had not seen the drownings.

Who could read the stars? The night was clear, and sisterworld, now much waned, had not yet risen; they shone in glory. Perhaps old Bloodyfinger could have, but he had never asked. He reminded himself that this was why the pit was called The Other Eye. Somewhere across the river Eastwind and Lastvoice would be studying the stars as well. Fretfully he rolled from side to side; the next time he would dive into the river and try to escape. Free, he might be able to help the others. If there remained others after the next time. He thought of Cedar Branches Waving being pushed beneath the surface (her face seen in agony through the ripples), then tried to put the thought aside. He wished that Seven Girls Waiting or Sweetmouth would come and lie with him and distract him, but they lay side by side, hands outstretched and touching, both asleep. The Tear Song rose and fell, then faded and died; Sandwalker sat up. 'Old Wise One! Can you read the stars?'

The Old Wise One came across the sand to him. He seemed fainter than ever, but taller, as if his illusion had been stretched. 'Yes,' he said. 'Although I do not always read there what your kind do.'

'Can you walk among them?'

'I can do whatever I choose.'

'Then what do they say? Will more die?'

'Tomorrow? The answer is both no and yes.'

'What does that mean? Who?'

'Someone dies every day,' the Old Wise One answered. And then, 'I am what you call a Shadow child, remember. If the stars speak to me it is of our own affairs they speak. But it is all foolish divination – the truth is what one believes.'

'Will it be Cedar Branches Waving?'

The Old Wise One shook his head. 'Not she. Not tomorrow.'

Sandwalker lay back, sighing with relief. 'I won't ask about he others. I don't want to know.'

'That is wise.'

'Then why walk among stars?'

'Why indeed? We have just sung the Tear Song for our dead. You were full of thoughts of the others who died, so we are not angry that you did not join – but the Tear Song is better than such thoughts.'

'It won't bring them back.'

'Would we wish it?'

'Wish what?' Sandwalker found, with a certain wrench of surprise, that he was angry, and angry at himself for being so. When the Old Wise One did not answer immediately he added, 'What are you talking about?' The constellations flashed with icy contempt, ignoring them both.

'I only meant,' the Old Wise One said slowly, 'if our song could call back Hatcher and Hunter, would we sing? Returned from death, would we not kill them?' Sandwalker noticed that the Old Wise One seemed younger than he had previously. Ghosts were strange.

And easily offended he remembered. 'I'm sorry if I sounded discourteous,' he said as politely as he could. 'Hatcher and Hunter were your friends' names? They were my friends too if I am a shadowfriend, and Bloodyfinger, and Leaves-you-can-eat. We should do something for them too – sit around and tell stories about them until late – but this doesn't seem like a place where you can do it. I don't feel good.'

'I understand. You yourself resemble the man you called Bloodyfinger to a marked degree.'

'His mother's mother and my mother's were probably sisters or something.'

'You are looking at my comrades, the other Shadow children. Why?'

'Because I never thought of Shadow children having names. I only thought of them as the Shadow children.'

'I know.' The Old Wise One was staring at the sky again, reminding Sandwalker that he had said he could walk there. After what seemed a long time (Sandwalker lay down again, turning on his belly and resting his head on his arms, where he could smell, faintly, the salt tang of his own flesh), he said, 'Their names are Foxfire, Swan, and Whistler.'

'Just like people.'

'We had no names before men came out of the sky,' the Old Wise One said dreamily. 'We were mostly long, and lived in holes between the roots of trees.'

Sandwalker said, 'I thought we were the ones.'

'I am confused,' the Old Wise One admitted. 'There are so many of you now and so few of us.'

'You hear our songs?'

'I am made of your songs. Once there was a people using their hands – when they had hands – only to take food; there came among them another who crossed from star to star. Then it was found that the first heard the songs of the second and sent them out again – greater, greater, greater than before. Then the second felt their songs more strongly in all their bones – but touched, perhaps, by the first. Once I was sure I knew who the first were, and the second; now I am no longer sure.'

'And I am no longer sure of what it is you're saying,' Sandwalker told him.

'Like a spark from the echoless vault of emptiness,' the Old Wise One continued, 'the shining shape slipped steaming into the sea . . . ' But Sandwalker was no longer listening. He had gone to lie between Sweetmouth and Seven Girls Waiting, reaching out a hand to each.

*

The next morning, before dawn, the liana was flung down the side of the pit again. This time there was no need for the marsh men to come down into The Other Eye to drive the hill-people up. Someone shouted from the rim and they came, though slowly and unwillingly. At the top Eastwind stood waiting, and Sandwalker, who had climbed with the three remaining Shadow children, asked him, 'How were the stars last night?'

'Evil. Very evil. Lastvoice is disturbed.'

Sandwalker said: 'I thought they looked bad myself – Swift right in the hair of Burning Hair Woman. I don't think Leaves you-can-eat and old Bloodyfinger delivered the message you gave them. Leaves-you-can-eat would always do about what anybody asked him, but old Bloodyfinger's probably been telling everyone you deserve worse than you've been getting. That's what I'm going to do myself if you send me.'

Eastwind exclaimed, 'Fool!' and tried to knock him down. When he could not, two of the marshmen did.

It was misty, and because of the mist dark. Sandwalker (when he got up) thought that the darkness and cold fog, which he knew would be thickest a few feet above the water of the river, would be excellent for escape; but apparently the marshmen thought so as well. One walked on either side of him, holding his arms. Today it seemed a long way to the river. He stumbled, and his guards hurried him along to catch up with the others. Ahead the small, dark backs of the Shadow children and the broad, pale ones of marshmen appeared and vanished again.

'A good eating last night,' one of the marshmen said. 'You weren't invited, but you'll be there tonight.'

Sandwalker said bitterly, 'But your stars are evil.'

Fear and fury rushed into the man's eyes, and he wrenched Sandwalker's arm. Ahead, in the mist, there were not quite human screams, then silence.

'Our stars may be evil,' the other marshman said, 'but our bellies will be full tonight.' Two more came walking back the way they had come, each carrying the limp body of a Shadow child. Sandwalker could smell the river – and hear, in the uncanny silence of the fog, the sound its ripples made against the bank.

Lastvoice stood as he had before, tendrils of white vapor twining about his tall figure. The marshmen wore necklaces and anklets and bracelets and coronets of bright green grass today, and danced a slow dance on the bank; women, children, and men all winding like a serpent, mumbling as they danced. Eastwind relieved one of the guards and muttered in Sandwalker's ear, 'This may be the last muster of the marsh. The stars are very evil.' Sandwalker answered contemptuously, 'Are you so afraid of them?' Then Eastwind was gone, and the guards were thrusting him, with the last Shadow child, his mother, and the two girls into a shivering group. Pink Butterflies was crying, and Seven Girls Waiting rocked her back and forth, comforting her with some nonsense and asking things of God. Sandwalker put his arm around her and she buried her face in his shoulder.

The last Shadow child stood next to Sandwalker, and Sandwalker, looking down, saw that he trembled. The Old Wise One stood beside him, so thin in the mist that it seemed no one except Sandwalker could possible see him. Unexpectedly the last Shadow child touched Sandwalker's arm and said, 'We will die together. We loved you.'

'Chew harder,' Sandwalker told him, 'and you won't believe that.' And then, because he was sorry to have hurt a friend at such a time he added more kindly, 'Which one are you – aren't you the one who showed me what it is you chew?'

'Wolf.'

Lastvoice had begun his chant. Sandwalker said, 'Your Old Wise One told me last night your names were Foxfire, Whistler, and something else I forget – but there was none of that name.'

'We have names for seven,' the Shadow child said, 'and names for five. The names for three you have heard. My name now is the name for one. Only his name, the Old Wise One's name, never changes.'

'Except,' the Old Wise One whispered, 'when I am called – as occasionally I once was – the Group Norm.' The Old Wise One was only a sort of emptiness in the mist now, a man-shaped hole.

Sandwalker had been watching the guards, and he saw, as he thought, an opening – a moment of relaxation of vigilance as they listened to Lastvoice. The mist hung everywhere and the river was wide and hidden. If God so willed, he might reach the deep water . . .

God, dear God, good Master . . .

He bolted, feet splashing, then slipping as he tried to dive his supple body between two marshmen. They caught him by the hair and smashed his face with fists and knees before pushing him back among the others. Seven Girls Waiting, Sweetmouth, and his mother tried to help him, but he cursed them and drove them away, bathing his face in the bitter river water.

'Why did you do that?' the last Shadow child asked.

'Because I want to live. Don't you know that in a few minutes they're going to drown us all?'

'I hear your song,' the Shadow child said, 'and I wish to live too. I am not, perhaps, of your blood, but I wish to live.'

'But we must die,' the voice of the Old Wise One whispered.

'*We* must die,' Sandwalker said harshly, 'not you. They won't pick your bones.'

'When this one dies, I die,' the Old Wise One said, indicating the last Shadow child. 'Half I am of your making and half of his, but without him to echo, your mind will not shape me.'

Softly the last Shadow child said again, 'I, too, wish to live. It may be that there is a way.'

'What?' Sandwalker looked at him.

'Men cross the stars, bending the sky to make the way short. Since first we came here – '

'Since first *they* came here,' the Old Wise One corrected him gently. 'Now I am half a man, and know that we were always

100

ere listening to thought that did not come; listening without nought of our own to be men. Or it may be that all are one stock, alf-remembering and dwindling, half-forgetting and flourishing.'

'The song of the girl with the little child is in my mind,' said ne last Shadow child, 'and the one they call Lastvoice is chanting. And I do not care if we are two or one. We have sung to hold the tarcrossers back. We desired to live as we wished, unreminded f what was and is; and though they have bent the sky, we have ent their thought. Suppose I now sing them in, and they come? he marshmen will take them, and there will be many to choose rom. Perhaps we will not be chosen.'

'Can one do so much?' Sandwalker asked.

'We are so few that among us even one is no mean number. And the others sing so the starcrossers will not see what they vish to see. For a heartbeat my song will clear their sight, and he bent sky is near here at many points. They will be swift.'

'It is evil,' the Old Wise One said. 'For very long we have valked carefree in the only paradise. It would be better if all here vere to die.'

The last Shadow child said firmly, 'Nothing is worse than that should die,' and something that had wrapped the world was ;one. It went in an instant and left the river and the mist, the haking, dancing marshmen and chanting Lastvoice and them-elves all unchanged, but it had been bigger than everything nd Sandwalker had never seen it because it had been there ilways, but now he could not remember what it had been. The ky was open now, with nothing at all between the birds and the un; the mist swirling around Lastvoice might reach to Burning lair Woman. Sandwalker looked at the last Shadow child and aw that he was weeping and that his eyes held nothing at all. He elt that way himself, and turning to Cedar Branches Waving isked, 'Mother, what color are my eyes now?'

'Green,' Cedar Branches Waving answered. 'They look gray n this light, but they are green. That is the color of eyes.' Behind ler Seven Girls Waiting and Sweetmouth murmured, 'Green.' And Seven Girls Waiting added, 'Pink Butterflies's eyes are green oo.'

Then, glowing red as old blood through the fog, a spark ippeared – high overhead to the north, where Ocean moved like in eel under the grayness. Sandwalker saw it before anyone else. t grew larger, more angry, and a whistling and humming came over the water; on the bank one of the dancing women screamed ind pointed as the gout of red fire came hissing down. It made

the noise heard when lightning kills a tree. There were two mor
red stars falling with it already, and the shrieking of all the peopl
followed them down, and when they struck, the marshmen fled
Sweetmouth and Seven Girls Waiting threw their arms aroun
Sandwalker and buried their faces in his chest. The marshme
who had guarded them were running, tearing away their gras
bracelets and crowns.

Only Lastvoice stood. His chant had stopped, but he did no
flee. Sandwalker thought he saw in his eyes a despair like that o
the exhausted beast that at last turns and bares its throat to th
jaws of the tire-tiger. 'Come,' Sandwalker said, pushing asid
the girls and taking his mother's arm; but in his ear the Old Wis
One said, 'No.'

Behind them feet were splashing in the river water. It wa
Eastwind, and when Lastvoice saw him said, 'You ran.'

Eastwind answered: 'Only for a moment. Then I remembered.
He sounded shamed. Lastvoice said, 'I shall speak no more,
and turned his back on them all, looking out to Ocean.

Sandwalker said: 'We're going. Don't try to stop us.'

'Wait.' Eastwind looked at Cedar Branches Waving. 'Tell hin
to wait.'

She said to Sandwalker, 'He, too, is my son. Wait.'

Sandwalker shrugged and asked bitterly, 'Brother, what dc
you want of us?'

'It is a matter for men, not women; and not,' Eastwind looked
at the last Shadow child, 'for such as he. Tell them to go to the
bank and upriver. No marshman, I swear, will hinder them.'

The women went, but the last Shadow child only said, 'I wil
wait on the bank,' and Eastwind, defeated, nodded.

'Now, *Brother*,' said Sandwalker, 'what walks here?'

'While the stars remain in their places,' Eastwind answered
slowly, 'the starwalker judges the people; but when a star falls
the river must be clouded with his blood, that it may forget. His
disciple does this, aided by all nearby.'

Sandwalker looked a question.

'I can strike,' Eastwind said, 'and I will strike. But I love him,
and I may not strike hard enough. You must help me. Come.'

Together they swam the river, and on the farther bank found
a tree of that white-barked kind Sandwalker had once dreamed
grew in a great circle about Eastwind. The roots trailed in the
bitter water, and selecting a branching one less thick than a
finger, Eastwind bit it through, pulled it up dripping to give to
Sandwalker. It was as long as his arm, the lower part heavy with

all shellfish and smelling of ooze. While Sandwalker examined Eastwind took another for himself, and with them they flogged stvoice until no further blood ran as he floated, though the arp little shells sliced the white flesh of his back. 'He was a ll-man,' Eastwind said. 'All starwalkers must be born in the gh country.'

Sandwalker dropped his bloody flail into the water. 'Now hat?'

'It is over.' Eastwind's eyes were wet with tears. 'His body is ot eaten, but allowed to drift to Ocean, a total sacrifice.'

'And you rule the marsh now?'

'My head must be burned as his was. Then – yes.'

'And why should I let you live? You would have drowned our other. You are no man, and I can kill you.' Before Eastwind uld answer Sandwalker had seized him, bending him backward y the hair.

'If he dies,' the Old Wise One's voice whispered to Sandalker, 'something of you dies with him.'

'Let him die. It is a part of me I wish to kill.'

'Would he slay you thus?'

'He would have drowned us all.'

'For what was in his mind. You slay him now for hate. Would e have slain you so?'

'He is like me,' Sandwalker said, and he bent Eastwind back ntil the water was on his forehead and lapping at his eyes.

'There is a way to know,' the Old Wise One said, and Sandalker saw that the last Shadow child had come out into the iver again. When he saw Sandwalker looking at him, he repeated, There is a way.'

'Very well, how?'

'Let him up,' the Shadow child said, and to Eastwind, 'You at us but you know we are a magic people.'

Gasping, Eastwind answered, 'We know.'

'By our power I made the stars to fall; but I now do a greater nagic. I make you Sandwalker and Sandwalker you,' said the hadow child, and as quickly as a striking snake darted forward nd plunged his teeth into Eastwind's arm. While Sandwalker vatched, his twin's face went slack and his eyes looked at things nseen.

'That which swam in my mouth swims in his veins now,' the Shadow child said, wiping Eastwind's blood from his lips. 'And ecause I spoke to him and he believed me, in his thought he is ou.'

Sandwalker's arm was sore from flogging Lastvoice, and he rubbed it. 'But how will we know what he does?'

'He will speak soon.'

'This is a game for children. He should die.' Sandwalker kicked Eastwind's feet so that he fell into the water, and held him there until he felt the body go limp. When he straightened up he said to the last Shadow child, 'I spoke.'

'Yes.'

'But now I don't know if I am Sandwalker or Eastwind in his dream.'

'And neither do I,' said the Shadow child. 'But there is something happening down there on the beach. Shall we go and see?'

The mist was burning away. Sandwalker looked where the Shadow child pointed and saw that where the river joined moaning Ocean a green thing was bobbing in the water. Three men with their limbs wrapped in leaves stood on the sand near it pointing at the stranded body of Lastvoice and talking a speech Sandwalker did not understand. When he came close to them they extended their hands, open, and smiled; but he did not understand that open hands meant (or had meant, once) that they held no weapons. His people had never known weapons. That night Sandwalker dreamed that he was dead, but the long dreaming days were over.

V.R.T.

But don't think that I am at all interested in you. You have warmed me, and now I will go out again and listen to the dark voices.

Karel Čapek

It was a brown box, a dispatch box, of decayed dark brown leather with brass reinforced corners. The brass had been painted a brownish green when the box was new; but most of the paint was gone, and the dying sunlight from the window showed dull green tarnish around the bright scars of recent gouges. The slave set this box carefully, almost soundlessly, beside the junior officer's lamp.

'Open it,' the officer said. The lock had been broken a long time ago; the box was tied shut with hard-reeved ropes twisted from reclaimed rags.

The slave – a high-shouldered, sharp-chinned man with a shock of dark hair – looked at the officer and the officer nodded his close-cropped head, his chin moving a sixteenth of an inch. The slave drew the officer's dagger from the belt over the back of his chair, cut the ropes, kissed the blade reverently and replaced it. When he had gone the officer rubbed his palms on the thighs of his knee-length uniform trousers, then lifted the lid and dumped the contents on to his table.

Notebooks, spools and spools of tape. Reports, forms, letters. He saw a school composition book of cheap yellow paper, the cover half torn off, picked it up. An unskilled hand had monogramed it: V.R.T. The initials were ornate and very large but somehow wrongly formed, as though a savage had imitated them from letters indicated to him on a sign.

Birds I have seen today. I saw two birds today. One was a skull-shrike, and the other was a bird that the shrike had ...

The officer tossed the composition book to the back of the table. His eyes, straying, had identified amid the clutter the precise, back-slanted writing favoured by the Civil Service.

SIR: The materials I send you ...
    ... is my own opinion.
    ... from Earth.

The officer raised his eyebrows slightly, put down the letter, and picked up the composition book again. At the bottom of the cover, in smudged, dark letters, he read: Medallion Supplies, Frenchman's Landing, Sainte Anne. *Inside the back cover:*

Rm E2S14 Seat 18
name

Armstrong School
school

Frenchman's Landing
city

Taking up one of the spools of tape, he looked for a label, but there was none. The labels lay loose among the other materials, robbed by the humidity of their adhesion, though still neatly titled, dated and signed.

Second Interrogation.

Fifth Interrogation.

Seventeenth Interrogation – Third Reel.

The officer allowed them to sift between his fingers, then chose a spool at random and set it up on his recorder.

A: Is it going now?
Q: Yes. Your name, please.
A: I have already given you my name, it is on all your records.
Q: You have given us that name a number of times.
A: Yes.
Q: Who are you?
A: I am the prisoner in cell 143.
Q: Oh, you are a philosopher. We had thought you an anthropologist, and you don't seem old enough for both.
A:
Q: I am instructed to familiarize myself with your case. I could have done that without calling you from your cell – you realize that? I am subjecting myself to the danger of typhus and several other diseases for your sake. Do you want to return underground? You seemed to appreciate the cigarette a moment ago. Isn't there anything else you'd like?
A: (*Eagerly*) Another blanket. More paper! More paper, and something to write on. A table.

The officer smiled to himself and stopped the tape. He had enjoyed the eagerness in A's voice, and he now found pleasure in speculating to himself about the answer A would receive. He rewound a few inches of tape, then touched the PLAY button again.

Q: Do you want to return underground? You seemed to appreciate the cigarette a moment ago. Isn't there anything else you'd like?
A: (Eagerly) Another blanket. More paper! More paper, and something to write on. A table.
Q: We've given you paper, a great deal of it. And look at the use you've made of it: filled it with scrawlings. Do you realize that if the records in your case are ever forwarded to higher authority it will be necessary to have them transcribed? That will be weeks of work for somebody.
A: They could be photocopied.
Q: Ah, you'd like that, wouldn't you?

The officer touched the volume control, reducing the voices to murmurs, and poked at the litter on his table. An unusual and exceptionally sturdy notebook caught his eye. He picked it up.

It was perhaps fourteen inches by twelve, an inch thick, bound in stout canvas of a dun shade time and sun had turned to cream at the edges. The pages were heavy and stiff, ruled with faint blue lines, the first page beginning in the middle of a sentence. Looking more carefully, the officer saw that three leaves had been cut from the front of the book, as though with the blade of a razor or a very keen knife. He drew his dagger and tested its edge against the fourth. The dagger was sharp – the slave kept it so – but would not cut as cleanly as the edge someone had employed before him. He read:

. . . a deceptive quality even to daylight, feeding the imagination, so that I sometimes wonder how much of what I see here exists only in my own mind. It gives me an unbalanced feeling, which the too-long days and stretched nights don't help. I wake up – I did even in Roncevaux – hours before dawn.

Anyway it's a cool climate, so the thermometer tells me; but it does not seem cool – the whole effect is of the tropics. The sun, this incredible *pink* sun, blazes down, all light and no heat, with so little output at the blue end of the spectrum that it leaves the sky behind it nearly black, and this very blackness is – or at least seems to me – tropical; like a sweating African face, or the green-black shadows at noon in a jungle; and the plants, the animals and insects, even this preposterous jerrybuilt city, all contribute to the feeling. It makes me think of the snow langur – the monkey that lives in the icy valleys of the Himalayas; or of those hairy elephants and rhinoceros that during the glaciations held on to the freezing edges of Europe and North America. In the same way, here they had bright-colored birds and wide-leaved, red-and yellow-blossomed plants (as if this were Martinique or Tumaco) in profusion wherever the ground is high enough to free it from the monotonous grasp of the salt reeds of the meadowmeres.

Mankind collaborates. Our town (as you see, a few days in one of these new-built, falling-down metropolises makes you an old resident, and I was considered an Early Settler before I had transferred the contents of my bags to the splintering dresser in my room) is largely built of logs from the cypress-like trees that dot the lowlands around it and roofed with plastic sheet, corrugated – so that all we need is the throbbing of native drums in the distance. (And wouldn't it make my job easier to hear a few! Actually some of the earliest explorers farther south are supposed to have reported signal drumming on the standing trunks of hollow trees by the Annese; they are said to have used no drum-sticks, striking the trunk with the open hand as if it were a tom-tom, and like all primitives they would presumably have been communicating by imitating, with the sound of their blows, their own speech – 'talking drums.')

The officer riffled the stiff leaves with his thumb. There were pages more of the same kind of material, and he tossed the notebook aside to take up a portion of a loose sheaf of papers bound at their point of origin (he glanced at the top of the cover letter – (Port-Mimizon) with a flimsy tin clasp which had now fallen off. These were in the neat writing of a professional clerk; the pages were numbered, but he did not trouble himself to find the first of them.

Now that I have paper again it has proved possible, just as I predicted, to decipher the tappings of my fellow prisoners. How? you ask. Very well, I will tell you. Not because I must, but in order that you may admire my intelligence. You should, you know, and I need it.

By listening to the tapping it was not difficult to separate code groups which, as I realized, each represented a letter. I was greatly helped, I admit, by the knowledge that this code was meant to be understood, not to baffle, and that it must often be employed by uneducated men. By marking tallies I could determine the frequency of use of each group; so much was easy, and anyone could have done as well. But what were the frequencies of the letters? No one carries that information in his head except a cryptographer, and here is where I thought out a solution I flatter myself you would never have arrived at if you had had to sit in this cell, as it seems I must, until the walls crumble away to sand: I analyzed my own conversation. I have always had an excellent memory for what I have heard said, and it is even better for what I have said myself – I can still recall, for example, certain con-versations I had with my mother when I was four, and the oddity is that I comprehend now things she said to me which were perfectly opaque at the time, either because I did not know even the simple words she used or because the ideas she expressed, and her emotions, were beyond the apprehension of a child.

But I was telling you about the frequencies. I talked to myself – like this – sitting here on my mattress; but to prevent my un-conscious favoring certain letters I wrote nothing down. Then I printed out the alphabet and went back, in my mind, over all that I had said, spelling the words and putting tallies beneath the letters.

And now I can put my ear to the sewer pipe that runs down through my cell, and understand.

At first it was hard, of course. I had to scribble down the taps, then work it out, and the fragment of message I had been able to record often conveyed no meaning: YOU HEARD WHAT THEY . . .

Often I got less than that. And I wondered why so much of what was being said was in numbers: TWO TWELVE TO THE MOUNTAINS . . . Then I realized that they, we, call ourselves usually by our cell number, which gives the location and is the most important thing, I suppose, about a prisoner anyway.

The page ended. The officer did not look for the next in sequence, but stood up and pushed back his chair. After a moment he stepped through the open doorway; outside there was a faint breeze now, and Sainte Anne, high over his head, steeped the world in sad green light; he could see, a mile or more away in the harbor, the masts of the ships. The air held the piercing sweet smell of the night-blooming flowers the previous commandant had ordered planted around the building. Fifty feet away under the shadow of a fever tree the slave squatted with his back to the trunk, sufficiently hidden to support the fiction that he was invisible when he was not wanted, sufficiently close to hear if the officer called or clapped his hands. The officer looked at him significantly and he came running across the dry, green-drenched lawn, bowing. 'Cassilla,' the officer said.

The slave ducked his head. 'With the major . . . Perhaps, Maître, a girl from the town –'

Mechanically, the officer, who was younger than he, struck him, his open left hand smacking the slave's right cheek. Equally mechanically, the slave dropped to his knees and began to sob. The officer pushed him with his foot until he sprawled on the half-dead grass, then went back into the small room that served him for an office. When he was gone the slave stood, brushed his threadbare clothing, and took up his station beneath the fever tree again. It would be two hours or more before the major was finished with Cassilla.

There was a native race. The stories are too widespread, too circumstantial, too well documented, for the whole thing to be a sort of overgrown new-planet myth. The absence of legitimate artefacts remains to be explained, but there must be some explanation.

To this indigenous people, humankind and the technological culture must have proved more toxic than to any other aboriginal group in history. From rather ubiquitous if thinly scattered primitives they have become something less than memory in a period of not much more than a century – this without any specific catastrophe worse than the destruction of the records of the first French landing parties by the war.

My problem, then, is to learn all there is to be learned about some very primitive people who have left almost no physical traces at all (as far as anyone knows) and some highly embroidered legends. I would be disheartened if it were not that the parallel with those paleolithic, Caucasoid Pygmies who came to be called the Good People (and who survived, as was eventually shown, in Scandinavia and Eire until the last years of the eighteenth century) were not almost exact.

How late, then, did the Annese hang on? Though I have been questioning everyone who will stand still for it, and listening to every tale they wanted to tell (thirdhand, n^{th}hand, I always think I might pick up something, and there's no use making an enemy of anyone who might later direct me to better information), I have been especially alert for firsthand, datable accounts. I have everything on tape, but it may be wise to transcribe a few of the more typical, as well as some of the most interesting, here; tapes can be lost or ruined after all. I give all dates by local calendar to avoid confusion.

March 13. Directed by Mr Judson, the hotelkeeper, and bearing a verbal introduction from him, I was able to talk to Mrs Mary Blount, a woman of eighty who lives with her granddaughter and the granddaughter's husband on a farm about twenty miles from Frenchman's Landing. The husband warned me before I was taken in to meet the old lady herself that her mind sometimes wandered, and instanced, to prove his point, that she at times claimed to have been born on Earth, but at others insisted that she had been born aboard one of the colonizing ships. I began the interview by asking her about this; her answer shows, I fear, how little elderly people are listened to in our culture.

Mrs Blount: 'Where was I born. On the ship. Yes. I was the first that was born on the ship and the last born on the old world

111

– how d'you like that, young man? Women that was expecting wasn't to come on board, you see, though lots of them did as it turned out. My Ma, she wanted to go, and she decided not to say anything about her condition. She was a heavy woman, as you may imagine, and I guess I was a small little baby. Yes, they had physical examinations for all that was going, but that had been months and months before, because the blasting-off was delayed, you see. All the women was to wear these coveralls that they called space clothes, just like the men, and Ma felt I was coming and told them she wanted hers loose, and the Devil take style. So they didn't know. She was having pains, she said, when she come up in the gantry, but the doctor on the ship was one of them and didn't say nothing to anybody. I was born and he put her and me to sleep the way they did and when we woke up it was twenty-one years afterward. The ship we come on was the nine-eight-six, which was not the first one, but one of the more earlier of them. I've heard that before they used to have names for them, which I think would be prettier.

'Yes, there was still quite a few French left here when we came, most all except the littlest children had their arms or legs gone or was scarred terrible. They knowed they had lost and we knowed we had won, and our men just took land and stock, whatever they wanted, that's what Ma told me later. I was just small, you know, and didn't realize nothing. When I was growing up those little French girls that had been too small to fight was growing up too, and weren't they the cutest things? They got most of the handsome boys, you know, and all the rich ones. You could go to a dance in your prettiest dress, and one of those Frenchies would come in, just in rags you know, but with a ribbon and a flower in her hair, and every boy's head would turn.

'Annese? What's the Annese?

'Oh, them. We called them the abos or the wild people. They weren't really people, you know, just animals shaped like people.

'Of course I've seen them. Why when I was a child I used to play with the children, the little ones, you know. Ma didn't want me to, but when I was out playing alone I'd go out to the back of our pasture and they'd come and play with me. Ma said they'd eat me,' (Laughs) 'but I can't say how they ever tried. Wouldn't they steal, though! Anything to eat, they were always hungry. They got to taking out of our smokehouse, and one night Pa killed three, right between the smokehouse and the barn, with his gun. One was one I had played with sometimes, and I cried; that's the way a child is.

112

'No, I don't know where he buried them or if he did; just dragged them out back for the wild animals, I'd suppose.'

A brother officer came in. The officer laid the notebook aside, and as he did so a puff of wind swayed the pages.

'Feel that,' the brother officer said. 'Why can't we have that during the day when we need it?'

The officer shrugged. 'You're up late.'

'Not as late as you are – I'm going to bed now.'

'You see what I've got.' The officer's lips bent in a small, sour smile. He gestured at the jumble of papers and tapes on the table.

The brother officer stirred them with one finger. 'Political?'

'Criminal.'

'Tell them to knock the dust off their garrotte and get yourself some sleep.'

'I have to find out what it's all about first. You know the commandant.'

'You'll be ready for the spade tomorrow.'

'I'll sleep late. I'm off anyway.'

'You always were an owl, weren't you?'

The brother officer left, yawning. The officer poured a glass of wine, no cooler now than the room, and began to read again where the wind had left the book.

'I don't know. Might be fifteen years ago, or it might not. Our years are longer here – did you know that?'

Self: 'Yes, you don't have to explain that.'

Mr D: 'Well, those Frenchmen used to have all kinds of stories about them; most of them I never believed.

'What kinds of stories? Oh, just nonsense. They're an ignorant people, the French are.'

(End of Interview)

I had been told that one of the last survivors of the first French settlers had been one Robert Culot, now dead about forty years. I inquired about him and learned that his grandson (also named Robert Culot) sometimes referred to stories he had heard his grandfather tell of the early days on Sainte Anne. He (Robert Culot the younger) appears to be about fifty-five (Earth) years of age. He operates a clothing store, the best in Frenchman's Landing.

M. Culot: 'Yes, the old one frequently told tales concerning those you call the Annese, Dr Marsch. He had many stories of them, of all the different sorts.

'That is correct, he felt them to be of many races. Others, he said, might think them to be all one, but the other knew less than he. He would have said that to the blind, all cats are black. Do you speak French, Doctor? A pity.'

Self: 'Can you tell me the approximate date on which your grandfather last saw a living Annese, Monsieur Culot?'

M. C: 'A few years before he died. Let me think . . . Yes, three years I think before his death. He was confined to his bed the year following, and his death took him two years after.'

Self: 'About forty-three years ago, then?'

M. C: 'Ah, you do not believe an old man, do you? That is cruel! These French, you say to yourself, cannot be trusted.'

Self: 'On the contrary, I am intrigued.'

M. C: 'My grandfather had attended the funeral of a friend, and it had depressed his spirit; so he went for a walk. When he had been but a little younger he had walked a great deal, you comprehend. Then only a few years before the last illness he ceased to do so. But now because his heart troubled him he walked again. I was playing draughts with my father, his son, and was present when he returned.

'What did he say his *indigène* looked like? Ah!' (Laughs) 'I had hoped you would not ask that. You see, my father laughed at him as well, and that made him angry. For that to my father he spoke his bad English much, to make my father angry in return; and he said my father sat all day and consequently saw nothing. My father had both his legs gone in the war; it is fortunate for me, is it not, that he did not lose certain other things as well?

'I asked then that question you have asked me – how did it appear? I will tell you what it was he responded, but it will cause you to distrust him.'

Self: 'Do you think he may have been simply teasing you, or your father?'

M. C: 'He was a most honest old man. He would not tell lies to anyone, you understand. But he might – speak the truth in such a way as to make it sound impertinent. I asked him how the creature appeared, and he said sometimes likes a man, but sometimes like the post of a fence.'

Self: 'A fence post?'

M. C: 'Or a dead tree – something of the sort. Let me recollect myself. It may have been that he said: "Sometimes like a man,

114

sometimes like old wood.'' No, I cannot really tell what he meant by that.'

M. Culot directed me to several other members of the French community around Frenchman's Landing who he said might be willing to cooperate with me. He also mentioned a Dr Hagsmith, a medical doctor, who he understood has made some effort to collect traditions regarding the Annese. I was able to arrange an interview with Dr Hagsmith the same evening. He is English-speaking, and told me that he considered himself an amateur folklorist.

Dr Hagsmith: 'You and I, sir, we take opposite tacks. I don't mean to disparage what you're doing – but it isn't what I'm doing. You wish to find what is true, and I'm afraid you're going to find damned little; I want what is false, and I've found plenty. You see?'

Self: 'You mean that your collection includes a great many accounts of the Annese?'

Dr H: 'Thousands, sir. I came here as a young physician, twenty years ago. In those days we thought that by now this would be a great city; don't ask me why we thought it, but we did. We planned everything: museums, parks, a stadium. We felt we had everything we needed, and so we did – except for people and money. We still have everything.' (Laughs)

'I started writing down the stories in the course of my practice. I realized, you see, that these legends about the abos had an effect on people's minds, and their minds affect their diseases.'

Self: 'But you have never seen an aborigine yourself?'

Dr H: (Laughs) 'No, sir. But I am probably the greatest living expert on them you'll find. Ask me anything and I can quote chapter and verse.'

Self: 'Very well. Do the Annese still exist?'

Dr H: 'As much as they ever did.' (Laughs)

Self: 'Then where do they live?'

Dr H: 'What locality, you mean? Those that live in the back of beyond pursue a wandering existence. Those living about farms generally have their habitations in the farthest parts, but occasionally one or two may take up residence in a cowshed, or under the eaves of the house.'

Self: 'Wouldn't they be seen?'

Dr H: 'Oh, it's quite unlucky to see one. Generally, though, they take the form of some homey household utensil if anyone looks – become a bundle of hay, or whatever.'

Self: 'People really believe they can do that sort of thing?'

Dr H: 'Don't you? If they can't, where'd they all go?' (Laughs)

Self: 'You said most Annese live "in the back of beyond"?'

Dr H: 'The wilderness, the wastelands. It's a term we have here.'

Self: 'And what do *they* look like?'

Dr H: 'Like people; but the color of stones, with great shocks of wild hair – except for the ones that don't have any. Some are taller than you or I, and very strong; some are smaller than children. Don't ask me how small children are.'

Self: 'Supposing for the moment that the Annese are real, if I were to go looking for them where would you advise me to look?'

Dr H: 'You could go to the wharves.' (Laughs) 'Or the sacred places, I suppose. Ah, that got you! You didn't know they had sacred places, did you? They have several, sir, and a well-organized and very confusing religion too. When I first came I used to hear a great deal about a high priest as well – or a great chief, whichever you wanted to call him. At any rate, a more than usually magical abo. The railway had just been built then, and of course the game hereabouts wasn't accustomed to it and a good many animals were killed. This fellow would be seen walking up and down the right-of-way at night, restoring them to life, so people called him Cinderwalker, and various names of that sort. No, not Cinderella, I know what you're thinking – Cinderwalker. Once a cattle-drover's woman had her arm cut off by the train – I suspect she was drunk, and lying on the tracks – and the drover rushed her to the infirmary here. Well, sir, they got a frozen arm out of the organ bank in the regular way and grafted it on to her; but Cinderwalker found the one she had lost and grew a new woman on that so that the drover had two wives. Naturally the second one, the one Cinderwalker made, was abo except for the one arm, so she used to steal with the abo part, and then the human part would put back what she'd taken. Well, finally, the Dominicans here got on the poor drover for having too many wives, and he decided that the one Cinderwalker made would have to go – not having two human arms she couldn't chop firewood properly, you see ...

'Am I surprising you, sir? No, not being really human, you see, the abos can't handle any sort of tool. They can pick them up and carry them about, but they can't accomplish anything with them. They're magical animals, if you like, but only animals. Really,' (Laughs) 'for an anthropologist you're hellishly ignorant of your subject. That's the test the French are supposed to have applied at the ford called Running Blood – stopped every man that passed and made him dig with a shovel . . .'

A cat leaped on to the splintering sill of the officer's window. It was a large black tom with only one eye and double claws – the cemetery cat from Vienne. The officer cursed it, and when it did not go away, began reaching, very slowly and carefully so as not to disturb it, toward his pistol; but the instant the fingers touched the butt the cat hissed like a hot iron dropped into oil and leaped away.

M. d'F: 'Sacred places, Monsieur? Yes, they had many sacred places, so it was said – anywhere a tree grew in the mountains was sacred to them, for example; especially if water stood at the roots, as it usually did. Where the river here – the Tempus – enters the sea, that was a very sacred spot to them.'

Self: 'Where were some others?'

M. d'F: 'There was a cave, far up the river, in the cliffs. I don't know that anyone has ever seen that. And close to the mouth of the river, a ring of great trees. Most of them have been cut now, but the stumps are there still; Trenchard, the beggar who pretends to be one of them, will show you the place for a few sous, or have his son do it.

'Did you not know of him, Monsieur? Oh, yes, near to the docks. Everyone here knows him; he is a fraud, you comprehend, a joke. His hands' (Holds up his own hands) 'are crippled by the arthritis so that he cannot work, and so he says he is an abo, and acts like a madman. It is thought to bring luck to give him a few coins.

'No, he is a man like you and me. He is married to a poor wretched woman one hardly ever sees, and they have a son of fifteen or so.'

The officer turned twenty or thirty pages and began to read again where an alteration in the format of the entries indicated some change in the nature of the material recorded.

One heavy rifle (.35 cal.) for defense against large animals. To be carried by myself. 200 cartridges.

One light rifle (.225 cal.) for securing small game for the pot. To be carried by the boy. 500 cartridges.

One shotgun (20 gauge) for small game and birds. Packed on the lead mule. 160 shells.

One case (200 boxes in all) of matches.

Forty lb. of flour.

Yeast.

Two lb. tea (local).

Ten lb. sugar.

Ten lb. salt.

Kitchen gear.

Multivitamins.

Aid kit.

Wall tent, with repair kit for, and extra pegs and rope.

Two sleeping bags.

Utility tarp to use as ground cloth.

Spare pair of boots (for myself).

Extra clothing, shave kit, etc.

Box of books – some I brought from Earth, most bought in Roncevaux.

Tape recorder, three cameras, film, and this notebook. Pens.

Only two canteens, but we will be traveling with the Tempus all the way.

And that's everything I can think of. No doubt there are a great many things we'll wish we had brought, and next time I'll know better, but there has to be a first time. When I was a student at Columbia I used to read the accounts of the pith helmet and puttee expeditions of the Victorians, when they used hundreds of bearers and diggers and what not, and, filled with Gutenberg courage, dream of leading such a thing myself. So here I am, sleeping under a roof for the last time, and tomorrow we set out: three mules, the boy (in rags), and me (in my blue slacks and the sport shirt from Culot's). At least I won't have to worry about a mutiny among my subordinates, unless a mule kicks me or the boy cuts my throat while I sleep!

*

April 6. Our first night out. I am sitting in front of our little fire, on which the boy cooked our dinner. He is a capital camp cook (delightful discovery!) though very sparing of firewood, as I gather from my reading that frontiersmen always are. I would find him quite likeable if it were not for something of a sly look in those big eyes.

Now he is already asleep, but I intend to sit up and detail this first day's leg of our trip and watch alien stars. He has been pointing out the constellations to me, and I think I may already be more familiar with Sainte Anne's night sky than I ever was with Earth's – which wouldn't take much doing. At any rate the boy claims to know all the Annese names, and though there's a good chance they're just inventions of his father's, I shall record them here anyway and hope for independent confirmation later. There is Thousand Feelers and The Fish (a Nebula which seems to be trying to grasp a single bright star), Burning Hair Woman, The Fighting Lizard (with Sol one of the stars in The Lizard's tail), The Shadow Children. I can't find The Shadow Children now, but I'm sure the boy pointed them out to me – two pairs of bright eyes. There were others but I've forgotten them already; I'm going to have to start recording these conversations with the boy.

But to begin at the beginning. We started early this morning, the boy helping me load the mules, or rather, me helping him. He is very clever with ropes, and ties large, complicated-looking knots that seem to hold securely until he wants them loose, then fall apart under his hand. His father came down to see us off (which surprised me) and treated me to a great deal of untenanted rhetoric designed to pry me loose from a little more money to compensate him for the boy's absence. Eventually, I gave him a bit for luck.

The mules led well, and all seem so far to be good sturdy animals and no more vicious than could be reasonably expected. They are bigger than horses and much stronger, with heads longer than my arm and great square yellow teeth that show when they skin back their thick lips to eat the thorn beside the road. Two grays and one black. The boy hobbled them when we stopped, and I can hear them all around the camp now, and occasionally see the smoke of their breath hanging like a pale spirit in the cold air.

*

April 7. Yesterday I thought we were well begun on our trip, but today I realize that we were merely trekking through the settled – or at least half-settled – farmland around Frenchman's Landing, and might, almost certainly, if we had climbed one of the little hills near last night's campsite, have seen the lights of a farmhouse. This morning we even passed through a tiny settlement the boy called 'Frogtown', a name I suppose would not much recommend itself to the inhabitants. I asked if he weren't ashamed to use a name like that when he is of French descent himself, and he told me with great seriousness that, no, he was half of the blood of the Free People (his name for the Annese) and that it was with them that his loyalties lie. He believes his father, in short, though he is perhaps the only person in the world who does. Yet he is a bright boy; such is the power of parental teaching.

Once we were beyond 'Frogtown', the road simply disappeared. We had come to the edge of 'the back of beyond', and the mules sensed it at once, becoming less obstinate and more skittish, in other words less like people and more like animals. We are cutting west as well as north, I should explain, on a long diagonal toward the river instead of directly toward it. In this way we hope to avoid most of the meadowmeres (at the hands of the old beggar I have already seen enough of them not to want to try and walk across them!), and strike the little streams that feed it often enough to satisfy our needs for water. In any event the Tempus, or so I am told, is too brackish to drink for a long way back from the coast.

I should have mentioned yesterday (but forgot) that when we set up the tent I discovered we had not brought an ax, or any other sort of implement with which to drive the tent pegs. I chided the boy about this a little, but he only laughed and soon set the matter straight by pounding them in with a stone. He finds plenty of dead wood for the fire and snaps it over his knee with surprising strength. To build the fire he makes a sort of little house or bower of dead twigs, which he fills with dry grass and leaves, doing the whole construction in less time than it has already taken me to write this. He always (that is, last night and tonight) asks me to light it for him, apparently considering this a superior function to be performed only by no less a person than the leader of the expedition. I suppose there is something sacred about a campfire, if God's writ runs so far from Sol; but, perhaps so as not to overwhelm us with the holy mystery of smoke, he piously keeps ours so small that I am amazed that he is able to cook over it. Even so, he burns his fingers pretty often, I notice and each time boylike thrusts them into his mouth and hops around the fire, muttering to himself.

*

April 8. The boy is the worst shot I have ever seen; it is almost the only thing I have found thus far he doesn't do well. I have been having him carry the light rifle, but after watching him trying to shoot for three days I have taken it away from him – his whole idea seems to be to point the gun in the general direction of whatever animal I indicate to him, shut his eyes, and pull the trigger. I honestly think that in his heart of hearts (if the boy has such a thing) he believes it is the noise that kills. Such game as we've gotten so far I have shot myself, either snatching the light rifle away from him after he had fired once and making a second (running) shot before whatever he had missed was out of sight, or by using the heavy rifle, which is a waste of expensive ammunition as well as of meat.

On the other hand, the boy (I don't really know why I call him that, except that his father did; he is nearly a man, and now that I come to think of it, only eight or nine years younger, physiologically at least, than I am) has the best eye for wounded game I have ever seen. He is better than a good dog, both at locating and retrieving – which is saying a good deal – and has traveled often in the 'back of beyond', though he's never been as far upriver as the (I hope not mystical) sacred cave we're looking for. At any rate he seems to have lived in the wilderness with his mother for long periods – I get the impression she didn't care much for the kind of life her husband made for them in Frenchman's Landing, for which I can't say I much blame her. However that may be, with the boy's nose for blood and my shooting, I don't think we'll run short of meat.

What else today? Oh yes, the cat. One had been following us, apparently at least since we passed through Frogtown. I caught a glimpse of it today about noon, and (the sun-shimmer reinforcing the deceptive and fantastic quality extension has in the green landscape under this black-sky) thought for an instant that it was a tire-tiger. My bullet went high, naturally, and when I saw it kick up dust, everything snapped back into perspective: my 'scrub trees' were bushes, and the distance which I had thought at least 250 yards away was less than a third of that – making my 'tire-tiger' only a big domestic cat of Terrestrial stock,

121

no doubt a stray from some farm. It seems to follow us quite deliberately, staying, now, about a quarter mile behind us. This afternoon I took a couple of rather long-ranged (200 to 300 yards) shots at it, which upset the boy so much that I regretted my felicidal intentions and told him that if he could get the animal into camp he could keep it as a pet. I suppose it is following us for the scraps of food we leave behind. There will be plenty for it tomorrow – I got a dew-deer today.

*

April 10. Two days of uninterrupted hiking during which we have seen a good deal of game but no sign of any still-extant Annese. We have crossed three small streams which the boy calls the Yellow Snake, the Girl Running, and the End-of-Days; but which my map tells me are Fifty Mile Creek, the Johnson River, and the Rougette. No trouble with any of them – the first two we are able to ford where we struck them, the Rougette (which painted my boots and the legs of the boy and the mules), a few hundred yards upstream. I expect to see the Tempus (which the boy calls simply 'The River') tomorrow, and the boy assures me that the Annese sacred cave must lie a good deal farther up; he says, indeed, that the banks we have bypassed by our route are mud, not stone, and could not hold a cave.

It finally occurred to me that if the boy has lived (as he says) a good part of his life in the wild country, he may be – despite the corrupting influence of his father and his own consequent belief that he is himself partly Annese – an excellent source of information. I have the interview on tape, but as I have tried to make it a practice to do with the more interesting material, I transcribe it here.

Self: 'You've told me that you and your mother have often lived, you say in spring and summer particularly, "in back of beyond" – sometimes for months at a stretch. I have been informed that fifty or more years ago Annese children often came to play with human children on the remote stock farms. Did anything of that sort ever happen to you? Did you ever see anyone out here besides your mother and yourself? After all, we've seen no one in four days.'

V. R. T.: 'We saw a great many people almost every day, many

122

animals and birds, trees that were alive, just as you and I have traveling, as you say for these four days – though this is still not the back of beyond where one sees gods come floating down the river on logs, and trees gone traveling, the gods with large and small heads, and blossoms of the water hydrangea in their hair; or the elk-men whose heads and hair and beards and arms and bodies were like those of men, whose legs were the bodies of red elk so that they needed to mate with the cow-women once as beasts and once as men do, and fought shouting all spring on the hillsides, then when the black mereskimmers flew back from the south were at once friends again and went away with their arms around each other and stole eggs from the pine-thrashers or kicked stones at me; and The Shadow Children of course came to steal by evening, riding up in the bubbles and the foam from the springs – then my mother would not let me go out from beneath her hair – this was when I was very small – after the sun set, but when I was larger I would go out and shout and make them run! – they believe – they always believe – that they'll get all around, and then they'll all run in at once, biting; but if you turn quickly and shout, they never do, and there are never as many of them as they think, because some are only in the minds of the others so that at the time to fight they fade back into each other and become one lonely.'

Self: 'Why haven't you and I seen any of these strange things?'
V. R. T.: 'I have.'
Self: 'What have you seen – I mean, while you've been with me.'
V. R. T.: 'Birds and animals and trees living, and The Shadow Children.'
Self: 'You mean the stars. If you see anything extraordinary you'll tell me, won't you?'
V. R. T.: (Nods)
Self: 'You're an unusual boy. Do you ever go to school when you're with your father in Frenchman's Landing?'
V. R. T.: 'Sometimes.'
Self: 'You're almost a man now. Have you given any thought to what you're going to do in a few years?'
V. R. T.: (Weeps)

There was no reply to that last question; the boy broke into tears, embarrassing me so acutely that after putting my arm around his shoulders for a moment, I had to walk away from the fire, leaving him there sobbing for half an hour or more while I blundered around in the brush where huge worms, luminous but of the livid color of a dead man's lips, writhe underfoot at night. I confess it was a miserably stupid question; what *is* he going to do, a beggar's son, no better than half-educated? He does read well – he's borrowed some of my anthropology texts, and I've asked him questions and gotten better answers than I would have expected from the average university student; but his hand-writing is miserable, as I've seen from an old school notebook (one of his very few pieces of personal baggage).

*

April 11. An eventful day. Let me see if I can cure my habit of skipping back and forth and give everything of interest in the order in which it occurred. When I came back into camp last night (I see that at the close of yesterday's entry I left myself blundering about in bushes), the boy was asleep in his bag. I put more wood on the fire and played back the tape and wrote the stuff on the last page, then turned in. About an hour before dawn we were both roused by a commotion among the mules and went running out to see what the trouble was, myself with a flashlight and the heavy rifle, the boy with two burning sticks from the fire. Didn't see anything, but smelled a stink like rotten meat and heard some big animal, which I really don't believe could have been one of the mules, making off. The mules, when we found them, were covered with sweat, and one had broken its hobble – fortunately it didn't go far, and as soon as it got light the boy was able to catch it, though it took him the best part of an hour – and the two that were still with us seemed very glad to claim the protection due domestic animals.

By the time we had thrashed around long enough to decide there was nothing to find, further sleep was out of the question. We struck the tent, loaded the mules, and then at my insistence spent the first hour in backtracking our path of the day before to see if we could turn up the spoor of any large predatory animal. We saw the cat (which growing bolder now that I've stopped shooting at it) and some tracks of what the boy calls a fire-fox and which, by comparing his description with my *Field Guide to the Animals of Sainte Anne*, I have decided is most probably Hutchesson's fennec, a fox or coyote-like creature with immense ears and a liking for poultry and carrion.

After this little interlude of backtracking we made good progress, and about an hour before noon I made the best shot of the trip to date, dropping a huge brute – not described in the *Field Guide* – similar to the carabao of Asian Earth; this with a single brain shot from the heavy rifle. I paced the distance when the animal was down and found it to be a full three hundred yards!

Naturally I was proud as hell and carefully examined the result of my shot, which had struck the big fellow just in back of the right ear. Even there the skull was so massive that the bullet had failed to penetrate completely; so that the animal had probably been alive for a good part of the time while I was pacing off the distance to it; there seemed to have been a heavy flow of lachrymal fluid that left broad wet streaks in the dust beneath each eye. I lifted one of the eyelids with my fingers after I had looked at the wound and noticed that the eyes were double-pupiled, like those of certain Terrestrial fish; the lower segments of one eye moved slightly when I touched it with my finger, indicating that the animal may have been hanging on a bit even then. The double pupils don't seem characteristic of most life here; so I suppose they must be an adaptation induced by the creature's largely aquatic habits.

I longed to have the head mounted, but that was out of the question; as it was the boy was almost in tears (his own eyes, which are large, are a startling green), imagining that I would want to load the entire carcass, which must have weighed a good fifteen pounds, on to the mules, and assuring me that they could not be expected to carry so much. Eventually I was able to convince him that I intended to leave behind the entrails, the head (though how I regretted those horns!) and the hide and hoofs, as well as the ribs and, in fact, all but the choicest meat. The mules, even so, appreciated neither the added weight nor the smell of blood, and we had more difficulty with them than I had anticipated.

About an hour after we got them going again, we reached the bank of the Tempus. It is a very different river from the one I saw when the boy's father showed me the Annese 'temple'. There it was nearly a mile wide, brackish, and had hardly a trace of current, the mouth itself being not a single river but a serpent cluster of dull streams meandering through a choking delta of mud and reeds. Here everything is changed: the water has hardly any yellow coloration, and flows fast enough to whisk a stick out of sight in a few seconds.

The meadowmeres are entirely behind us now, and this new, swift, clear Tempus runs among rolling hills covered with emerald grass and dotted with trees and thickets. I see now that my original plan of ascending the river by boat was – as my acquaintances in Frenchman's Landing warned me – completely impractical, no matter how convenient it would have been to search for riverbank caves that way. Not only is the water so swift even here that we would be spending most of our fuel just to fight the current, but the river shows every sign of falls and rapids farther up in the mountains. A hovercraft would perhaps be ideal, but with Sainte Anne's small industrial capacity there are probably not more than two dozen on the whole planet, and they are (typically) the sacred prerogative of the military.

But I will not complain. In a hovercraft we might already have found the cave, but with what chance of making contact with any Annese who may yet survive? With our small and I hope not frightening party moving slowly and living off the country, we can hope for contact, if any Annese remain.

Besides, let me confess now, I enjoy it. When we had struck the river and gone a mile or so upstream the boy became very excited and told me we had reached an important point which he had often visited with his mother. It seemed to me to be in no way unusual – a slight bend with a few (very large) overhanging trees and a somewhat oddly shaped stone – but he insisted that it was a beautiful and special locality, showing me how comfortable the stone was, on which one could sit or lie in various positions, how the trees shaded the sun and would give protection from rain and even, covered with snow, form a sort of hut in winter. There were deep pools at the foot of the stone that always had fish – we could find mussels and edible snails (that French mother!) – along the bank here, and in short it was a veritable garden spot. (After listening to him talk in this way for a few minutes I realized that he looks upon the outdoors – at least on certain special areas or parts of it such as this – in the way that most people are accustomed to looking at buildings or rooms, which is an odd idea.) I had been wanting to be alone for a few minutes anyway; so I decided to pamper his harmless enthusiasm, and asked him to take the mules on ahead while I remained behind to contemplate the beauty of the wonderful place to which he had introduced me. He was delighted, and in a few minutes I was more utterly alone than it is ever given most of us born on Earth to be, with only the wind and the sun and the sighing of the great trees that trailed their roots in the murmuring water before me.

Alone I should say except for our camp-follower cat, who

came meowing up and had to be chased after the mules with rocks.

It gave me time to think – about that carabao-like animal I got this morning (which would surely be a record trophy of some sort if only I had been able to take the skull back to civilization) and about this entire trip. Not that I am not as eager as I was before to show that the Annese are not yet extinct, and to record as much as I can of their customs and mode of thought before they fade from humanity's knowledge altogether. I am, but for new reasons. When I landed here on Sainte Anne, all I really cared about was acquiring by field work enough reputation to get a decent faculty post on Earth. Now I know that field work can be, and should be, an end in itself; that those highly distinguished old professors I used to envy for their reputations were not seeking (as I thought) to go back into the field – even if it were just to work over poor old played-out Melanesia once more – to enhance their academic dignity; but rather that their standing was a tool they employed to secure backing for their field work. And they were right! Each of us finds his way, his place; we rattle around the universe until everything fits; this is life; this is science, or something better than science.

By the time I caught up to the boy he had already made camp (early), and I think was rather concerned about me. Tonight he has been trying to dry a part of the carabao meat over the fire to preserve it, though I have told him we can simply throw aside any that spoils before we can eat it.

Forgot to mention that I got two deer while I was catching up to the boy.

The officer laid the canvas-bound notebook aside, and after a moment, rose and stretched. A bird had blundered into the room and he now noticed it for the first time, perched silent and bewildered on the frame of a picture high on the wall opposite the door. He shouted at it, and when it did not move, tried to strike it with a broom the slave had left standing in a corner. It flew, but instead of going out the open door it struck the lintel, fell half-stunned to the floor, then flopped past his face to resume its perch on the picture frame, brushing his cheek with the dark feathers of one wing as it passed. The officer cursed and sat down, picking up a handful of loose pages, these at least decently transcribed in good clerical script.

I should have an attorney – that much is clear. I mean, in addition to the one the court will assign. I feel certain the university will advance me funds to fee a private attorney, and I have asked my court-appointed one to contact the university and arrange the thing for me. That is, I will ask him.

It seems to me that the following questions are involved in my own case. I will write them down here and discuss the possible interpretations, and this will prepare me for the trial. First, then, is the question of the concept of guilt which is central to any criminal proceeding. Is the concept broadly valid?

If it is not broadly valid, then there will exist certain classes of persons who cannot under any circumstance be punished by reason of guilt, and a little reflection convinces me that such classes do in fact exist, viz.: children, the weak of intellect, the very rich, the disturbed of mind, animals, the near relations of persons in high positions, the persons themselves, and so on.

The next question, then, Your Honor, is whether I, the prisoner at the bar, do not in fact belong to one (or more) of the exempted classes. It is clear to me that I do in fact belong to all the classes I have designated above, but I will here – in order to conserve the court's valuable time – concentrate on two: I am exempt by reason of being a child and by reason of being an animal; that is to say, by reason of belonging to the first and fifth of the classes to which you have just consented.

This leads us to the third question: what is meant (in terms of the exempted classes already outlined) by the designation 'child'. Clearly we must rule out in the beginning any question of mere age. Nothing could be more absurd than to suppose a defendant innocent though he committed some abominable act on Tuesday, but guilty were he to have committed it Wednesday. No, no, Your Honor, though I myself am only a few years past twenty, I confess that to think in that way is to invite a carnival of death just prior to each young man's or woman's reaching whatever age you determine shall be deciding. Nor can childhood be based on *internal* and subjective evidence, since it would be impractical to determine whether such interior disposition existed or not. No, the fact of childhood must be established by the way society itself has treated the individual. In my own case:

I own no real property, and have never owned such property.

I have never taken part in, or even witnessed, a legally binding contract.

I have never been called upon to give evidence in a court of law.

I have never entered into marriage or adopted another child.

I have never held a remunerative position on the basis of work performed. (You object, Your Honor? You cite my own testimony with regard to my connection with Columbia against me? The prosecution cites it? No, Your Honor, it is a clever sophistry, but invalid; my tutorial position at Columbia was a manifest sinecure given me to enable me to complete my graduate work, and for my expedition to Sainte Anne I received my expenses only. You see? And who would know better than I?)

Then surely, Your Honor, it is clear from all these points – and I could make a thousand more – that at the time of the crime, if in fact I am charged with any crime, which I doubt, I was a child; and by these proofs I am a child still, for I have still not done any of these things.

As for my being an animal – I mean an animal as opposed to being a human being, an animal as a mere beast – the proof is so simple that you may laugh at me for troubling to present it. Are those who are permitted to run free in our society the animals? Or are they human beings? Who are confined in stalls, sties, kennels, and hutches? Which of the two great divisions sleeps upon bedding thrown upon the floor? Which upon a bed standing above the floor? Which is given bathing facilities and a heated sleeping compartment, and which is expected to warm itself with its own breath and clean itself by licking?

I beg your pardon, Your Honor; I did not intend to offend the court.

*

Forty-seven has been knocking on the pipe – shall I tell you what he said? Very well.

ONE FORTY-THREE, ONE FORTY-THREE, IS THAT YOU? ARE YOU LISTENING? WHO IS THE NEW MAN ON YOUR FLOOR?

I have filled in the punctuation myself. Forty-seven does not use punctuation, and if I have misrepresented his intention, I hope he will forgive me.

I sent: WHAT NEW? It would be very useful to have a stone – or a metal object as Forty-seven does (he says he uses the frames of his glasses) with which to tap the pipe. It hurts my knuckles.

I SAW HIM THIS MORNING THROUGH MY DOOR.

OLD, LONG WHITE HAIR. DOWNSTAIRS TO YOU.
WHICH CELL?
DON'T KNOW.

If I had a stone I could rap on the walls of my cell loudly
enough for those on either side to hear. As it is, the prisoner to
my left raps to me – I do not know with what, but it makes every
sort of strange noise, not just a rapping or ticking – but does not
know the code. The wall on my right is silent; possibly there is no
one there, or, like me, he may have nothing with which to speak.

Shall I tell you how I was arrested? I was very tired. I had
been to the Cave Canem, and as a result was up very late – it
was nearly four. At noon I had an appointment with the president,
and I felt quite certain I would be officially placed at the head of
a department, and on very favorable terms. I intended to go to
bed, and left a note for Madame Duclose, the woman at whose
house I was lodging, to wake me at ten.

Forty-seven sends: ONE FORTY-THREE, ARE YOU
CRIMINAL OR POLITICAL?
POLITICAL. (I wish to hear what he will say.)
WHICH SIDE?
YOU?
POLITICAL.
WHICH SIDE?
ONE FORTY-THREE, THIS IS RIDICULOUS. ARE
YOU AFRAID TO ANSWER MY QUESTION? WHAT
MORE CAN THEY DO TO YOU? YOU ARE ALREADY
HERE.
I rap: WHY SHOULD I TRUST YOU IF YOU DO NOT
TRUST ME? YOU BEGAN. (Hurting my knuckles.)
OF THE FIFTH OF SEPTEMBER.
WHEN I GET ROCK. HAND HURTS.
COWARD! (So sends Forty-seven, very loudly. He will break
his glasses.)

Where was I? Yes, my arrest. The whole house was quiet – I
thought this was only because of the lateness of the hour, but I
now realize that most of them must have been awake, knowing
that they were waiting in my room for me, lying in their beds
hardly daring to breathe while they waited for the shots or
screams, Madame Duclose, particularly, must have been concerned for the large, gilt-framed mirror in my room, which she

130

had cautioned me about repeatedly. (Mirrors, I have found – I mean good ones of silvered glass, not polished bits of metal – are quite expensive in Port-Mimizon.) And thus there was no snoring, no one stumbling down the corridor to the lavatory, no muffled sighs of passion from Mlle Etienne's room while she entertained herself with the fruits of imagination and a tallow candle.

I did not notice. I scrawled my note (others think my hand very bad, but I do not think so; when I receive my appointment I will – if I have to teach classes at all – have my students write on the chalkboard for me, or distribute notes for my classes already printed in purple ink on yellow paper) for Mme Duclose and went up, as I thought, to bed.

They were quite confident. They had a light burning in my room, and I saw the stripe of radiance at the bottom of my door. Surely if I had in fact committed some crime I would have turned and fled on tiptoe when I saw that light. As it was, I thought only that there had been some letter or message for me – perhaps from the president of the university, or possibly from the brothelkeeper at the Cave Canem who had earlier that evening asked my help in dealing with his 'son'; and I decided that if it were he, I would not answer until the evening following; I was very tired and had drunk enough brandy to feel let down now when it was flickering out, and I was conscious of the inefficiency of my motions as I got out my key and then discovered that my door was not locked.

There were three of them, all seated, all waiting for me. Two were uniformed; the third wore a dark suit which had once been good but was now worn and stained with food grease and the oil from lamps and, moreover, was a little too small for him, so that he had the appearance of the valet of a miser. He sat in my best chair, the chair with the needlepoint seat, with one arm hanging quite carelessly over the back of it, and the lamp with the globe painted with roses and the fringed shade at his elbow as though he had been reading. Mme Duclose's mirror was behind him, and I could see that his hair was cut short and that he had a scarred head, as though he had been tortured or had had an operation on his brain or had fought with someone armed with some tearing weapon. Over his shoulder I could see myself in the tall hat I had bought here in Port-Mimizon after landing, and my second best cape and my stupid, surprised face.

One of the uniformed men got up and shut the door behind me, throwing the night bolt. He wore a gray jacket and gray trousers and a peaked cap, and around his waist a broad brown pistol belt with a very large, old-fashioned looking revolver in a holster. When he sat again, I noticed that his shoes were ordinary workmen's shoes, not of much quality and already quite worn. The second uniformed man said, 'You may hang up your hat and coat, if you like.'

I said, 'Of course,' hanging them, as I usually did, on the hooks on the back of the door.

'It will be necessary for us to search your person.' (This was still the second uniformed man, who wore a short-sleeved green jacket with many pockets and loose green trousers with straps about the ankles, as though he were intended to ride a bicycle as part of his duties.) 'We will do this in either of two ways, depending on your own preference. You may, if you like, disrobe; we will then search your clothing and allow you to dress yourself again – however, you must disrobe before us so that you have no opportunity to secrete anything you may have on your person. Or we will search you here and now, as you are. Which do you prefer?'

I asked if I were under arrest and if they were the police. The man in the needlepoint chair answered, 'No, Professor, certainly not.'

'I am not a professor, at least, not at present as far as I know. If I am not under arrest, why am I being searched? What am I supposed to have done?'

The man who had shut the door said, 'We're going to search you to *see* if there's any reason to arrest you,' and looked at the man in the black suit for confirmation. The other uniformed man said: 'You must choose. How will you be searched?'

'And if I will not submit to being searched?'

The man in black said: 'Then we will have to take you to the citadel. They will search you there.'

'You mean that you will arrest me?'

'Monsieur . . . '

'I am not French. I am from North America, on Earth.'

'Professor, I urge you – as a friend – not to force us to arrest you. It is a serious matter here, to have been arrested; but it is possible to be searched to be questioned, to be – as it may be – even held for a time – '

'Perhaps even to be tried and executed,' the man in the green jacket finished for him.

' – without having been arrested. Do not, I beg you, force us to arrest you.'

'But I must be searched.'

'Yes,' said both the uniformed men.

'Then I prefer to be searched as I am, without undressing.'

The two uniformed men looked at one another as though this were significant. The man in black looked bored and picked up the book he had been reading, which I saw was one of my own – *A Field Guide to the Animals of Sainte Anne*.

The man with the pistol belt came over, half-apologetically, to search me, and I noticed for the first time that his uniform was that of the City Transit Authority. I said: 'You' e a horsecar driver, aren't you? Why are you carrying that gun?'

The man in black said: 'Because it is his duty to carry it. I might ask why you yourself are armed.'

'I'm not.'

'On the contrary, I have just been examining this book of yours – there are tables of figures penciled on the flyleaves in the back, you see? Can you tell me what they are?'

'They were left there by some former owner,' I told him, 'and I have no idea what they are. Are you accusing me of being some sort of spy? If you'll look at them you'll see they're nearly as old as the book and badly faded.'

'They are interesting figures; pairs of numbers of which the first is given in yards and the second in inches.'

'I've seen them,' I said. The man in the City Transit uniform was patting my pockets; whenever he found anything – my watch, my money, my pocket notebook – he handed it with an obsequious little gesture to the man in black.

'I am of the mathematical turn of mind.'

'How fortunate for you.'

'I have analyzed these figures – they approximate quite well the conic section called a parabola.'

'That means nothing to me. As an anthropologist I am more often concerned with the normal distribution curve.'

'How fortunate for you,' the man in black said, repaying me for my sarcasm of a moment before. He motioned to the two uniformed men, who came to him. For a moment the three whispered together, and I noticed how similar their faces were, all three with pointed chins, black brows and narrow eyes, so that they might have been brothers, the man in black the eldest and probably the cleverest as well, the City Transit man the least imaginative, but all three of a family.

'What are you talking about?' I said.

'We were speaking of your case,' the man in black said. The City Transit man left the room, shutting the door behind him.

'And what were you saying?'

'That you are ignorant of the law here. That you should have an attorney.'

'That's probably true, but I don't believe you were saying that.'

'You see? An attorney would advise you against contradicting us in that tone.'

'Listen, are you from the police? Or the prosecutor's office?'

The man in black laughed. 'No, not at all. I am a civil engineer from the department of public works. My friend here,' he indicated the man in green, 'is an army signalman. My other friend as you divined, is a horsecar driver.'

'Then why have you come to arrest me as though you were police?'

'You see how ignorant you are of our ways here. On Earth, as I understand, it is different; but here all public employees are of one fraternity, if you follow me. Tomorrow my friend the horsecar driver may be picking up garbage – '

The man in green interrupted to snicker, 'You may say he's doing that tonight.'

' – my friend here may be a crewman on one of the patrol boats and I may be an inspector of cats. Tonight we have been sent to get you.'

'With a warrant for my arrest?'

'I must tell you again that it is best for you if you are not arrested. I say to you frankly that if you are arrested it is very improbable that you will ever be released.'

As he completed this sentence the door opened behind me, and I saw in the mirror Mme Duclose and Mlle Etienne, with the horsecar driver standing behind them. 'Come in, ladies,' the man in black said, and the horsecar driver herded them into the room, where they stood side by side in front of the washstand, looking frightened and confused. Mme Duclose, an old, gray-haired woman with a fat stomach, wore a faded cotton dress with a long skirt (whether because the horsecar driver had allowed her to put it on before summoning her or because she had been using it for a night-gown, I do not know). Mlle Etienne – a very tall girl of twenty-seven or -eight – might have been not the sister, but possibly the half-sister or cousin of the three men. She had the sharply pointed face and the black eyebrows, but hers had been plucked thin to form arches over her eyes, which were, mercifully, not the dark, narrow eyes of the men but large and blue-purple like the dots of paint on the face of a doll. Her hair was a mop of brown curls, and she was, as I have said, exceedingly tall her legs stiltlike in their elongation, rising on thin, straight bones to hips broader than seemed consonant with the remainder of her physique, after which her body contracted again abruptly to a small waist, small breasts, and narrow shoulders. She boasted tonight a negligee of some gossamer fabric like a very thin cheesecloth, but this was gathered in so many layers and foldings and wraps as to be quite opaque.

'You are Mme Duclose?' the man in black asked that lady. 'The owner of this house? You rent the room we presently occupy to this gentleman here?'

She nodded.

'It will be necessary for him to accompany us to the citadel, where he will converse with various officials. You will close this room and lock the door when we leave, do you understand? You will disturb nothing.'

Mme Duclose nodded, wisps of gray hair bobbing.

'In the event that the gentleman has not returned within one week, you will apply to the Department of Parks, which will dispatch a reputable man to this address. In his company you will be permitted to enter this room to inspect it for rodent damage and to open the windows for the period of one hour, at the close of which you will be required to relock the room, and he will leave. Do you understand what I have just said?'

Mme Duclose nodded again.

'In the event that the gentleman has not returned by Christmas, you will apply to the Department of Parks as before. On the day following Christmas – or in the event that Christmas falls on a Saturday, on the following Monday – a reputable man will be dispatched as previously. In his company you will be permitted to change the bedding and, if you wish, air the mattress.'

'On the day after Christmas?' Mme Duclose asked in bewilderment.

'Or in the event that Christmas falls on Saturday, on the Monday following. In the event that the gentleman has not returned by one year from this date – which you may compute, for our convenience, as being the first of the current month, should you so choose – you may again apply to the Department of Parks. You may at that time – if you wish – place the gentleman's belongings in storage at your expense, or you may store them elsewhere in your home if you wish. They will be inventoried by the Department of Parks at that time. You may then use this room for other purposes. In the event that the gentleman has still not returned at a date fifty years distant from the date whose

135

calculation I have just explained to you, you – or your heirs or assigns – may again apply to the Department of Parks. At that time the government will claim any article falling under the following categories: articles made wholly or in part of gold, silver, or any other precious metal; moneys in the currencies of Sainte Croix, Sainte Anne, or Earth, or other worlds; antiques; scientific appliances; blueprints, plans, and documents of all sorts; jewelry; body linen; clothing. Any article not falling under these categories shall become the property of you, your heirs, and assigns. If tomorrow you find you do not clearly recall what I have just told you, apply to me at the Department of Public Works, Subdepartment of Sewers and Drains, and I will explain to you again. Ask for the assistant to the General Inspector of Sewers and Drains. You understand?'

Mme Duclose nodded.

'And now you, Mademoiselle,' the man in black continued, turning his attention to Mlle Etienne. 'Observe; I hand the gentleman a visiting pass.' He took a stiff card, perhaps six inches long and two wide, from the breast pocket of his greasy coat and handed it to me. 'He will write your name thereupon and give it to you, and with it you will be admitted on your own recognizance to the citadel on the second and fourth Thursdays of each month between the hours of nine and eleven p.m.'

'Wait a moment,' I said. 'I don't even know this young lady.'

'But you are not married?'

'No.'

'So your dossier informed me. In cases where the prisoner is unmarried it is the rule to give the card to the closest resident single woman of suitable age. It is, you will understand, based upon statistical probabilities. The young woman may transfer the card to whomever you wish, who may then use it in her name. That will be something for you to discuss – ' (he paused a moment in thought) ' – ten days from now. Not now. Write down her name.'

I was forced to ask Mlle Etienne's first name, which proved to be Celestine.

'Give her the card,' the man in black said.

I did so, and he laid one hand heavily on my shoulder and said, 'I hereby place you under arrest.'

*

136

I have been moved. I continue this record of my thoughts – if that is what it may be said to be – in a new cell. I am no longer my old self, one forty-three, but some new, unknown 143; this because that old number was chalked upon the door of this new cell. The transition must seem very abrupt to you, reading this; but I was not actually interrupted in the task of writing, as it must seem. The truth is that I grew tired of detailing my arrest. I scratched. I slept. I ate some bread and soup the warder brought me and found a small bone – the rib bone, I suspect, of a goat – in my soup and with this held long conversations with my neighbor upstairs, forty-seven. I listened to the madman on my left until it almost seemed to me that among his idiot scratching and scrapings I could discern my own name.

Then there was a rattling of keys at the door of my cell, and I thought that perhaps Mlle Etienne was to be permitted to see me after all. I tried insofar as I could to make myself clean, smoothing my hair and beard with my fingers. Alas, it was only the guard, and with him a powerfully built man wearing a black hood which concealed his face. Naturally I thought I was going to be killed, and though I tried to be courageous – and really felt that I was not especially fearful – I found that my knees had become so weak that I could only stand with great difficulty. I thought of escape (as I always do when they take me to be questioned; it's the only chance, because there's no escaping from these cells), but there was only the narrow corridor to run in, as always, without windows and with a guard posted at every stair. The hooded man took my arm and, without speaking, led me through passageways and up and down steps until I was completely confused; we must have walked for hours. I saw any number of miserable dirty faces like my own staring at me through the tiny glassed Judas windows in the doors of the cells. Several times we passed through courtyards, and I thought I was to be shot in each; it was about noon, and the bright sunlight made me blink and my eyes water. Then in a corridor much like all the others we halted before a door marked 143, and the hooded man raised a concrete slab from the center of the floor, showing me a narrow hole from which a steep iron stair descended. I went down and he followed me; the distance must have been fifty meters or more, and at the bottom it was only with a flashlight that we were able to grope our way down a corridor stinking of stale urine, until we reached the door of this cell into which a push from him sent me sprawling.

At the time I was happy enough to sprawl, for I thought, as I

137

have said, that I was about to be executed. I still do not know that it is not true; the man was certainly dressed as an executioner though that may have been merely to frighten me, and perhaps he has other duties.

The officer groped among the materials on his desk for the next page, but before he could locate it the brother officer entered the room a second time. 'Hello,' the officer said, 'I thought you were turning in.'

'I was,' said the brother officer. 'I have; I did. I slept for a while, then woke up and couldn't get back to sleep. It's the heat.'

The officer shrugged.

'How are you coming with your case?'

'Still trying to catalogue the facts.'

'Didn't they send a summary? They're supposed to.'

'Probably, but I haven't found it in this mess yet. There's a letter, and a fuller summary may be on one of these tapes.'

'What's this?' The brother officer had picked up the canvas-bound notebook.

'A notebook.'

'The accused's?'

'I think so.'

The brother officer raised his eyebrows. 'You don't know?'

'I'm not sure. Sometimes I think that notebook . . .'

The brother officer waited for him to continue, but he did not. After a moment the brother officer said, 'Well, I see you're busy. Think I'll wake up the surgeon and see if he won't give me something that will let me sleep.'

'Try a bottle,' the officer said as the brother officer went out When he had gone he picked up the canvas-bound notebook again and opened it at random.

'No, he is a man like you and me. He is married to a poo wretched woman one hardly ever sees, and they have a son o fifteen or so.'

Self: 'But he claims to be Annese?'

M. d'F: 'He is a fraud, you understand. Much of what he says o the abos is from his own head – oh, he will tell you wonderfu tales, Monsieur.'

(End of Interview)

138

Dr Hagsmith had also mentioned this beggar, and I have decided to find him. Even though his claim to be Annese is false – as I have no doubt it is – he may have picked up some real information in the course of his impersonations. Besides, the idea of finding even a counterfeit Annese appeals to me.

*

March 21. I have had a talk with the beggar, who calls himself Twelvewalker and claims to be a direct descendant of the last Annese shaman, and thus rightfully a king – or whatever distinction he may happen to covet at the moment. In my opinion his actual descent is Irish, very probably through one of those Irish adventurers who left their island for France at the time of the Napoleonic Wars. At any rate, his culture seems clearly French, his face certainly Irish – the red hair, blue eyes, and long upper lip are unmistakable.

Apparently even counterfeit Annese are elusive, and turning him up was more of a problem than I had anticipated; everyone seemed to know him and told me I could find him in such and such a tavern, but no one seemed to know where he lived – and, naturally, he was not to be found in any of the taverns where he 'always' was. When I discovered his hut at last (I cannot call it a house), I realized that I had passed it several times without realizing it was a human dwelling.

Frenchman's Landing, as perhaps I should mention here, is built on the banks of the Tempus about ten miles upstream of the sea itself. The waterfront is thus the muddy shore of the river, looking across the yellowish, salt-tinged flood toward a muddle of even less presentable buildings – La Fange – on the bank opposite. Sainte Anne's twin world of Sainte Croix creates fifteen-foot tides all over the planet, and these affect the river far upstream of Frenchman's Landing. At high tide the water is completely undrinkable and marine fish – so I am told – may be caught from the ends of the docks. Then the decking of these docks is only a few feet above the water, the air is fresh and pure, and the meadowmeres surrounding the somewhat higher ground on which the town stands have the appearance of an endless lacework of clear pools fringed with the brilliant green salt rushes. But in a few hours the tide is gone, and all vitality seems drained from the river and the country around it. The docks stand twelve-feet high on stilts of rotting timbers; the river shows a thousand islands of muck, and the meadowmeres are desolate salt flats of stinking mud over which, at night, wisps of luminous gas hover like the ghosts of the dead Annese.

The waterfront itself is not too different, I suppose, from the waterfront of a similar rivertown on Earth, except perhaps for the absence of the robot cranes one expects to see and the use of native building materials in place of Earth's all-pervasive compressed waste walls. Twelve years ago, I understand, old-fashioned thermonuclear ships were commonplace at the piers here, but now that the planet has been ringed with an adequate network of weather satellites, safe, modern sailing vessels are in use here as on Earth.

The beggar's hut, when I located it at last, was an old boat turned upside down and propped above the ground with every sort of rubbish. Still doubting that anyone could actually live there, I rapped on the hull with the handle of my pocketknife, and a dark-haired boy of fifteen or sixteen thrust his head out almost at once. When he saw me he ducked under the edge of the boat, but then, instead of standing, remained on his knees with both hands outstretched and began a sort of beggar's whine in which I could make out only occasional words. I assumed that he was mentally retarded, and it seemed possible that he could not even walk, since when I stepped away from him he followed me, still on his knees, with a sort of agile shuffle that seemed to imply that this was his normal gait. After half a minute of this I gave him a few coins in the hope of quieting him enough to ask him some questions, but the coins were no sooner out of my hand than the head of an older man, the red-haired beggar, as it turned out, appeared from under the boat (from where, I feel sure, he had been observing his son's technique).

'Bless you, Monsieur!' he said. 'I am not, you comprehend, a Christian, but may your generosity to my poor boy be blessed by Jesus, Mary, and Joseph, or in the eventuality that you are Protestant, Monsieur, by Jesus only and by God the Father and the Holy Ghost. As my own ten-times decimated people would say, may the Mountains bless you and the River and the Trees and the Oceansea and all the stars of Heaven and the gods. I speak as their religious leader.'

I thanked him, and for some reason I cannot quite explain gave him one of my cards, which he accepted with such a flourish that I felt for a moment that he had accepted with it the duty to second me in a duel or assist me in my love affairs. Afte glancing at it he exclaimed, 'Ah, you are a doctor! Look, Victor, our visitor is a doctor of philosophy!' and held the card for an instant in front of the boy's eyes, which were as large and sea green as his own were tiny and blue.

'Doctor, Doctor Marsch, I am not an educated man – you see that – but I yield to none in my respect for education, for scholarship. My house,' he waved toward the inverted boat as though it had been a palace and a quarter-mile distant, 'is yours! My son and I are entirely at your service for the remainder of the day – or the remainder of the month, should you wish it. And should you be disposed to tender some small emolument for our services, let me assure you in advance of any possible embarrassment that we do not expect from the temple of learning the golden munificence of commerce triumphant; and we are well aware of that blessed natural law by which the townsman's gilt buys more – more, haven't I said, (giving the boy a push) ' – than the merchant's gold. How may we serve you?'

I explained that I understood that he sometimes guided visitors to locations nearby that were supposed to have been important to the prediscovery Annese, and he immediately invited me into his home.

There were no chairs under the inverted boat, there being insufficient headroom for them; but old flotation cushions and folded squares of sailcloth served for seats, and they had a tiny table (such as might have served a poor Japanese family) whose top was hardly more than a double-hand's width above the tarpaulin that covered the ground. The older man lit a lamp – a mere wick floating in a shallow dish of oil – and ceremoniously poured me a small glass of what proved to be hundred-proof rum. When I had accepted it he said: 'You wish to see the sacred places of my fathers, the lords of this planet! I can show them to you, Doctor – indeed no one but I *can* show them to you properly or explain their significations and enter you yourself into the very spirit of that departed age! But it is already too late today, Doctor; the tide is already past the flood. If you could come tomorrow, in the middle of the morning – not too late – then we will skim across the meadowmeres as cheerfully as a gondola. With no effort at all on your part, Doctor, for my son and I will paddle and pole you wherever you may wish to go and show you everything worth seeing. You may take photographs – or do whatever you please – my son and I will be glad to pose.'

I asked him what the cost would be, and he named a sum which seemed reasonable enough, adding quickly, 'Remember,

Doctor, you will be receiving the labor of two men for five hours – and the use of our boat. For a unique experience! – no one but myself can properly show you what you wish to see.' I agreed to the price, and he said: 'There is one other thing – the lunch. We must have food for three. If you wish to leave funds with me, I will procure it.' I frowned at him, and he added at once, 'Or you may bring it yourself – but remember, it is to be a lunch for three. Perhaps a bottle of wine and a bird.

'But now, Doctor, I have some very choice things to show you. Wait a moment.' He reached into a packing box which lay beside his seat and took out a tin tray, with its surface covered with red flock. On it were two dozen or so projectile points chipped and ground from every sort of stone, and several which I am fairly sure had been made from common colored glass, probably from pieces of broken whisky bottles. They were new, as was shown by their razor-sharp edges (genuinely old flint or volcanic glass implements have always lost their keenness by friction with soil grit); and from their fantastic shapes – extremely broad, doubly or triply barbed – as well as their general crudeness, it seemed certain they had been made for display rather than use.

'Weapons of the abos, Doctor,' the beggar said. 'My son and I go looking for them when there's no one will hire us and our boat. Irreplaceable, and genuine souvenirs of the Frenchman's Landing country, where as you know the abos was found more thickly than anywhere else on this world, as it was my forefathers' sacred place like Rome or Boston would be to you, and a paradise of fish and animals and all sorts of things to eat, which you will hear me tell about tomorrow when we go out upon the meadow-meres, and if we have luck, the boy will even demonstrate the catching of fish or animals in the abo manner, without even using such delicate and now valuable implements as these I offer for sale to you here.'

I told him that I wasn't interested in buying any such things, and he said: 'You really should not be missing any such opportunity, Doctor. These have been bought by the museum at Roncevaux, and castings made from them so they could be sent all over the world, and even to Sainte Croix, so that you might say they're universally respected, at least as far as this system goes. Look at this one!' He held up the largest, a chipped flint core that might have been more effective if it were used to club the animal to death. 'I could put a pin on the back for you, so that a lady could wear it for a brooch. Make a nice conversation piece.'

I had seen the points at Roncevaux; I said: 'No thank you

142

But I have to admit that I admire your industry – since you obviously make these yourself.'

'Oh, no! Look,' he held up his hands, 'we abos can't do that kind of work, Doctor. See my hands.'

'I thought you just said the abos made these.'

The boy, who had been sitting quietly listening to us, said in an undertone, 'With their teeth.' The first words I had heard from him except for the unintelligible beggar's litany earlier.

'My hands is worse even than the others,' his father protested. 'You mock me – I who can scarcely tie his own shoes. It is all I can do, Doctor, to handle the boat pole.'

'Then your son makes them,' I said, but I saw as soon as I had said it that I had made a mistake. The boy's face showed the kind of pain so easily evoked in a sensitive adolescent, and the older man crowded with mirth.

'He! Doctor, he is worse even than I am myself, and good for nothing but to fight with the other boys, who always beat him, and to read his books from the library. He can't even remember the way to twist open the top of a jar.'

'Then I was right the first time – you make them yourself. Knapping flint requires a certain dexterity, but not of the same order as playing a violin. One hand holds the striker, the other the mallet, and it's a matter of where the point of the striker is placed and how hard it's hit.'

'From your sound, you have done it yourself, Doctor.'

'I have, and I've made better points than those.'

Unexpectedly the boy said: 'The Free People didn't use those things. They made nets by knotting vines and grasses, but if they wanted to cut something they used their teeth.'

'He is correct, you know,' the older man said in a new voice. 'But you will not give me away, Doctor?'

I told him that if the museum at Roncevaux asked my opinion I would give it to them, but that I didn't think he was an important enough fraud to waste time denouncing him otherwise.

'We must have something, you know,' he said, and for the first time I got the impression that he was not talking to wheedle money. 'Something we can sell, something they can hold in their hands. You can't sell the truth – that's what I used to tell my wife. That's what I tell my son.'

A few minutes after this I excused myself, promising again to meet the pair tomorrow morning. My impression of them both – impostors though they undoubtedly are – is somewhat better than I had anticipated. The older man certainly is not, as I had been led to expect, an alcoholic; no alcoholic would be sober, as he was, with a bottle of hundred-proof rum in his possession. No doubt he begs in taverns because he finds money freest there and drinks what is offered him. The boy seemed intelligent when he was no longer feigning imbecility for profit, and is handsome in a rather sensitive way, with his green eyes, pale complexion, and dark hair.

*

March 22. Met the two beggars, father and son, a few minutes before ten, this time remembering to bring my tape recorder, which I had neglected on the previous visit. (The account of our conversation I gave yesterday is true and correct to the best of my memory and was written immediately after the event, but I can promise no more.) Also a shotgun, bought locally yesterday, in case the meadowmeres afforded any edible waterfowl; it is a twenty gauge and thus rather too small for the purpose, but the only thing available except some poorly finished single-shots intended for sale to farmers. My landlord here recommended getting the gun and promised to cook anything I bagged in return for a half share of the meat.

(To anticipate slightly, I was fortunate and killed three good-sized specimen of a bird called the reed-hen, which the beggar pointed out to me as good to eat. It is slightly smaller than a goose and of a beautiful green color like a parrot or a parakeet; he claims they were a favorite article of diet among the Annese, and from my dinner tonight I believe him, though I am sure he knows no more about it than I do.)

All traces of the boat-hut were gone when I arrived, and the spot where it had stood was a mere corner of waste ground. The boy, bare-chested and barefooted, was leaning against a building nearby, and explained that his father was taking care of our vessel; he at once relieved me of the basket lunch I was carrying (which my landlord had prepared for us) and would have carried my tape recorder and gun as well if I had been willing to let him.

He led me some distance along the waterfront to a little floating jetty (which he called a stage), where I saw his father, in a blue shirt and an old red scarf, waiting in the boat that had been our roof the day before. The older man at once demanded the payment we had agreed upon, but settled, after an argument, for half – the remaining amount to be paid on the termination of our tour. I then clambered (rather cautiously, I admit) into the boat, the boy jumped in after me, and we were off, father and son each pulling an oar.

For five minutes or so we picked our way among the ships in the harbor, following an almost imperceptible curve in the river; then between the hulls of two big four-masters I saw, as though I were looking through a cleft rock into a valley of incredible green, the open, wild meadowmeres of Sainte Anne, which had been, before the coming of the first starcrossers from Earth (as the older man had truly said), the paradise of the Annese. Father and son laid harder to the oars; a sailor on one of the big ships gave us a few halfhearted curses, and we shot between them and out on to the broad water of the Tempus, now swollen by a high tide still making.

'Five kilometers farther to the Oceansea,' the beggar explained, 'and if the Doctor agrees – '

He was interrupted, as I saw, by something he had seen behind me. I twisted in my seat in the stern to look, but at first could see nothing.

'Just by the t'gallant yard of the ship on our left,' the boy told me softly. I saw it then, a silvery object in the sky that seemed no bigger than a blown leaf. In three minutes it was overhead, a shark-shaped military craft perhaps a mile and a half long. It was not really silver, but the color of a knife, and I could make out tiny dots lining the sides that might have been observation ports or laser muzzles or both. The beggar said, 'Do not wave,' then whispered something to the boy of which I caught only the beginning and end: '*Faîtes attention . . . français!*' I think the meaning must have been, 'Remember that you are French.' The boy answered something I could not hear and shook his head.

First we visited the ocean, which the beggar claimed was itself a sacred object in the Annese religion, wending our way through one of the serpentine throats of the Tempus. Our little boat behaved better than I would have expected in the choppy surf, and we landed a mile or so north of the northernmost mouth on a sandy beach. 'Here,' the old man said, 'is the actual spot.' He showed me a small stone marker with an inscription in French attesting to the fact that the first human party to reach Saint Anne had splashed down twenty-five kilometers out to sea and landed their boats where we stood. On this stretch of beach I think I was more conscious than I have ever been before of being on a world foreign to my own; the sand was littered everywhere with seashells, with something alien about them all, so that I believe that even if I had found one on a Terrestrial beach I would have known that it had never been washed up by any ocean of Earth's.

'Here,' the older man said, 'they landed – the first French. You say, Doctor, that many do not believe the abos ever to have existed, but I tell you that when the boats came ashore they found a man – '

'One of the people of the meadowmeres,' his son put in.

'Found him floating on his face in the Oceansea. He had been beaten until dead with scourges of little shells tied together – such was their custom, to sometimes so sacrifice men. They found him here, and that great ancestor of mine who is sometimes called The Eastwind came down to make a peace with them. You do not know, and the log of that first ship was burned in the fusing of Saint-Dizier, but I have talked to a man, an old man, who sixty years ago knew well one of them who was in that first little air-filled boat, and I know.'

We walked inland and visited the great sinkhole in the sand, which is now called the Hourglass, and where the beggar told me the Annese sometimes imprisoned their fellows. The boy slid down into it to show me that a man could not escape unaided, but I thought he was exaggerating the difficulty and scrambled in myself, so that his father had to rescue us both by throwing down the end of a rope he had carried from the boat for the purpose. The sides are not at all steep, but the sand is so soft that they cannot be climbed by an unaided man.

After seeing the Hourglass we returned to our boat, and re-entering the river by a different mouth, moved out on to the meadowmeres proper, my guides poling us through still tidal pools among waving clumps of salt reeds. I got my three reed-hens here, the boy swimming after the birds for me – I was about to write 'as well as any retriever', but the truth is that he swam better than that, almost like a seal; so that I was ready to believe his father when he told me he sometimes caught un-wounded birds by swimming beneath them and seizing their feet. He (the boy) told me there was good fishing here when the tide was out, and his father added, 'But you cannot get anything for them in the town, Doctor – too many there fish for themselves.' The boy said, 'Not fish to sell, fish to eat.'

The Annese temple (or observatory) has now been ruined by the settlers' need for timber, all the trees cut except a few half-rotten ones. From the stumps, however, it is fairly easy to reconstruct the way it must have appeared in prediscovery times. There were four hundred and two trees (the number of days in Sainte Anne's year) spaced approximately a hundred and ten feet apart so that they formed a circle about three miles in diameter. The stumps show that the trunks of most were more than twelve feet in thickness, thus at the time they were destroyed, the foliage of each tree may almost have touched the next; certainly from a distance they must have appeared to form a continuous wall except for the portion immediately ahead of the observer. The interior of this ring seems to have been cleared of any further planting or other object. I would conjecture that the Annese used the trees to keep count of days, perhaps by moving some sort of marker from tree to tree, hanging it on the limbs; but it seems doubtful that any more sophisticated astronomy was carried out here. (To say, however, as some scholars on Earth do, that the Annese 'temple' is possibly of natural growth is absurd. It was certainly intelligently planned, and undoubtedly predated the splashdown of the first French ship by a century or more. I counted the rings of four stumps and found the average age to be a hundred and twenty-seven Annese years.)

I have made a sketch-map showing the locations of the stumps and the approximate size of each; they are decaying rapidly now, and in a decade more, it will be impossible to trace their position.

Though the tide was ebbing by the time I completed my map we made our way up the river for a few miles and stopped to look at a stone outcrop – one of the very few to be found in the meadowmeres – which the beggar claimed was originally in the form of a seated man. There is, so he told me, a superstition current among the people of Frenchman's Landing and La Fange that indecent and perverse acts committed while sitting or lying in the lap of this natural statue are invisible to God. The belief is supposed to be of Annese origin, though the boy denied this. The stone is now almost completely worn away.

As we made our way back to town I reflected on the rumors I have heard of a sacred cave a hundred miles or more up the river. It is one of the failures of science here – at least, to date – that, though a native Annese race surely existed and perhaps still exists, no skull or positively identifiable bone has ever been described. To some like me, raised on accounts of Windmill Hill Cave and the rock shelter of Les Eyzies, the grottoes of the

Périgord and the cave paintings of Altamira and Lascaux, the idea of an Annese sacred cave is irresistible. A swamp like the meadowmeres will, except maybe in one case out of ten thousand, completely destroy the skeleton of any creature that dies there; but a cave will, again except in one case out of ten thousand, preserve it. And why shouldn't the Annese have used the depths of such a cave for burials, as primitive people did all over Earth? It is even possible that there may be paintings, though the Annese do not seem to have reached the tool-making stage. Tonight, even as I write this, I find myself making plans to search for the cave, which is supposed to have its opening in the rocky walls rising above the Tempus. We will need a boat (or perhaps more than one), light enough for portage around any falls or rapids and equipped with an engine with enough power to make good time against the current. We should have enough people to allow one man to stay with the boat (or boats) while at least three (for safety) enter the cave. One of us besides myself ought to be an educated man, capable of appreciating the importance of what we may find; and, if possible, one or more should be familiar with the mountain country we'll be going into. Where I can find people like that – or if I can afford them if I find them – I don't know; but I will keep the possibility in mind as I conduct my interviews.

Nearly forgot to mention a conversation I had with the beggar and his son while they rowed me back to Frenchman's Landing. Because of the man's claim to be Annese (unquestionably spurious), any information from that source must be regarded as tainted, but I thought it was interesting, and I am glad I taped it.

R. T.: 'Speaking of the abos as you was, Doctor, I hope you'll mention to any of your friends who wish to come here that we gave you satisfaction showing you the sacred places.'

Self: 'Certainly. Is this much of a source of income for you?'

R. T.: 'Not as much as we would like, you may be sure. To tell you the truth, Doctor, it used to be better than at present. Then there was more trees standing, and the statue was more presentable. My family – we did not, you comprehend, live always as you saw yesterday. We do not now, not in winter when the wolf-snow blows from the mountains. We could not.'

V. R. T.: 'When my mother was here, we had a house, sometimes.'

Self: 'Has your wife passed on, Trenchard?'

V. R. T.: 'She isn't dead.'

R. T.: 'What do you know, *imbécile*? You have not seen her.'

V. R. T.: 'My mother and I used to go, when I was small, into the hills in summer, Monsieur. There we lived as the Free People did, and only came back here when it began to be too cold for me. My mother used to say that among the Free People many children died each winter, and she did not wish for me to die, and so we came back.'

R. T.: 'She was a useless woman, you understand, Doctor. Ha! She could not even cook. She was a – ' (Spits over side of boat).

The boy flushed at this, and for a few minutes nothing more was said. Then I asked him if it were while he was living in the hills with his mother that he had learned to swim so well.

V. R. T.: 'Yes, in the back of beyond. I would swim in the river, and my mother also.'

R. T.: 'We abos all swim well, Doctor. I could myself before I grew old.'

I laughed at the old faker and said that I understood that he was an abo but that I'd have to find another before my search was over. Since we talked about the projectile points he has known that he is not really deceiving me, so he simply grinned back at me (showing a good many missing teeth) and said that in that case it was half complete, since his son was half abo.

V. R. T.: 'You believe nothing, Doctor, but it is true. And it is not true what he says of my mother, who was his wife. She was an actress, a very fine one.'

Self: 'Did she teach you to behave like an Annese, to get money from people? I'll have to admit, when I first met you I thought you were retarded mentally.'

R. T.: (Laughing) 'Sometimes I think so still.'

V. R. T.: 'She taught me a great many things. Yes, to behave like those you call abos.'

R. T.: 'I cursed her a moment ago, Doctor, you comprehend, because she left me, though I drove her away. But what my son says is true, she was a fine actress. We used to go about perform-

149

ing, she and I. You would not believe the things she could do! She could talk to a man, and he would believe her a girl, a virgin, hardly out of school. But then if she did not like him she would become an old woman – a matter of the voice, you understand, and the muscles of the face, the way she walked and held her hands–'

V. R. T.: 'Everything!'

R. T.: 'When I married her, Doctor, she was a fine woman. And you may forget what you have heard! My son is legitimate; we were married by the priest at the church of St Madeleine. Then she was truly beautiful, magnificent.' (Kisses his fingers, releasing the oar with one hand) 'That was not acting. But later when she slept, she could not conceal; every woman is her true age when she sleeps. You are not married? Remember that.'

Self: (To the boy) 'But if she taught you how to behave like an Annese she must have seen some.'

V. R. T.: 'Oh, yes.'

R. T.: 'You comprehend that they must remain hidden, the abos.'

Self: 'Then you seriously believe, Trenchard, that living Annese still exist.'

R. T.: 'Why should they not, Doctor? In the back of beyond there is still land, thousands of hectares, where no one ever goes. And there are animals to eat, and fish there, as before. The abos can no longer come to the sacred places in the meadowmeres, it is true; but there are other sacred places.'

V. R. T.: 'The wetland people were never the Free People of the mountains. These places were not sacred to the Free People.'

R. T.: 'That may be. We say "the abos", Doctor. But the truth is that they were many people. Now you say, "Where are they?" but would they be wise to show themselves? Once all this world of Sainte Anne was theirs. A farmer thinks: "Suppose they are men like me after all? That Dupont, he is a clever lawyer. What if they engage him, eh? What if he spoke to the judge – the judge who has no French and hates us – and said, *This man you call abo has nothing, but Augier's farm was his family's – you make Augier to show the bill of sale?*" What do you think the farmer does then if he sees an abo on his land, Doctor? Will he tell anyone? Or will he shoot?'

So it comes to that. The Annese, if there are any left, are hiding because they are afraid, no doubt with good reason; and many people who have seen them or know where they might be are not likely to report it or even admit it under questioning.

150

As for their being 'many people,' it reminds me of the man who said what he saw was sometimes like a man and sometimes like old wood. The truth is, in fact, that the reports are very contradictory. Even in the interviews I have, it's often difficult to believe that two subjects are talking about the same thing, and the reports of the early explorers – such of them as have survived – show even less agreement. Certainly some of the more fantastic must be pure myth, but there remain a great many reports of a native race so similar to human beings that they might almost have been the descendants of an earlier wave of colonization. So similar, in fact, that old Trenchard can deceive the credulous with his claim to be Annese, and on a planet where we find plants, birds, and mammals so near the Terrestrial types, a form strikingly like man is surely not impossible – the manlike form may be optimal for this biosphere.

The officer laid the notebook on his table once more, and rubbed his eyes with the heels of his hands. As he straightened up, the slave said softly from the doorway, 'Maître . . .'

'*Yes, what is it?*'

'*Cassilla. . . . Does Maître still wish –*' *At the officer's look he hurried away, returning a few seconds later with a girl whom he pushed into the room. She was tall and slender amd peculiarly graceful, with a long neck and a round head; she wore a faded gingham work-dress much too small for her, with (as the officer knew) nothing beneath it; and she looked tired.*

'*Come in here,*' *he said.* '*Sit down. There is wine if you wish it.*'

'*Maître . . .*'

'*Yes, what is it?*'

'*It's already very late, Maître. I must rise an hour before the soldier's reveille to help with breakfast –*'

The officer was not listening to her. He had picked up one of the spools of tape and was fitting it into the machine. '*Duty,*' *he said.* '*We shall listen while we enjoy ourselves. Put out the lamp, Cassilla.*'

Q: Do you understand why you have been brought here?

A: To this prison?

Q: You know quite well what you have done. To this interrogation.

A: I do not even know the charges against me.

Q: Don't think you are going to misdirect us with that sort of thing. Why did you come to Sainte Croix?

A: I am an anthropologist. I wished to discuss certain findings I had made on Sainte Anne with others of my profession.

Q: Are you trying to tell me that there are no anthropologists on Sainte Anne?

A: No good ones.

Q: You think that you know what we want, don't you? You believe yourself clever. It is your opinion that the political situation vis-à-vis the sister planet is such that your hostility to it will buy your freedom; is that correct?

A: I have been in your prison long enough to learn that nothing I can say will buy my freedom.

Q: Is that so?

A: What are you writing?

Q: It does not concern you. If you believe that, why do you answer my questions?

A: It would be equally valid to ask why you ask them, if you plan never to release me.

Q: You forget that I might answer, 'You may have accomplices!' Would you like a cigarette?

A: I thought you didn't do that anymore.

Q: I am not teasing you – look, here is my cigarette case. The offer is made in good faith.

A: Thank you.

Q: And a light from my lighter. I would advise you not to inhale too deeply – you have not smoked in some time.

A: Thank you. I'll be careful.

Q: You are always careful, are you not?

A: I don't know what you mean.

Q: I had understood it was a trait of the scientific mind.

A: I'm careful in taking data, yes.

Q: But you leaped to a conclusion concerning your relations with the government of Sainte Anne.

A: No.

Q: You came from Sainte Anne only a year or so ago, and you believe war is at the loading point.

A: No.

Q: Do you also believe their victory will release you?

A: You think I'm a spy.

Q: You are a scientist – at least for the moment I will assume you are. Is that agreeable?

A: I'm accustomed to the assumption.

Q: I have examined your papers, and letters follow your name. I shall call you:

> 'A Polish Count, a Knight Grand Cross,
> Rx. and Q.E.D.;
> Grand Master of the Blood Red Dirk,
> and R.O.G.U.E.'

You seem to me very young.

A: It was thought that there was no use sending an old man out from Earth.

Q: I propose to your young and elastic but scientific mind a hypothesis in political science: that a murderer would make an excellent spy and that a spy might find many occasions to murder. You would find that difficult to contradict?

A: I am an anthropologist, not a political scientist.

Q: So you never tire of telling us; but an anthropologist is concerned with the folkways of the less complex societies. Do they never spy upon one another?

A: Most primitive people only make war to show their courage. That's why they lose.

Q: You are wasting my time.

A: May I have another cigarette?

Q: Finished already? Certainly. And a light.

A: Thank you.

Q: Whom had you planned to assassinate here? Not the man you killed – that has the look of spur-of-the-moment necessity. Someone you could not get close to; someone well guarded.

A: Whom am I supposed to have killed here?

Q: I have told you that I am not here to answer your questions. To answer would imply that we conceded some slight possibility of truth to your assertions of innocence, and we do not concede that. Truth is something which is to be had from us, not from you. Ours is the most remarkable government in the history of mankind; because we, and only we, have accepted as a working principle what every sage has taught and every government has feigned to accept; the power of the truth. And because we do, we rule as no other government has ever ruled. You have often asked me what your crime is, why we detain you. It is because we know you are lying – do you understand what I am telling you?

A: When I was arrested a certain girl, a Mlle Etienne, was given

153

a card which was to have admitted her to see me on certain specific days. You say you honor your promises, but she has not been admitted.

Q: Because she has not applied:

A: Do you know that?

Q: Yes! Don't you understand? That is our secret, that is truth. You tell me she was given the card, which is always given to someone in any event. *Therefore* I know that if you have not seen her it is because she has not made application. You realize that she may later – when we had come to understand your obstinacy and the full seriousness of your case – have been warned of unpleasant consequences which might follow her visit, but if she had applied she would have been admitted.

We are the only government upon whose word every man may rely absolutely, and because of that we command infinite credit, infinite obedience, infinite respect. If we say to anyone, 'Do this and your reward will be such and such,' there is no doubt in his mind that he will be rewarded. If we say villages breaking a certain ordinance will be burned to the ground, there is no doubt. We speak little, but every word drops like a weight of iron –'

The girl, Cassilla, asked, 'What's the matter?'

'The tape broke,' the officer said. 'Never mind. I'm going to start another one – remember what I told you I wanted you to do.'

'Yes, Maître.'

Q: Sit down. You are Dr Marsch?

A: Yes.

Q: My name is Constant. You are newly come from the mother world by way of Sainte Anne; is that correct?

A: From Sainte Anne, a matter of a year and a few months.

Q: Precisely.

A: May I ask why I have been arrested?

Q: The time has not yet come to discuss that. We have only – thus far – established your name, the identity under which you have traveled. Where were you born, Doctor?

A: In New York City, on Earth.

Q: Can you prove that?

A: You have taken my papers.

154

Q: You are telling me you cannot prove it.

A: My papers prove it. The university here will vouch for me.

Q: We have already spoken to them; unfortunately I am not permitted to disclose the results of other investigations. I can only say, Doctor, that you should expect no more help there than you have already received. They have been contacted, and you are where you find yourself. You left Earth how long ago?

A: Newtonian time?

Q: I will rephrase my question. How long has it been since – according to your claim – you came to Sainte Anne?

A: About five years.

Q: Sainte Croix years?

A: Sainte Anne years.

Q: They are the same for practical purposes. In the future in our discussions you will use Sainte Croix years. Describe your activities after arriving on Sainte Anne.

A: I splashed down at Roncevaux – that is to say, out to sea about fifty kilometres from Roncevaux. We were towed into the port in the usual way, and I went through customs.

Q: Continue.

A: When I had cleared customs I was questioned by the military police. That was strictly a formality – it lasted about ten minutes as I recall. I was then issued visitor's papers. I checked into a hotel –

Q: Name the hotel.

A: Let me think ... the *Splendide*.

Q: Go on.

A: I then visited the university, and the museum, which is attached to it. The university has no Department of Anthropology. Natural History tries to cover the area, and on the whole does a poor job of it. The anthropology displays in the museum – of which they are quite proud – are a mixture of secondhand information, fraud, and pure imagination. I required their support, of course, so I was as polite as I could honestly be. May I ask why that man went out of the room?

Q: Because he is a fool. You then left Roncevaux?

A: Yes.

Q: How?

A: By train. I took the train to Frenchman's Landing, which lies about five hundred kilometers up the coast from Roncevaux, north and west. I might have gone by ship as easily – more easily – but I wished to see the countryside, and I am some-

155

what subject to motion sickness. I chose Frenchman's Landing to begin my work because what little is known about the aboriginal people of Sainte Anne indicates that they were most numerous in the meadowmeres there.

Q: I am told it is a city set in a swamp.

A: Hardly a city. The ground to the south rises after twenty kilometers or so, and there is agricultural land there – Frenchman's Landing exists because it is a port for the farmers and stock-raisers.

Q: You spent a great deal of time in that area?

A: In the farming area? No. I went upriver. The land rises there too, but there aren't many settlers.

Q: One would think there would be; they could send their produce to market by water.

A: The river is very shallow through the meadowmeres, and there are sandbars and mudbanks. A channel is kept dredged from the sea to Frenchman's Landing, but that is as far as it goes. Besides, as soon as the hills rise above the meadowmeres there are rapids.

Q: You have a fine eye for geography, Doctor, which is what I wished to ascertain by these questions. No doubt you could tell me a great deal about Port-Mimizon as well.

A: The way in which a population supports itself is basic to anthropology. A fishing culture, for example, will be quite different from a hunting culture, and both different from an agricultural culture. Noticing that sort of thing becomes second nature.

Q: A useful second nature it must be; a wise general might send you ahead of his army. Tell me –

Q: Here you are, sir.

Q: Ah! Do you know what my colleague has brought me, Doctor?

A: How could I?

Q: It is a file on the *Hôtel Splendide*. He wishes me to ask you questions concerning the hotel, not realizing that nearly any lapse of memory might be excused by five years' absence, and that a spy might have lodged there as easily as a scientist. But we will exert ourselves to make him happy. Do you recall, for example, the name of your bellman?

A: No. But I remember one thing about him.

Q: Oh?

A: I remember that he was free. Most of the menials I've seen here have been slaves.

156

Q: So. You are not only a spy, but an ideologically motivated spy – is that it, Doctor?

A: Of course I'm not a spy. And I am from Earth; if I am motivated by any ideology it is hers.

Q: Doctor, Sainte Croix and Sainte Anne are called planetary twins; the phrase refers to more than their rotation about a common center. Both our worlds remained unknown when planets more distant from Earth had been colonized for decades. Both were originally found and settled by the French.

A: Who lost the war.

Q: Precisely. But now we had done with similarities; we begin to deal with differences. Do you know, Doctor, why we on Sainte Croix possess slaves while Sainte Anne does not?

A: No.

Q: When the fighting was over, the military commander here – to our good fortune – made a decision which proved to have great consequences. Perhaps I should say he made two. First, he decreed that every conquered Frenchman and French-woman was subject to compulsory labor to rebuild the installations destroyed by the war – but he allowed those who could raise the money to purchase exemptions, and he set the price sufficiently low for most to do so.

A: That was generous of him.

Q: Not at all; the price was calculated to produce the maximum revenue. After all, a banker and his wife can stack cement bags – and will, under the whip – but what is their labor worth? Not a great deal. And, secondly, he ordered that continuity be maintained in all civilian administration below the central planetary government. That meant that many provinces, cities, and towns retained their French governors, mayors, and councils for years after the end of the war.

A: I know. I saw a play about it last summer.

Q: In the park? Yes, so did I; just children, of course, but they were charming. But the point of that play, Doctor, though you did not realize it and perhaps even the young actors did not, was that after losing the war it was still possible for the better French elements to retain a measure of power. They were never wholly stripped of authority, and now they are an influential element once more in the life of our world. At the same time they were regaining lost ground it became customary to increase the number of unremunerated workers from other sources, principally criminals and orphaned children. so that the slave caste lost its exclusively French character. On Sainte Anne every man of French descent is the bitter enemy of the government, with the result that Sainte Anne has become a camp armed against itself, where a colossal military establishment threatens citizens of every class. Here on Sainte Croix the French community is not hostile to the government – its leaders are a part of that government.

A: Possibly my views are influenced by the fact that that government is holding me a prisoner.

Q: It is a dilemma, is it not? You are hostile to us because you are a prisoner. But if you were no longer hostile, if you were willing to tender your full cooperation, you would be a prisoner no longer.

A: You have my full cooperation. I've answered every question you've asked.

Q: You are willing to confess? To name your contacts here?

A: I haven't done anything wrong.

Q: Perhaps we had better talk some more then. Forgive me, Doctor, but I have lost my place; what was it we were discussing?

A: I believe you were telling me that it was better to be a slave on Sainte Croix than free on Sainte Anne.

Q: Oh, no. I would never tell you that, Doctor – it is not true. No, I must have been telling you that on Sainte Croix some men are free – in fact, most men are free. While on Sainte Anne and, for that matter, Earth, most are slaves. They are not called by that title, possibly because they are worse off. A slave's owner has a sum of money tied up in him, and is obliged to take care of him – if he becomes ill, for example, to see that he receives treatment. On Sainte Anne and on Earth, if he does not have sufficient cash to pay for his own treatment he is left to recover or die.

A: I believe that most of the nations of Earth have government programs to provide medical care for the people.

Q: Then you see who their owners are. But aren't you certain, Doctor? We thought you came from Earth.

A: I was never ill there.

Q: No doubt that explains it. But we have left our subject far behind. You journeyed by rail to Frenchman's Landing. Did you remain there long?

A: Two or three months. I interviewed people concerning the aborigines – the Annese.

158

Q: You recorded these conversations.

A: Yes. Unfortunately I lost the tapes while I was in the field.

Q: But you had transcribed the more interesting interviews into your notebook.

A: Yes.

Q: Continue.

A: While I was at Frenchman's Landing I visited the sites actually or supposedly associated with the Annese. Then, with a local man I employed to assist me, I went into the field; specifically, into the hills above the meadowmeres and the mountains from which the Tempus rises. I found –

Q: I don't think we are much interested in your supposed discoveries on Sainte Anne, Doctor. In any case I have full reports on the talks you gave at the university. For how long did you remain, as you call it, 'in the field'?

A: For three years. That was in my talks.

Q: Yes, but I wished to have it confirmed by your own lips. You are telling us that for three years you lived in the Temporal Mountains, winter and summer?

A: No, in winter we – I, after my assistant died – came down into the foothills. Many of the Free People did as well.

Q: But you remained isolated from civilization for three years? I find that difficult to believe. And when you returned you did not go back to Frenchman's Landing, from which you had set out. You appeared instead – I believe *appeared* is the right word – at Laon, much farther down the coast.

A: By going south I covered a good deal of ground that had been unfamiliar to me. If I had returned to Frenchman's Landing I would have been passing over the same country I had seen on my way up.

Q: Let us concentrate on the time between your appearance at Laon and the present; but I will make one last digression to point out that had you returned to Frenchman's Landing, you could have notified the family of your late assistant in person of his death. As it was, you merely sent a radiogram.

A: That happens to be true, but I would like to know how you know it.

Q: We have – shall I call him a correspondent? – in Laon. You have not commented on my digression.

A: My assistant's family, for which you feel this tender concern, consisted exclusively of his father – a dirty, drunken beggar. His mother had fought free of her husband years before.

Q: There is no need to become angry, Doctor. No one likes to

159

be the bearer of bad news. In addition to sending the radiogram, what did you do in Laon?

A: Sold the one pack mule that had survived, and such of my
equipment as was still serviceable. Bought new clothes.

Q: And left for Roncevaux, this time by ship?

A: Exactly.

Q: And at Roncevaux?

A: I audited several courses in the graduate school and attempted
to interest the faculty in the results of my three years' work.
Since you will ask, I will tell you that I had little success;
at Roncevaux they are convinced that the Free People are
extinct, and so are uninterested in preserving those that
remain, and much less in securing for them the minimum
human rights; I wasn't helped by the fact that they believe
them to have had a paleolithic culture, which is also incorrect – the aboriginal culture was, and is, dendritic, the
stage preceding the paleolithic. One might almost say
predendritic.

I also took up smoking, put on eight kilos – mostly fat –
and had my beard trimmed by the only man I've ever found
who could do it correctly.

Q: How long did you remain at Roncevaux?

A: About a year; a little less.

Q: Then you came here.

A: Yes. At Roncevaux I had had the opportunity to catch up on
the literature of my profession. I was anxious to talk to anyone in this system who was interested by its anthropological
puzzles. The situation there was hopeless, so I boarded the
starcrosser. We splashed down, out beyond the Fingers.

Q: And you have remained here in Port-Mimizon ever since. I
am surprised you did not proceed to the capital.

A: I have found a great deal here to interest me.

Q: Partly at six sixty-six Saltimbanque Street?

A: Partly there, yes. As you are so fond of pointing out, I am
young, and a scientist has desires like other men.

Q: You found its proprietor remarkable?

A: He is an unusual man, yes. Most medical men seem to em-
ploy their skill mostly to prolong the lives of ugly women, but
he has found better things to do.

Q: I am aware of his activities.

A: Then perhaps you are also aware that his sister is an amateur
anthropologist. That was what originally attracted me to the
house.

160

Q: Really.

A: Yes, really. Why do you ask me questions if you don't believe anything I tell you?

Q: Because experience has taught me that you must occasionally let slip some fragment of truth. Here, do you recognize this?

A: It looks like a book of mine.

Q: It is a book of yours: *A Field Guide to the Animals of Sainte Anne*. You carried it with you even when you left Sainte Anne and came here, although the rates for baggage in excess of ten pounds are quite high.

A: The rates from Earth are much higher.

Q: I doubt that you know that from experience. I suggest to you that the reason you carried this book with you had nothing to do with the book itself – that is, the printed matter and the illustrations. I suggest to you that you brought it for the sake of the numbers written on the last flyleaf.

A: I suppose you're about to tell me you've broken the code.

Q: Don't make jokes. Yes, we've broken the code, in a sense. These numbers describe the trajectory of a rifle bullet – the number of inches above or below the point of aim the bullet will strike when the rifle is sighted for three hundred yards. The table covers distances from fifty to six hundred yards – an impressive range. Shall I show you? See, at six hundred yards your bullet would strike eight inches below the place you aim at. It seems like quite a lot, but if you had this table you could still rely on shooting your man in the head at six hundred yards.

A: I could, possibly, if I were a good shot. I'm not.

Q: Our ballisticians are even able to calculate, simply from examining this table, what sort of rifle it was intended for. You planned to use a .35 caliber rifle of high velocity, a type commonly employed here by those hunting wild boars. It is not difficult for a reputable person here to secure a permit for such a rifle if he has an interest in hunting.

A: I had a rifle like that on Sainte Anne. I lost it in a deep pool of the Tempus.

Q: Most unfortunate – but then you were planning to come here in the event, and it would have been impossible to ship. No matter, you could replace it after you landed.

A: I have not applied for a permit.

Q: We apprehended you too soon – do you expect to quote our own efficiency against us? You have referred to your notebook, to your supposed profession of anthropology.

161

A: Yes.

Q: I have read your notebook.

A: You must be a fast reader.

Q: I am. It is a tissue of fabrications. You speak of a habe[r]
dasher named Culot – do you think we do not know th[at]
culotte is the French for short trousers? It is an obsession [of]
yours that physicians serve merely to keep ugly women ali[ve]
– you referred to it only a moment ago. And in your not[e]
book you give us a Dr Hagsmith. You appeared two yea[rs]
ago at Laon, where our agent saw you. You wore a hea[vy]
beard, as you do now, which would serve to conceal your re[al]
identity from any chance acquaintance you might meet. Y[ou]
said you had been living in the mountains for three years; a[nd]
yet some of the equipment you sold was suspiciously ne[w,]
including a pair of boots that had never been worn. Never [in]
three years.

And here you sit, and tell me lies about Earth, where yo[u]
have clearly never been, and pretend you do not understan[d]
that it is only by possessing slaves that any man can be tru[ly]
free. All this, the captivity, the deceptions, the questioning[,]
are new to you now; but they are old to me. Do you kno[w]
what is going to happen to you? You will be returned to you[r]
cell, and afterward you will be brought here again, and I wi[ll]
talk to you again as I am doing now, and when I am finishe[d]
I will go home and have dinner with my wife, and you will g[o]
back to your cell. In this way the months will go past, and th[e]
years. My wife and my children and I will go to the island[s]
next June, but when we return you will be here still, mor[e]
pallid and dirty and thin than ever. And in time, when th[e]
best part of your life is over and your health is ruined, we wi[ll]
have the truth, and no more lies.

Take him. Bring in the next.

*There was nothing more on the tape. It spun in silence while th[e]
officer washed himself. He always washed when he had had [a]
woman, not just his genitals, but beneath his arms and up and dow[n]
his legs. He used a perfumed soap he reserved only for that pur[-]
pose, but the same common enameled basin that would hold hi[s]
morning shaving water. The washing was not only a prophylacti[c]
precaution, but a sensual experience. Cassilla's saliva had streake[d]
his body; now he felt pleasure in removing it.*

Now they have brought me more paper, a whole thick pad of cheap paper and a bundle of candles. The first time they gave me paper, and the second, I felt certain they would read whatever I wrote, so I was very careful and wrote only what I believed would help my case. Now, I wonder. I have, in the past, put out little feelers, little tests. But they are never referred to in the interrogations. My handwriting is abominable I know, and I write so very much. It is possible that someone is simply too lazy to decipher it all.

Why is my hand so poor? My teachers, those ugly old women with their crabbed minds, had an immediate explanation: I held (and still hold) my pen incorrectly. But this, of course, is an explanation that does not explain. Why do I hold my pen badly? I remember very well the first day we were taught to write in school. The teacher showed us just how the pencil should be, then went to each seat and placed our own fingers on our own pencils. Holding mine as she showed me I could do nothing except draw – by dragging my whole arm across the page – weak and wiggling lines. I was paddled for it repeatedly, of course. When I came home my mother would take my trousers to the river, walking upstream for hours to get away from the sewers, and wash the blood out of them, leaving me ashamed and afraid, with an old blanket or a torn piece of sail wrapped around me. Eventually, by experimentation, I learned to hold the pencil as I now do this pen, clamped between my second and third fingers with my thumb quite free to do whatever it wishes. I was no longer the boy who could not write, but merely the boy whose penmanship was worst, and since there must be one such boy (it is never a girl) in each class I was no longer beaten.

The answer, then, to why I hold the pen badly is that I cannot write if I hold it well. I have just been trying that system, for the first time in years, and find I still cannot do it.

Do you know Dollo's Law? From his studies of the carapaces of fossil turtles, the great Belgian formulated the Law of the Irreversibility of Evolution: *An organ which degenerates during evolution never reacquires its original size, and an organ which disappears never reappears; if the offspring return to a mode of life in which the vestigial organ had an important function, the organ does not return to its original state, but the organism develops a substitute.*

*

163

I have been thinking about the location of this underground cell. I have often passed the citadel, both on foot and in a chase, and though it is large, it is not large enough to allow of any such straight underground passage as that we traversed. My cell, then, is technically outside the walls. Where then? The citadel fronts what is called the Old Square. To its right is a canal; I cannot be there because this cell, however chill, is dry. Behind it is a clutter of shops and tenements. (I bought a brass implement in one of the shops there once, because it fascinated me; a thing of clamps and toothed jaws and cruel little hooks. I am still unable to guess its use unless it was employed in the practice of veterinary medicine; I imagine it in the opened belly of a great dray horse, pushing away the liver, thrusting down the small intestine, and cramping the spleen to the spine while it gnaws at a diseased pancreas.) It seems highly unlikely that they would build cells under these, since it would make it far too easy for the prisoner's friends (I am assuming a prisoner possessed of friends) to release him.

To the left, however, is a complex of government offices; a tunnel connecting these with the citadel would seem a very reasonable construction and would allow the clerks and bureaucrats there to take refuge in the event of a civil disturbance without exposing themselves to attack on the streets. Once such a tunnel had been built it would surely seem logical – if more facilities or more secret facilities were needed for prisoners – to excavate cells in its side walls. I am almost surely, then, beneath one of those brick government buildings – possibly the Ministry of Records.

*

I have been asleep and had all sorts of dreams and let my candle burn out. I must be more careful; that they gave me candles and matches this time is no guarantee that they will be replaced when the present supply is gone. Inventory: eleven candles, thirty-two matches, a hundred and four sheets of still unused paper, and this pen which manufacturers its ink by drawing moisture from the air and with which a patient man so-minded could paint black the four walls of this cell. Fortunately I have never been a patient man.

What did I dream of? The howling of beasts, the ringing of bells, women (when I can remember what I have dreamed I have nearly always dreamed of women, which I suppose makes me unusually blessed), the sounds of shuffling feet, and my own execution, which I dreamed of as having taken place in a vast deserted courtyard surrounded by colonnades. Five of the stalking robots used as guards in the prison camps above the city, which I have sometimes observed overseeing labor gangs at work on the roads, were my executioners. A crisp command from invisible lips – blinding blue-white light from the lasers – myself falling, my hair and beard on fire.

But the dream of women – actually, of a woman, a girl – has set my mind again upon a theory I formulated when I was living in the mountains. It is so simple a theory, so obviously true, so self-evident that it seemed to me at that time that everyone must have thought of it; but I mentioned it several times to various people at the university at Roncevaux, and most of them looked at me as if I were mad. It is simply this: that all the things we consider beautiful in a woman are merely criteria for her own survival and thus the survival of the children we shall father in her. In the main (ah, Darwin!) those who followed these criteria in their ambushes of the female (for we do not really pursue them, do we? We are not swift enough. We leap upon them from cover, having lulled their suspicions) populated the worlds – we are their descendants; while those who flouted them saw, in the long prehistory of man, their children torn by bears and wolves.

And so we seek long-legged girls, because a long-legged girl is swift to fly danger; and for the same reason a girl who is tall, but not too tall – a girl will be swiftest at a height of about a hundred and eighty centimeters, or a little more. Thus, men will crowd around a girl as tall as an ordinary tall man (and her shorter sisters will lengthen the heels of their shoes and thicken the soles to seem like her). But a girl too tall will run clumsily, and one of, say, two hundred and twenty centimeters will almost never find a husband.

In the same way the femal pelvis must be wide enough to pass living infants (but not too wide or, again, she will be slow) and every man gauges the width of those bones when the girl has passed. Breasts there must be or our children will starve as babes so our instincts tell us still, and though a thin girl can run well, one too thin will have no milk when there is no food.

And the face. It has troubled artists ever since the fading of superstition allowed human portraiture – they decide what shall be beautiful, then marry a woman with crooked teeth in a wide mouth. When we look at their pictures of the great beauties of history, the idols of the populace, the mistresses of kings, the great courtesans, what do we see? That one has mismatched eyes and another a large nose. The truth is that men care nothing for any of these things, and want vivacity and a smile. (Will she see the danger, will she kill the son of my loins in her rage?)

The girl in my dream, you ask, what of her? Shadowy, but as I have described. Naked. No woman arouses me who wears even a wisp of clothing; and once at Roncevaux when I tried to slake my passion with a girl who did not divest herself of a sort of halter, I was a sad failure. I wanted to tell her what was wrong, but was afraid she would laugh, then at last I did and she laughed, but not as I had feared, and told me of a man who made her wear a ring – which he brought in his pocket, and took from her finger as soon as possible, since it was a valuable one – and could do nothing without it; (and since I have been here on Sainte Croix I have heard of a man who, being unable to penetrate the walls of a convent, clothes a girl in the habit of a nun and then disrobes her). When we had both made fun of that, she did as I asked, and I found she wore her halter to conceal a scar, which I kissed.

As for the girl in my dream, I will write only that we did nothing which, recounted here, would excite passion at all – in dreams a look, or the vision of a thought, is enough.

*

So. I have candles now, and matches, a pen and paper. Does that mean a relaxation in the official attitude toward me? This cell does not indicate it – it is worse than the 143 where I was before, and I know that that 143 was not a good cell. In fact, from what Forty-seven (who used to tap messages to me when I was in that cell) told me, his was a better cell than mine; it was larger, and had a cover for the sanitary pail; and he said there were other cells that had glass windows inside the bars to keep out the cold and a few with curtains and chairs. When I had the rib bone found in my soup one day, I could converse very well with Forty-seven. Once he asked me about my political beliefs – because I had told him I was a political prisoner – and I told him I belonged to the Laissez-Faire Party.

YOU MEAN THAT YOU BELIEVE BUSINESS SHOULD BE ALLOWED TO OPERATE WITHOUT INTERFER ENCE? I SEE – YOU ARE AN INDUSTRIALIST.

NOT AT ALL. I BELIEVE GOVERNMENT SHOULD BE LET ALONE. WE OF THE LAISSEZ-FAIRE TREAT OFFICIALS AS DANGEROUS REPTILES: THAT IS, WE GIVE THEM GREAT RESPECT, BUT AS WE CANNOT KILL THEM, WE HAVE NOTHING TO DO WITH THEM. WE NEVER ATTEMPT TO OBTAIN A CIVIL SERVICE POST, OR TELL THE POLICE ANYTHING UNLESS WE ARE CERTAIN OUR NEIGHBORS HAVE TOLD THEM ALREADY.

THEN IT IS YOUR FATE TO BE TYRANNIZED.

I rapped: IF WE LIVE ON THE SAME WORLD, CAN THERE BE TYRANNY OVER YOU AND NOT OVER ME?

BUT I RESIST.

IT IS ENERGY WE RESERVE FOR OTHER PURPOSES.

AND LOOK WHERE...

Poor Forty-seven.

This cell. Let me describe this cell, now full of yellow candle-light. It is only a trifle over a meter high – say, one meter, ten centimeters. When I lie on this gritty floor (which I do a great deal, as you may imagine), I can almost touch the ceiling with my feet without raising my hips. This ceiling, as I should have said before, is concrete; also the walls (no tapping here, not even the scrapings and creakings of the poor madman next to me when I was above ground; it may be that the cells to either side of mine are empty; or possibly the builders left a thickness of earth between the walls to muffle sound) and my floor are concrete. My door is iron.

But my cell is larger than you might think. It is wider than I can spread my arms, and longer than I am when I lie with my arms stretched over my head; so it is no torture box, though it would be nice to be able to stand up. There is a sanitary pail (with no lid), but no bedding; there are no windows, of course – wait, I retract that – the door has a little Judas, though since it is always dark in the corridor outside, it does me no good, and it may be that I was given the candles only so they could observe me, and the paper only so that I would burn them. There is an opening at the bottom of the door like a very large letter slot, through which I pass my food bowl. I have my matches and candles, paper and pen; the candle flame is making a black spot on the ceiling.

What is the progress of my case? That is the question. That I have been put in this cell suggests that it is going badly, that I

167

have been given candles and writing materials leads me to hope. It may be that there are two opinions about me on that level (whatever it is) where opinions matter: one thinks me innocent, wishes me well, sends the candles; the other, thinking me guilty, orders me confined here.

Or possibly it is the one who thinks me guilty who wishes me well. Or the candles and paper (and this is what I fear) may be only a mistake; soon the guard may come to take them away.

*

I have made a discovery! A real discovery. I know where I am. After writing that last, I blew out my candle and lay down and tried to sleep again, and with my ear against the floor I could hear the sound of bells. If I took my ear from the floor I could not hear them at all, but if I pressed against it they were there, for as long as the ringing lasted. The corridor outside my door, then, runs under the Old Square toward the cathedral; and I must be near its foundations with the sound transmitted by the stones of the bell tower. Every few minutes now, I press my ear to the wall and listen again. For all the time I lived in the city I cannot remember how often the cathedral bells rang, except that I know they did not strike the hours like a clock.

At home there was no cathedral, but several churches, and for a time we lived close to that of St Madeleine. I remember the bells ringing at night – I suppose for a midnight mass – but it did not frighten me as other sounds did. Often the ringing did not wake me, but if it did I would sit up in my bed and look for my mother, who would also be sitting up, her beautiful eyes shining like shards of green glass in the dark. Any sound woke her, but when my father came stumbling home she would pretend to be asleep and make herself as unattractive as possible, something she could do without your noticing – even if you were watching her – with the muscles of her face. I have the same ability, though not to the extent she did; but I chose to cover everything with this beard instead, because I was afraid of it – frightened of myself – and needed only to make my voice like his and look older. But it does not do to be too clever, and I suppose I have been here more than long enough to have a beard now even if it had been clean-shaven when I was arrested.

I suppose, too, I grew my beard for my mother, to show her – if I were ever to find her again (and there seemed to be some

168

reason to think, at Roncevaux, that she had come here) – that I am now a man. She never told me, but I know now that among the Free People a boy remains a boy until his beard sprouts. When he has enough to protect his throat from the teeth of the other men he is a man. (What a fool I was. I thought when she left, and for many years after, that she had gone because she was shamed by me, having found me with that girl; I know now that she had only been waiting until the milk-task was done. I had wondered why she smiled at me then.)

*

I had thought she would go into the hills and so went there myself when the chance came, but she did not. She should have, and I, when I found myself there, should have stayed. But it is terribly hard; half the children die, and no one lives to be old. And so we – my mother and I come down to the town, together or separately, when winter is coming. So see where I am, I who laughed at poor Forty-seven.

*

Much later. A meal, tea and soup, the soup in the old battered tin bowl they gave me here (above ground, utensils came with the meal and had to be returned afterward) and the tea, black tea with sugar in it, in the same bowl after I had emptied it, with the thin grease from the soup floating on top. When he gave me my soup the guard said: 'There's tea. Let's have your cup.' I told him I didn't have one, and he just grunted and went on, but when he came back from feeding the cells farther along, he asked me if I had finished my soup, and when I said I had, he told me to put out my bowl again and I got the tea.

Is it this guard who, acting on his own initiative, gave me the candles and paper? If so, it may be only that he feels sorry for me, and that must be because I am going to be executed.

*

The bells have rung three times since I wrote last. Vespers? Nones? The Angelus? I don't know. I have slept again, and dreamed. I was very small and my mother – at least I think the

169

girl was my mother – was holding me on her lap. My father was rowing us on the river, as he often did then, while he was still fond of fishing; I saw the reeds bowing to the wind all about us, and there were yellow flowers floating around the boat, but the odd thing about my dream was that I knew everything that I was to learn later, and I looked at my father, who seemed a red-bearded giant, and knew what would happen to his hands so that he could no longer follow his trade. My mother – yes, I am sure it was she, though I never understood how one of the Free People could bear a child to my father – had been buttoned into her yellow dress by him, and had the happy, tumbled look of a woman who had been dressed by a man; she smiled when he spoke, and I laughed; we all smiled. I suppose it was only some memory come back in the dream, and in those days he must have seemed an ordinary man, possibly a little more fond of talk than most, who lived on bread and meat and coffee and wine; it was only when he hadn't them anymore, not for himself or to give to us, that we found he lived on words.

*

No, I have not been sleeping. I have been lying here for hours in the dark, listening to the cathedral bells and polishing my bowl, in the dark, with my poor torn trousers.

They were very good trousers once. I bought them last spring, not having brought any summer clothes – or any clothes at all except the ones I had on – from Sainte Anne. It is not economical to do so, and it would be more sensible if everyone crossed naked and bought all new on Sainte Croix. As it is, the clothing worn on board is free weight, and so everyone (at least in winter, when I came) buys the heaviest possible winter suit for the crossing. There is also a small allowance of free baggage weight, but I used that to bring the books I had had with me in the back of beyond.

But these were very good summer trousers, part of a good summer suit, with silk from the southern continent blended with linen in the weave. This silk is a native product (as opposed to the linen, which is grown from seed brought from Earth), and we do not have it on Sainte Anne. It is produced by the young of a kind of mite which, when they have hatched from the egg sac, wait on blades of grass until they sense an updraft, then spin an invisibly slender thread which, rising like a fakir's rope, eventually lifts them high into the air. Those who light elsewhere in the

170

grasslands are safe and begin new lives, but every year a great many are blown out to sea, where these tangled threads, like lost memories floating on time past, form great mats as much as five kilometers long and covering hundreds of hectares. The mats are collected by boats and brought to factories ashore where they are fumigated, carded, and spun into thread for the textile industry. Since the mites are extremely resistant to fumigation – I have been told that they can survive for as long as five days without oxygen – and live as parasites in the cardiovascular systems of warm-blooded hosts, the slaves who do the work are not long-lived. Once when I was at the university here, I was shown films of a new model housing area for them. A cemetery dating from French times had been destroyed to make way for it, and the whitewashed walls were all of rammed earth and bones.

My object in polishing my bowl was not cleanliness but the hope of seeing my own reflection. I have called it tin, but it is (I think) actually pewter, and although no one is more helpless with tools than I, I can hold a rag and scrub something with it; and so I have been doing that, up until a short while ago, as I lay here in the dark, shivering and listening to the bells. I polished it inside and out, very hard. Of course I couldn't see how shiny it was getting, or if it was getting shiny at all, and I didn't want to waste the candle looking – besides, I had plenty of time. Once the guard brought some boiled barley and I ate it quickly, both because I hoped there might be tea afterward if I did (there was not) and because I wanted to get back to my polishing. Finally I became tired and wanted to write instead, and so I set the bowl down and struck a match to light my candle. I thought, then, that my mother was somehow in my cell with me, for I saw her eyes in the dark. I dropped the match and sat hugging my knees and crying while all the bells rang, until the guard came kicking my door and asking what the trouble was.

When he had gone I lit the candle. The eyes, of course, were the reflections of my own in my polished bowl, which shines now like dull silver. I should not have cried, but I really think that in some way I am still a child. This is a terrible thing, and I have sat here and thought about it for a long time since I wrote the last sentence.

How could my mother have taught me to become a man? She knew nothing, nothing. It may be that my father never allowed her to learn. She did not think it wrong to steal, I remember; but I believe she seldom took anything unless he told her – occasionally food. If she had eaten she wanted nothing, and then

171

if someone wanted her to go with him, my father had to force her. She tried to teach me all I would need to know to live where I was not living and am not living now. How am I to know what there was of this place and that place I did not learn? I do not even know what human maturity is, except that I do not possess it and find myself among men (smaller, many of them, than I) who do.

At least half of me is animal. The Free People are wonderful, wonderful as the deer are or the birds or the tire-tiger as I have seen her, head up, loping as a lilac shadow on the path of her prey; but they are animals. I have been looking in the bowl at my face, pulling my beard back as much as I could with my hands, wetting it from the sanitary pail so that I could see the structure of myself, and it is an animal's mask I see, with a muzzle and blazing animal eyes. I can't speak; I have always known that I do not really speak like others, but only make certain sounds in my mouth – sounds enough like human speech to pass the Running Blood ears that hear me; sometimes I do not even know what I have said, only that I have dug my hole and passed to run singing into the hills. Now I cannot speak at all, but only growl and retch.

Later. It is colder, and I can hear the bells even when I drive my hands against my ears. If I press my ear to the stone I hear shovels scraping, and the shuffling of feet; and so I know where it is I am. This cell is beneath the cathedral floor itself, and since they bury the dead in that floor, with their gravestones paving the aisles and pews, the graves are above me, and it may be my own that they are digging; there, once I am safely dead, they will say masses for me, the distinguished scientist from the mother world. It is an honor to be buried in the cathedral, but I would wish instead a certain dry cave high in one of the cliffs that overlook the river. Let the birds build their nests in the front of my cave, and I will lie in mine at the back, until the pink sun is always red, with dark scars across her face like the coal of a cigarette going out.

April 12. A very disturbing thing has happened, and one of the most disturbing elements . . .

Never mind. Let me describe the day. We followed the river-bank, as planned, for most of the day, although it was plain that we were unlikely to find any sort of cave among the sandbanks of its margin, and the boy insists that we are still much too far

172

ownstream. About the middle of the afternoon the weather
egan to look bad, the first bad weather we have had on the trip.
oiled the guns as we walked along, and buttoned them into
heir covers; ahead we could see the great black thunderheads
uilding up, and it was obvious that the course of the storm
vould be east and south – that is, straight down the valley of the
'empus toward us. At the boy's suggestion we left the river and
vent a mile or more at right angles to the channel, since he felt
here was the possibility of a flash flood. When we reached the
op of a knoll we stopped and set up the tent, I not relishing the
dea of doing it later in the rain. We had no more than gotten
verything staked down when the first howling wind came, then
elting rain and hail. I told the boy that we would cook after the
torm was over, got into my bag, and for God knows how long
ay there wondering if the tent was going to hold. I have never
n my life heard another wind that howled like that one, but
ventually it died down until there was just the rain pounding
he fabric of the tent, and I went to sleep.

When I woke the rain had stopped; everything seemed very
quiet, and the air had that fresh, washed smell that follows a
torm. I got up and discovered that the boy was gone.

I called once or twice, but there was no answer. After casting
about for a few minutes it occurred to me that the most probable
explanation was that when he had begun to prepare our supper
ne had missed some article of kitchen gear and had decided to
retrace a few miles of our route in the hope of finding it. Accord-
ngly I took a flashlight and (don't ask me why, except that I was
n a hurry) the light rifle, and went looking for him myself. The
un was low, but not yet down.

Ten minutes' hard walking brought me to the river, and I saw
he boy standing there with the water a little past his waist,
scrubbing himself with sand. I called to him and he called back,
superficially very innocent, but with an underlying confusion I
could sense. I asked him why he had left camp without telling
ne, and he said simply that he felt dirty and wanted a bath, and
besides, he needed more water for cooking than we had in the
canteens, and had not wanted to waken me. It all sounded reasonable enough, and I still cannot show that that is not exactly what
happened and, in fact, all that happened; but I am certain in my
own mind that he is lying, and that someone – other than the
two of us – was in camp while I slept; the boy has, transparently,
been with a woman. It shows in everything he says and does. I
believe that twenty pounds or so of our smoked meat is missing,

173

and while I have no objection to his giving it to his maidenlove – we have plenty after all – it is properly mine and not his. I intend to get to the bottom of this.

At any rate, after I had questioned the boy for five minutes or so without getting anything more satisfactory from him than the answers I have outlined above, we began to make our way back to camp, the boy carrying a kitchen pot full of water. The sun had set by this time, though there was still some light. We were almost within sight of the tent when I heard one of the mules scream – a horrible noise, as though a big powerful man were being flayed alive and had broken completely under the pain.

I ran toward the sound, while the boy (very sensibly) made for the tent to get the other rifle. As nearly as I could make out, the mule was on the far side of clump of brush near the base of the knoll. Instead of running around the brush – as no doubt I should have – I went crashing through it, and came face to face with the most hideous animal I have ever seen, a creature patched of hyena, bear, ape, and man, with short, extremely powerful jaws and human eyes that looked straight at me with precisely the savage, stupid, skid row murder expression of a fighting mad, broken-bottle-swinging derelict. It had huge, high-hunched shoulders; forelegs as thick as a man's body, ending in stubby fingers studded with claws like tenpenny nails, and the whole animal reeked of filth and rotting flesh.

I fired three times with the light rifle without bothering to bring it to my shoulder, and the brute spun away from me and made off through the brush with great bounding leaps like an ape. By the time the boy came running up with the heavy rifle, it was gone. I feel certain I hit it, and more than once, but how much damage the little high-velocity bullets may have done to a beast like that, I can't guess – I'm afraid not much.

My *Field Guide to the Animals of Sainte Anne* leaves no doubt as to what our marauder was – a ghoul-bear (interestingly, the boy knows this animal under the same name). The *Field Guide* calls it a scavenger, but one paragraph of the description indicates that it is more than willing to destroy livestock if the opportunity offers:

> . . . so called because of its habit of despoiling any recent burial not protected by a metal casket. It is a powerful digger, and will move large stones in order to reach a body. If confronted boldly it will usually flee,

174

often carrying the disinterred corpse under one foreleg. It may enter farmyards where animals have been recently butchered, at which time it is likely to attack cattle or sheep.

I had to shoot the mule (one of the grays), which had been too badly mauled to survive. We have redistributed its load among the other two, over which the boy and I will stand alternate guards with the heavy rifle.

*

April 15. We are far up into the hills now. No more disasters since I wrote last, but no discoveries either. We now have a tire-tiger following us as well as the wounded ghoul-bear (which we have seen twice since I shot it). We hear the tiger screaming, usually an hour or two after midnight, and the boy positively identifies it. The day after the mule was killed (the thirteenth) I backtracked two hours in the hope of catching the ghoul-bear over the body. I was too late; the dead mule had been torn to bits, and everything but the hoofs and the largest bones consumed, also some of the carabao meat we had abandoned to lighten the animals. Where the mule's carcass had been I saw hundreds of footprints left by a number of species. Some very small tracks might have been those of human children, but I cannot be sure. No more signs of the girl who (I am still certain) visited the boy, and he will say nothing about her.

*

April 16. We have lost one camp follower at least – this by converting her into an expedition member. The boy has succeeded in luring the cat into camp and more or less taming her with scraps of food; and with little fish, which he catches very dextrously with his hands. She is still too shy to allow me to come close, but I wish we could take care of the tire-tiger as easily.

An interview with the boy:
Self: 'You say that you have often met living Annese – other

175

than yourself – when you and your mother were staying in the back of beyond. Do you think that if we met any they would show themselves to us? Or would they run away?'

V. R. T.: 'They are afraid.'

Self: 'Of us?'

V. R. T.: (Silent)

Self: 'Is it because the settlers have killed so many?'

V. R. T.: (Very quickly) 'The Free People are good – they do not steal unless others have plenty – they will work – they can herd cattle – find horses – scare away the fire-fox.'

Self: 'You know I wouldn't shoot one of the Free People, don't you? I only want to ask them questions, to study them. You've read Miller's *Introduction to Cultural Anthropology*. Didn't you notice that the anthropologists never harm the people they're studying?'

V. R. T.: (Stares at me)

Self: 'Do you think the Free People are frightened of us just because I shoot game to eat? That doesn't mean I would shoot one of them.'

V. R. T.: 'You leave the meat on the ground; you could hang it in the trees so that the Free People and the Shadow children could climb and get it. Instead you leave it on the ground and the ghoul-bear and tire-tiger follow us.'

Self: 'Oh, is that what's bothering you? If there is any more meat and I give you some rope, will you hang it up for me? For them?'

V. R. T.: 'Yes. Dr Marsch . . . '

Self: 'Yes, what is it?'

V. R. T.: 'Do you think I could ever become an anthropologist?'

Self: 'Why yes, you're an intelligent young man, but it would take a great deal of study, and you would have to go to college. How old are you?'

V. R. T.: 'Sixteen now. I know about college.'

Self: 'You seem older than that – would say seventeen at least. Are you counting in Earth years?'

V. R. T.: 'No, Sainte Anne years. They are longer here, and besides we of the Free People grow up very fast. I can look older than this if I want to, but I didn't want to change too much from when you first saw me and hired our boat. You don't really think I could go to college though, do you?'

Self: 'Yes, I do. I didn't say I thought you could go *directly* into college; your preparatory work probably hasn't been good enough, and you would have to study for several years first, and learn at least the rudiments of a foreign language – but I forgot, you already have some French.'

V. R. T.: 'Yes, I already know French. Would it be mostly reading?'

Self: (Nods) 'Mostly reading.'

V. R. T.: 'I know you think I'm uneducated because I talk strangely, but I only do it because it's the way my father taught me – to get money from people; but I can talk any way I wish. You don't believe me, do you?'

Self: 'You're talking very well now – I think you're imitating me, aren't you?'

V. R. T.: 'Yes, I've taught myself to speak as you do. Now listen; do you know Dr Hagsmith? I'll do Dr Hagsmith.' (In an excellent imitation of Hagsmith's voice:) ' "It's all falsity; everything ls false, Dr Marsch. Wait, let me tell you a story. Once in the iong dreaming days when Trackwalker was shaman of the abos, there was a girl called Three Faces. An abo girl, you see, and she used the colored clays the abos found by the river to paint a face on each breast – one face, sir, forever saying *No!* – that was the left breast – and the other, the right, painted to say *Yes!* She met a cattle-drover in the back of beyond who fell very much in love with her, and she turned her right breast toward him! Well, sir, they lay together all night in the pitch darkness that you find at night in the back of beyond, and he asked her to come and live with him and she said she would, and learn to cook and keep house and do all the things human women do. But when the sun rose he was still asleep, and when he got up later she had gone and washed herself in the river – that's for forgetfulness in the tales, you see – and had only her one, natural face; and when he reminded her of all the things she had promised in the dark, she stood and stared at him and wouldn't talk, and when he tried to take hold of her, she ran away." '

Self: 'That's an interesting bit of folklore, Dr Hagsmith. Is that the end of the story?'

V. R. T.: ' "No. When the drover began to dress himself – after the girl was gone – he found he had the images of the two faces on his own chest, the *Yes!* face on his left side and the *No!* face on his right. He put his shirt on over them and rode into Frenchman's Landing where there was a man who did tattoos and had him trace them with the tattoo needle. People say that when the drover died the undertaker skinned his chest inside the coat, and that he has the two faces of Three Faces preserved, rolled with cardamom in his desk drawer in the mortuary and tied with a black ribbon; but don't ask me if it's true – I haven't seen them." '

*

April 21. The strain of staying up half the night to protect our animals has become unbearable. Tonight – now – I am going to kill at least one of the predators who have been following us for the last ten days. I have shot a prance-pony – not killing it, but just breaking one leg; it is tethered in the clearing below me. As I write this, I am sitting in the fork of a tree, thirty feet or so above the ground, with the heavy rifle and this notebook to keep me company; the night is very clear; Sainte Croix hangs in the sky like a great blue light.

Now about two hours later. Nothing except a glimpse of a H. fennec. The thing that bothers me is that I know, I feel absolutely certain – call it telepathy or whatever you like – that while I am up here, the boy is with the woman who visited him before. He is supposed to be guarding the mules. That girl is Annese; I suspected it before and now I know it; he told that story to rub my nose in it, and no one else would live in these God-forsaken hills anyway. All that he would have to do would be to tell her that I wouldn't harm her, and the expedition would be a success and I would be famous. I could climb down and catch them together (I *know* she is with him, I can almost hear them), except that I can smell the ghoul-bear somewhere near. They would tie, the two of them – when the boy was washing I noticed he wasn't circumcised. If they were like that when I came, I think I would shoot them both.

Later. There is a new prisoner, I think about five cells down from mine. Seeing him brought in, has, I think, saved me from losing my mind; for that I do not thank him – sanity, after all, is only reason applied to human affairs, and when this reason, applied over years, has resulted in disaster, destruction, despair, misery, starvation, and rot, the mind is correct to abandon it. This decision to discard reason, I see now, is not the last but the first reasonable act; and this insanity we are taught to fear consists in nothing but responding naturally and instinctively rather

178

than with the culturally acquired, mannered thing called reason; an insane man talks nonsense because like a bird or a cat he is too sensible to talk sense.

Our new prisoner is a middle-aged fat man, very probably a businessman of the kind who works for others. My candle had burned out, and I was sitting here with my head on my knees when the faint sounds – we don't have the soundproof, shatterproof glass in the spy holes down here that all the doors had on the upper floors, but only a wire grille – reached me through the Judas. I thought it was the guard with food, and knelt at the door to watch him coming: there were two guards this time, the usual one with his flashlight and a uniformed stranger who might have been a soldier, the two of them holding our gross, frightened man between them and going crabwise in the narrow corridor, with him looking so white I laughed at him (which frightened him more); because the Judas is so small I could only show my eyes or my lips, not both together; but I let them have them alternately, less than waist-high to him as they took him past my door, and I shouted to him, 'What have you done? What have you done?' and he sobbed, 'Nothing, nothing!' which made me laugh more, not only at him but at myself because I could speak again, and most of all because I knew he had *nothing* to do with me, was not a part of me in any way, not of Sainte Anne, not of the university or the lodginghouse here or the Cave Canem or the dusty shop where I bought my brass implement, but simply a gross, frightened man who meant *nothing* and would be my neighbor now but nothing else at all to me.

*

I have been interrogated again. Not the usual thing. Something different was in the air, and I don't know what. He began with the regular bullying, then became friendly, offered me a cigarette – something he has not done in weeks – and even unbent so far as to recite a satirical little verse ridiculing academic degrees, which for him meant it was a party. I decided to take advantage of the jollity and asked for another cigarette; to my own astonishment I got it, and after that instead of more questions, a long lecture on the wonders of government on Sainte Croix, as though I had applied for citizenship. Then a short lecture pointing out that they had neither tortured me nor drugged me, both perfectly true. He attributed this to the nobility and humanity native to all

179

sharp-chinned, hunch-shouldered Croix-codiles, but my own opinion is that it is due to a sort of arrogance, a feeling that they don't need those things and can break me, or anyone, without them.

He said one thing in this connection that interested me: that a certain doctor whom they knew and who cooperated with them when they required him could have gotten everything they wanted from me in a few minutes. He seemed to expect me to react in some way to this remark. It might have meant they were no longer interested in my case, but this seemed unlikely since certain indirect questions had been scattered throughout the interview; or that they have already gotten information from some other source, but this also seems improbable since there is none to get. The best interpretation seemed to me to be that this doctor is no longer available, and since I thought, or at least suspected (whether by a flash of insight or because of something said earlier, I'm not certain now) that I knew who he was, I commented that it was too bad they hadn't questioned me under drugs while they could, since it would have proved my innocence, but that I was sure they'd find someone just as good soon.

'No. He was unique – an artist. We could find someone else, surely. But for someone half as skilled we have to send to the capital.'

I said: 'I know someone who might be able to help you. The man who operates a place called the *Maison du Chien*. He certainly doesn't seem too particular about what he does if he's paid well, and he has a great reputation.'

The look he gave me was answer enough. The whoremaster is dead.

I could have told him – though he would not have believed me – that he would have been dealing with the same man if he employed the son in his place; but no doubt the young one is under arrest by now; he might even be in another part of this building. His aunt – biologically his daughter, but I will use the same designation the family does to save confusion – will by this time be trying to get him out.

Perhaps (this is the first time I have thought of it) she is trying to secure my release as well; she possessed real intelligence as well as a fascinating mind, and we had a number of long talks – often with one or more of her 'girls', as she called them, for audience. Where are you now, *Tante Jeannine?* Do you even know they have me?

She believed, though she pretended not to, that the Annese

have devoured and replaced homo sapiens – Veil's Hypothesis, and she is Veil; it has been used for years to discredit other heterodox theories about the original population of Sainte Anne. But who, then, *Tante Jeannine*, are the Free People? Conservatives who would not desert the old ways? The question is not, as I once thought, how much the thoughts of the Shadow children influence reality; but how much our own do. I have read the interview with Mrs Blount – a hundred times while I was in the hills – and I know who I believe the Free People to be: I call it Liev's Postpostulate. I am Liev and I have left.

*

The new prisoner has been talking. He asked if there was anyone in the other cells and what their names were and when we would be fed and if it were possible to get bedding and a hundred other things. Of course no one answered him – anyone caught talking is beaten. After a while, when I realized the guard was away, I warned him. He was silent then for a long time, then asked me in a voice he thought very soft and secret, 'Who was the madman who laughed at me when they brought me here?' By that time the guard had returned, and that great fat man screamed like a rose-rabbit in a noose when they pulled him out of his cell for the whips. Poor bastard.

*

Incredible! You will never guess where I am! Go on – you may have as many guesses as you want.

That is foolishness, of course, but I feel foolish, so why not out with it. I am back in the other 143, my old place above ground, with a mattress and a blanket, and light that comes in through the window – even if there's no glass and the chill comes in, too, at night. It looks like a palace.

Forty-seven started tapping the pipe about an hour after I got here; he had heard some sort of gossip about my return and sent his greetings. He says this cell was empty while I was gone. I have lost the soupbone I used to use, but I replied as well as I could with my knuckles. The prisoner next to me knew I was back, too, and began tapping and scraping the wall between us in the old way, but still has not learned the code or is using a different one I cannot decipher. The sounds are so various I think sometimes he must be trying to talk with his noises.

*

Next day. Does this mean they are going to release me? The best meal last night since being arrested – bean soup, thick, with real pieces of pork in it. Tea with lemon and sugar. They gave me a big tin mug of it, and there was milk with the bread this morning. Then out of my cell for a bath in the shower room with five others, and insect powder for my hair, beard, and groin. I have a different blanket, fairly new and almost clean – better than the one I had before. I am writing now with it wrapped around my shoulders. Not because I am cold, but just to feel it.

*

Another interrogation, this one not by Constant but by a man I have never seen before who introduced himself as Mr Jabez. Fairly young, good civilian clothing. He gave me a cigarette and told me he was risking typhus by talking to me – he should have seen me before they let me wash. When I asked him for another blanket and more paper he showed me that he had some of the pages I had written earlier in his file, and complained about the work it would take to have them transcribed. Since I knew there was nothing harmful in them I suggested he have them photocopied instead if he wanted (as he implied he might) to send them to someone of higher rank; but I don't think I should let them take what I have here now. I let my imagination range pretty freely about my life with my parents on Earth – to tell the truth, I was thinking of doing a novel, a great many books have been written in prisons – and it would only confuse my case. I will destroy the pages at the first opportunity.

*

Midnight or past. Fortunately they let me keep my candles and matches, or I could not write this. I had gone to sleep when a guard came in, took me by the shoulder, and told me I wa 'wanted'. My first thought was that I was to die; but he wa grinning in a way that made that seem improbable, and I thought then that it was to be some nasty but half-funny indignity like getting my head shaved.

He took me to a room just at the edge of the cell area and shoved me in, and there waiting for me was Celestine Etienne, the girl from Mme Duclose's lodginghouse. It must be the height of summer outside now, for she was dressed as if to attend an evening mass on a summer Sunday – a pink dress without sleeves, white gloves, and a hat. I know I used to think her tall as a stork, but the truth is that she looked a pretty creature there, with her big, frightened, blue-violet eyes. She stood when I came in, and said, 'Oh, Doctor, how thin you look.'

There was one chair, a light we could not turn off, a wall mirror (which meant, I feel sure, that we were being observed from the next room) and an old, sagging bed with clean sheets stretched over a mattress it was probably better not to see.

And, surprisingly, a bolt on the inside of the door. We talked for a time afterward, and she told me that the day after I was arrested a man from the city treasurer's office had come to see her and told her that on Thursday of the following week – the day she was to see me – at eight p.m. precisely, she was to report herself to the Bureau of Licences. She had, and had been kept waiting until eleven, when an official told her she could see no one that night as they were closing the office, but to come back in two weeks. She had known very well, she said, what was being done, but had been afraid not to go every two weeks as they told her. Tonight she had no sooner sat down on the bench in the waiting room than the same official who had always dismissed her at eleven appeared and suggested that she go here to the citadel instead, adding that her presence at the Bureau of Licences would not be required again in the foreseeable future. She had stopped by Mme Duclose's to put on scent and changed her frock, and come here.

*

And that is enough. It has been a pleasure writing all this, seeing my pen leave its weeks'-long spidery trail of black, but the sight of my earlier writings in the new interrogator's file folder was somewhat disturbing. I am fairly certain the guard is asleep in the corridor outside, and I intend to burn everything, page by page, in the flame of my candle.

The transcription ended in the middle of a sheet with a notation giving the place, time, and date on which the originals had been confiscated from the prisoner.

You must excuse my writing in this entry, and I suppose some of the subsequent entries as well. An absurd accident has occurred which I will explain when the time comes. I have killed the tire-tiger and the ghoul-bear, the latter over the tire-tiger's body the night after. The tiger sprang at me when I climbed down from the tree, where I had waited for it all night. I suppose I should have been badly mauled, but I got nothing more than a few scratches from the thorns when the animal's body knocked me down.

The officer laid down the canvas-bound journal and rummaged for the tattered school composition book with the note about the shrike. When he found the book he glanced at the first few pages, nodded to himself, and picked up the journal again.

April 23. Came back to camp after shooting the tire-tiger as I described above and found no one with the boy except the cat that had been following us. The boy had enticed it into his lap and was sitting – as he always used to when he wasn't cooking – with his back to the fire and the cat on his knees. I was very excited about the tire-tiger, of course, and began talking about it, and went over and picked up the cat to show him where my shots had hit. The cat twisted her head around and sank her teeth into my hand. It wasn't bad yesterday when I got the ghoul-bear, but is sore today. I have bandaged it and applied an antibiotic powder.

*

April 24. Hand still bad, as you see from the writing. Without the boy I don't know what I'd do. He has done everything, most of the work, for the entire trip. We talked today about whether we should break camp and go on upstream, and ended deciding to stay here today and leave tomorrow unless my hand is worse. It is a good spot. There is a tree, which is always lucky, and

184

long grassy slope running down to the river; the river flows quickly here, with sweet, cold water. There is plenty of meat – we are eating the prance-pony and have hung a haunch from another tree two kilometers off for those who hunger. Farther upstream the river will be sunk into a gorge – that can be seen from here.

*

April 25. Broke camp today, the boy doing most of the work as usual. He has been reading my books and asks me questions, some of which I cannot well answer.

*

April 26. The boy is dead. I have buried him where he will never be found, because I find, looking at the dead face, that I do not believe in strangers looking into graves. It happened this way. About noon today we were leading the mules along a path that ran along the south rim of the gorge. It was about two hundred meters deep there, and narrow, with the water running swiftly in a deep channel at the bottom, bordered with red sand and broken stones. I reminded him that he had said we were still too far downstream to find the sacred cave of the Free People, but he said that there might be other such caves and climbed among the rocks anyway. I saw him fall. He tried to grasp a rock, then screamed and dropped down. I hobbled the mules and went back looking for him, hoping that in quieter water he would have been able to swim out. Downstream a long way, a big tree stood grasping the rock, with water at his feet, and had thrust out a root to catch my friend.

Let me confess now that I lied. The dates on this page and the one before are not correct. Today is the first of June. For a long time I did not write anything in this notebook, and then, tonight, I thought that I would keep it again and write down what had happened. As you see, my hand is still bad; I do not think it will ever be right again, although it looks healthy and there is no scar. I have trouble holding on to things.

I hid the dead boy's body in the cave in a sheer cliff beside the river. I think he would have liked that, and the ghoul-bears will not get it there; they can move big stones aside, but they cannot climb like a man. It took me three days to find the cave, with him strapped to one of the mules. The cat I killed and laid at his feet.

I find I am unused to writing like this – not just my hand, but writing down my thoughts. I wrote down the interviews, of course, and about seeing the sacred places, but not my thoughts. It has a fascination, and now there is no one else to talk to. No one else will read this anyway.

We – the two mules and I – move much more slowly than when he was alive. We walk only for three or four hours in the morning, and there is always something to stop for in these hills, a beautiful spot with shady trees and ferns or a place to look for the cave or a deep hole with fish in it. I have not killed any large animals since he died, only eating fish and a few small creatures for which I set nooses I make of the tail hair I comb from the mules. Several times these snares have been robbed, but I am not angry; I believe I know who steals.

There are many things to eat here besides fish and animals, though it is still too soon for fruits or all but the first berries. I believe that the Wetlanders, I should say the Annese of the meadowmeres, ate the roots of the salt reeds; I have tried them (you must first strip away the black underbark which is bitter and will kill fish if you pound a great deal of it between two stones), and they are good, though I think not very nourishing; it is best to eat them by Ocean so the white part can be dipped into the salt water after each bite.

There, in the meadowmeres, if you want to eat the roots you have only to pull some up, but there is very little else to eat besides fish and clams, or snails in the spring, unless you catch a bird. Here things are quite different and there are many foods, but all are hard to find. The shoots of certain plants are good, and worms you find in rotten wood. There is a fungus that grows only where no light comes that is very good.

As I said, I have not killed any large animals, though once I was very tempted. But the rifle makes so much noise – and the shotgun even more – that I am certain it would frighten away those I wish to find.

*

June 3. (This is the real date.) Higher up into the hills – the two mules and I. More stones and less grass. The deer do not look like cattle here.

June 4. No fire tonight. I have been making one every night since he died, more than a month. Tonight I began to collect the sticks as I always did, then wondered why. The dead boy used to, because there was meat to cook and tea to make; I like tea, but it is gone now, and I have already eaten, and had nothing that had to be cooked. Soon, though, the sun will set; and then until sisterworld is above the hills I will not be able to write. Sometimes I wonder who will read this and I think no one, and decide to put in all my innermost thoughts. Then I remember that I am supposed to be keeping a scientific notebook; and that even if no one reads it, it will be good practice.

But what is there to tell? I have stopped shaving. I sit here with the book in my lap and try to think about the life of the Free People here before men came from Earth. These hills are hard and bare, no one would live here if there were better land. It may be that the mountains – the Temporals, as they are called – are better, but for the present I have no way of knowing; certainly the low hills through which we have come were better, and even the meadowmeres. Why then did the Free People live in the mountains, as they surely did if the old stories are to be trusted? Did they ever come here? Do they come now? I believe they do, but that is another subject.

If ever they came here it was not often, because the stories always speak of the people of the mountains (the Free People) and the Wetlanders, the people of the meadowmeres. It is true that when the Wetlanders are made to speak in the stories they sometimes call the Free People 'hill-men', but only they do that, and these hills, I think, are empty as the marshes are not; there are no dead here, or few.

And the Marshmen. Why didn't they come here?

Let us begin with them; we know more about them. We know they were ever eager for meat, for the stories tell that they howled for the meat of sacrifice, even those who did not believe. Living in the meadowmeres they must have eaten the roots of the salt reeds, as I have said, and fish and waterfowl. Surely sometimes, wishing meat, they went into the low green hills above the marshes to hunt; but fishers and snarers of waterfowl cannot have hunted well. Then they would come (How many? ten? twenty and thirty?) into these hills to find victims for the river. I see them walking, one behind another, thickset men, stump-legged, splay-footed, white-skinned. Ten, twelve, thirteen, fourteen, fifteen. The Free People are better hunters, no doubt better fighters, long of leg and narrow of foot, but there cannot

187

be so many together or they would starve – there is not enough game. Possibly no more than ten together all told, women and children; and not more than three or four could be men of fighting age. How many must have been driven back across these empty, rocky hills toward the Hourglass and the Observatory and the River. How many? How long was human prehistory on Mother Earth? A million years? Some would say ten million. (Bones of my fathers.)

Later. Sisterworld is queen of the night sky now, and covers this page with her blue light, save where the shadow of my pen hand falls. Half dark and half light she is now, and in the region between I can see the Hand reaching out into the sea, and what must be Port-Mimizon, a tiny spark, where the thumb joins the palm; I have heard it called the worst city on either world.

Later. For a moment I thought I saw my cat flying like a shadow in the dark, and I wondered if she were really dead, though I broke her neck. The day before I found the burial cave for him, she brought me a little animal and laid it at my feet. I told her that she was a good cat and could eat it herself, but she only said, 'My master, the Marquis of Carabas, sends you greetings.' And disappeared again. The little animal had a pointed snout and round ears, but its teeth were the even, biting teeth of a human being, and it smiled in its agony.

Later. By sisterworld's light I have been looking among the rocks for implements – eoliths. I have found none.

*

June 6. We have behaved like explorers today, marched all day. On our right the river roars through walls of stone; ahead of us the mountains lift their blue wall. I will follow the river in; I know it rises in their heart.

*

June 7. Today a small stone came tumbling down the slope ahead of us. Dislodged by some animal, I am sure, but I could not see the animal. I thought that we were no longer followed since I have not been shooting game; my snares are seldom robbed now, and when they are there is often sign of the fire-fox. How strange I must look to them, with the mules. I wear no clothing except my shoes, which I need for the stones, but the mules must frighten them.

Much later. I do not know what time it is. Far after midnight, I think; sisterworld is half down the sky in the west, but she grows brighter and I can see far, far down the valley, and the great cliffs ahead glow with her blue light.

I will not say *Later*, for I only left this book for a few seconds to gather brush and dead grass for a fire. This is the first fire I have had in several days, but now that I am out of my sleeping bag I am cold, and I do not want to go back to sleep. I dreamed that naked people were crowding all around me as I slept. Children, twisted Shadow children that are neither children nor men, and a tall girl with long, straight hair that hung almost in my face when she bent over me.

It was the last entry in the canvas-bound journal. The officer closed it, tossed it aside, then for a moment tapped the stiff cover with his fingers. Dawn had come while he had been reading; he put out the feeble flame of his lamp, pushed back his chair, stood up and stretched. There was already a feeling of humidity and heat in the morning air. Outside, as he could see through the open door, the slave had left his post beneath the fever tree and no doubt was asleep in a corner somewhere. For a moment the officer considered looking for him and kicking him awake; then turned back to his table and, still standing, read for the second time the cover letter which had accompanied the file. It was dated almost a year past.

SIR: The materials I send you relate to prisoner #143, currently detained at this installation and purporting to be a citizen of Earth. The prisoner, whose passport (which may have been tampered with) states his identity as John V. Marsch, Ph.D., arrived here April 2nd last year and was arrested June 5th of the current year in connection with the murder of a GSPB Class AA Correspondent *Espion* in this city. The son of the man referred to has since been convicted, but there is considerable evidence, as you will see from the material I enclose, that #143 may be an agent of junta currently in power on the sisterworld; this is, in fact, my own opinion.

189

I call your attention to the circumstance that the execution of an agent of Sainte Anne would, at this time, have an excellent effect on public opinion here. On the other hand, if we are willing to accept the prisoner's claim that he is in fact from the mother world, his release, at least until he further incriminates himself, might have an equally favourable effect. People here, particularly the intellectual class, were very ready to welcome him when he came as a scientist from Earth.

'Maître . . .'

The officer looked up. Cassilla, yawning, stood at his elbow with a tray, the slave behind her. 'Coffee, Maître,' she said. In the bright daylight he could see fine wrinkles near her eyes; the girl was ageing. A pity. He took the cup she proffered, and as she poured, asked how old she was.

'Twenty-one, Maître.' The pot was one of the silver ones with Divisional decorations, which meant the slave had insisted on it in the kitchen; otherwise they would have given him one of the plain ones from the junior officer's tables.

'You should take better care of yourself.' The coffee was hot, and had been lightly scented with vanilla. He added a dollop of heavy cream.

'Yes, Maître. Will that be all?'

'You may go.'

'You,' he gestured to the slave. 'What is the next ship sailing for Port-Mimizon?'

'The Evenstar, *Maître. At high tide today. But it will put in at Coldmouth before it reaches the Hand, Maître, and perhaps do some trading in the islands. The* Slough Desmond *won't sail until next week, but it should make Port-Mimizon about a month sooner.'*

The officer nodded, sipped coffee, and went back to the letter.

Although a number of items in the prisoner's private papers appear significant, he has thus far admitted nothing. We are pursuing the usual policy of alternately lenient and severe treatment to produce a breakdown. Shortly after he was placed in the favorable cell, #47 on the floor above began a communication with him by means of coded knocks upon a pipe passing through both cells. As soon as the prisoner replied we persuaded #47 (who is political, and soft like all our home-grown politicals) to keep records of the conversations. He has done so (File #181) and checks have shown it to be accurate, but the subject matter appears unimportant. The prisoner in an adjacent cell, an illiterate woman who is a habitual petty thief, also appears to attempt to communicate with the prisoner by knocking, but the pattern is unintelligible and he does not reply.

Since there is a certain amount of pressure from the university for #143's release we would appreciate a prompt disposition of this case.

The officer opened the top of the dispatch box and dropped the letter back inside, following it with handfuls of loose pages in official transcript, the spools of tape, the canvas-bound journal, the school composition book. Then taking a few sheets of official stationery and a pen from the drawer of his table he began to write.

Director, GSPB
Citadel,
Port-Mimizon,
Department de la Main.
Sir: We have considered at length the case enclosed. Though this prisoner is of no importance, both the courses you propose appear to us completely untenable. If he were to be publicly executed it would be thought by many that he was in fact a citizen of the mother world as claimed, and had been burned as a scape-goat. Alternately, if he were to be released as cleared and subsequently re-arrested, the credibility of the government would be gravely damaged.

We are not concerned about the state of public opinion in Port-Mimizon, but since it is the only importance this case possesses we direct you to continue your efforts to secure complete cooperation; in passing we would warn you not to place a premature reliance upon his developing attachment to the girl C.E. Until complete cooperation is achieved we direct you to continue to detain the prisoner.

Adding his signature below, the officer dropped this, too, into the dispatch box and, calling the slave, instructed him to bind it closed as it had been before. When he had finished, the officer said: 'You are to put this aboard the Evenstar. For Port-Mimizon.'

191

'Yes, Maître.'

'You will be serving the commandant today?'

'Yes, Maître. From twelve. For the dinner, you know, Maître, for the general.'

'Possibly an opportunity – a graceful opportunity – to speak to him will occur. Most probably when he asks you to convey his thanks to me for the loan of your services.'

'Yes, Maître.'

'At that time you might contrive to inform him that I remained awake all night to deal with this case, and that I sent it off this morning by the first ship sailing for Port-Mimizon. Do you understand?'

'Yes, Maître. I do, Maître.'

For an instant the slave let slip his normal look of deference and smiled; and the officer, seeing that smile, understood that he would carry out the instruction if he could, that some secret love of intrigue and duplicity in him delighted in it. And the slave, seeing the officer's expression, knew that he would never have to return to the carding rooms and the looms, understanding that the officer knew that he would do everything he could, for the sheer love of it. He put the dispatch box on his shoulder to carry it to the wharf and the ship Evenstar, and they parted, both quite happy. When he had gone, the officer found a spool of tape where it had rolled behind the lamp on his table; he dropped it out the window into one of the neglected flower beds, among the sprawling angels'-trumpets.

On the following pages are other recent paperbacks
published by Quartet Books.
If you would like a complete catalogue of
Quartet's publications please
write to us at 27 Goodge Street, London W1P 1FD.

MICHAEL MOORCOCK

'Like Tolkien and Roger Zelazny, Moorcock has the ability to create a wholly imaginative world landscaped with vivid and sometimes frightening reality, and peopled with magicians, heroes and monsters who are far from the one dimensional creatures of fairy tales but who possess human warmth and interaction' – *The Times*

'One of the best fantasy writers in the language' – *Tribune*

Other titles by Michael Moorcock available in Quartet paperback editions are –

THE ENGLISH ASSASSIN – A Romance of Entropy featuring Jerry Cornelius.

THE WAR LORD OF THE AIR – A Captain Bastable adventure.

THE SLEEPING SORCERESS – An Elric story.

THE BULL AND THE SPEAR – the first volume of The Chronicle of Prince Corum and the Silver Hand trilogy.

THE OAK AND THE RAM – The Chronicle of Prince Corum and the Silver Hand, volume two.

THE LAND LEVIATHAN – A new Captain Bastable story.

THE SWORD AND THE STALLION – the third volume of The Chronicle of Prince Corum and the Silver Hand trilogy.

Soon to be available –

THE ADVENTURES OF CATHERINE CORNELIUS AND UNA PERSSON IN THE 20TH CENTURY

A SAILOR ON THE SEA OF FATE

THE PROTO PAPERS
Philip Oakes

Only three of them really know what is going on. Two are mad. The third is a huge, vicious chimpanzee

'Much more than immensely readable and exciting; it is intelligent and precision built ... we shall be lucky to get any novel this year or next as absorbing and as open-eyed as this one' – *The Times*

'As a piece of speculative fiction, imaginative though rooted in scientific fact, this is a very readable adventure, sharply written, with many poetic touches, and of course sexy touches too. Very intelligent and racy' – *Sunday Times*

Fiction 50p

CLONE
Richard Cowper
by the author of *Kuldesak*

'An outstanding piece of sf satire which clearly establishes Mr Cowper as one of the most accomplished writers in the genre ... this brilliant book is destined to become a science fiction classic' – *Sunday Times*

'*Clone* boasts an impressive parade of bizarre characters, each of whom deserves a novel in his or her own right' – *Times Literary Supplement*

Science Fiction 40p

THE SEEDBEARERS
Peter Valentine Timlett

Men and supernatural forces are locked in battle – and th
prize for the victors is the future of mankind.

The bloody story of an immense and violent struggle in th
Atlantis of occult legend.

Occult fantasy 40p

IN THE KINGDOM OF THE BEASTS
DAY OF WRATH
Brian M. Stableford

The second and third volumes in the famous *Dies Irae* trilogy

In the Kingdom of the Beasts is an epic novel set ten thousand
years in the future.

Day of Wrath is a tale of the universe in the aftermath of th
bloodiest battle in cosmic history.

The author of these two exciting sf volumes is a young Englis
scientist who has already attracted a huge audience for hi
exciting brand of science fantasy, especially in America.

Science Fiction 40p each
ORIGINAL PUBLICATIONS

A Master Storyteller
One of the Giants of Science Fiction
Winner of Hugo and Nebula Awards

PHILIP JOSÉ FARMER

It is almost impossible to categorize Philip José Farmer's writings in a simple way. He has written straight science fiction which has won reader applause. He has written avant-garde meaning-within-meaning fiction which has captured awards. He has written novels different from any science fiction before or since and has won more awards. He is a unique science fiction genius.

The following Philip José Farmer titles are available in Quartet paperback editions.

THE WIND WHALES OF ISHMAEL	40p
DARE	40p
TIMESTOP!	40p
THE GATE OF TIME	40p
THE IMAGE OF THE BEAST	90p
BLOWN	90p
A FEAST UNKNOWN	90p

CHAMIEL
Edward Pearson

'The writing is surely excellent . . . vivid unearthliness . . . bold and unusual' – C. Day Lewis

The massed forces of Evil, led by Zareal the Black Angel, face the brotherhood of Michael's Court, of Gabriel and Brigit and Og. And at Michael's side is Chamiel, the young one, whose exploits in battle and subsequent adventurous wanderings on Earth and in the Kingdom form the stuff of legend.

Fiction 35p

An original publication

These books are obtainable from booksellers and newsagents or can be ordered direct from the publishers. Send a cheque/postal order for the purchase price plus 15p postage and packing for the first book plus 5p per copy for each additional book ordered to Quartet Books Limited, PO Box 11, Falmouth, Cornwall TR10 9EN. Overseas customers please allow 20p for the first book and 10p per copy for each additional book.